E.D.HACKETT

Reinventing Amara Leventis

First edition

ISBN: 978-1-7374679-3-9

Cover art by Maryann G. Haraldsen
Editing by Amber Lambda

This book was professionally typeset on Reedsy.
Find out more at reedsy.com

This book is dedicated to my dog, Ellie, for motivating me to wake up before 5 a.m. every single day to get my story on paper.

Contents

Acknowledgement

This novel was a work of perseverance and determination. This was the novel I wrote by doing all the steps. I plotted and researched before I wrote my first word. I studied craft, listened to podcasts, and bounced ideas off fellow writers, my family, and friends.

I wanted this book to be the best novel I have written (yet) and I couldn't have done it without help. It takes a village to write a novel and this novel was no exception.

First off, thank you to my family for putting up with my constant time away, where I holed up in my little office to work on my craft.

Thank you to my beta readers and critique partners for giving me sound advice on my words, the story, and the dreaded cover process.

A special thank you to Andrea, Kris, Gail, and Jamie for helping me get this story ready for publication.

Thank you to Loucia, for being my research guide regarding Greek culture. Without your help, this book would be nothing. I hope I represented your culture authentically and made you proud.

Thank you to Amber, for editing my manuscript and making it as strong as it can be.

Thank you, Ellie, for waking up before 5 a.m. every morning, no matter the day of the week or season. Without those hours alone when everyone else was fast asleep, I would still be trudging away with a half-written novel.

Chapter 1

O
n the first night of freshman year of college, Amara had shimmied into Bethany's tight black pants and silver sequined halter top. It had been cold, but Amara didn't object. Anticipation coursed through her veins at the thought of new college experiences that might include finding a best friend in Bethany. Amara downed two shots of vodka, ran red lipstick over her lips, and hiked to the club, hoping her roommate knew where they were going and how to get home.

Six years later, Amara tossed her black, slinky cocktail dress to Bethany. "Here, Beth. This dress will hug all your curves. The guys won't leave you alone tonight."

Bethany grabbed the dress and handed Amara a glass of wine. "Thank you." She pulled her heeled boots out of Amara's closet. "I'm taking my shoes back."

Amara turned up the music and continued to get ready. "Bethany," she called down the hallway. "Are you sure it's okay with your sister if I come?"

"Yes!" Bethany appeared in Amara's bedroom doorway. "I told her you're my date. She knows we're inseparable. She doesn't care. Trust me, there are going to be so many people there. She'll probably say hi to us, and then we won't see her for the rest of the night."

Amara nodded and scrunched her hair. "I wish my hair were curly like yours. Mine is so straight and boring. It just hangs there."

Bethany handed Amara her curling iron. "Here, use this and spray it with hairspray."

Amara wrinkled her nose and scrunched her forehead. "Hairspray. What is this, 1985? Do we even have hairspray?"

"We do. It's in the bathroom, and I promise it'll hold." Bethany bounced out of the room.

"I'm so excited to celebrate with you," Amara called from the bathroom cabinet.

Bethany laughed. "You mean to celebrate with Mikayla's class?"

Amara took a sip of wine and grinned. "Yes! Do you think we're too old? I mean, she's graduating from college, and we should be responsible adults by now. Shouldn't we be more mature than her? Are we too old for frat house parties?" Self-doubt crept in and out like a flash of lightning.

Bethany grinned. "We deserve it. I promise to protect you from any creepy guys if you promise to do the same." She sat next to Amara and adjusted the clasp on her necklace.

Amara stuck out her pinky. "Promise. And I'll try to control my drinking."

Bethany's eyes narrowed, and Amara knew she was thinking back to their graduation party. "You better. It's my sister's party. I can't be attached to your hip, making sure you don't say or do something stupid."

Amara stuck out her tongue at Bethany. "I promise. Please don't hook up with any sketchy guys. I'd rather not scare them with my almost six-foot frame in three-inch heels when I have to save you from all the drunk men. Remember, I know self-defense, and I'll use it to protect you."

Bethany giggled. "Like freshman year when you came home from late-night studying and found Ronnie Mac in our room, naked?"

"I could've killed you that night."

"I couldn't get him to leave, so I left him there drunk and sleeping in my bed. Thank you, Amara. Even though we'd just met, that night solidified every thought I had about you being a great friend. You saved me from a jerk and probably a pervert."

"I saved both of us. There was something about him that I couldn't place, but he made my skin crawl. You're lucky I was there to save your life."

Amara remembered that night. She'd trudged home from the library carrying her messenger bag overflowing with books, binders, and papers. She had a midterm in six hours and felt completely unprepared. So much was riding on her grades. She was one bad moment away from breaking under pressure.

The quiet dorm hallways were well-lit, but the light under her door was faint. Amara assumed Bethany was sleeping since it was one o'clock in the morning. Amara dug her key out of her back pocket and slowly pushed open the door. Bethany lay in her bed under the covers, her steady quiet breathing interrupted by the occasional snore. Amara looked around the room, her eyes adjusting to the shadows, and noticed her roommate's usual dark hair was flaming red and short. Amara squinted her eyes, taking in the large mound under the blankets.

"Hey," a deep voice mumbled. Someone sat upright in Bethany's bed. Amara's throat constricted, and her heart pounded. She flipped the light on and saw a messy Ronnie Mac shirtless under Bethany's blankets.

Ronnie lived in their dorm on a different floor. His thick red hair and pale freckled face stared at Amara. "Ronnie." Amara shrieked. "Get out of my room!"

"Amara? Where's Bethany?" He stumbled out of bed and the scent of weed mixed with beer seeped out of him. He grabbed the crumpled throw blanket from the corner of the bed and wrapped it around his waist, looking for his pants.

"Ronnie, get out!" Amara eyed his jeans wedged between the corner of the bed and the closet and threw them to him. "Where is Bethany?" she hollered, not caring if the other girls on her floor woke up.

He dropped the sheet, and Amara turned, shielding her eyes.

She felt him breathing against the back of her neck, his sour breath climbing up her nostrils. She hid a gag and froze. When she heard the door click closed, she released her breath and ran out into the hallway. Ronnie was gone, and the hallway was empty.

A group of girls hanging around the common room looked over. Panic settled in Amara's chest as she searched for Bethany. "Hey, Claire, have you seen Bethany?" Amara asked the blond girl, studying in the corner.

"Yeah, I think she's in Ruby's room. I saw her a few minutes ago." Claire stood up and followed Amara.

Amara crept down the hall and debated whether she should knock on Ruby's door. She didn't know Ruby well, but Ruby and Bethany had many classes together. Amara leaned her ear up to the door and heard music beating on the other side. She knocked loudly. "Beth?"

A petite girl with spiky hair opened the door, her green eyes greeting Amara. "Hey." She pushed the door the rest of the way open and pulled Amara's arm. Claire followed and sat on Ruby's roommate's bed. Bethany sat huddled on Ruby's bed with Sharice and Maxine beside her. *It feels like we're in a sorority meeting.*

"Amara." Bethany jumped up and hugged her roommate. "You didn't go to our room, did you?"

Amara nodded. "What the hell, Bethany? Why was Ronnie Mac in our room? He was naked under your covers." Amara scrunched her

4

face, and all the girls in the room shrieked in repugnance.

"I'm so sorry. He showed up at our room, completely wasted. He asked if I had any extra water bottles. I walked over to the fridge, and when I turned around, he was sitting on my bed. He kicked his shoes off, told me he was hot, and pulled off his sweatshirt."

Amara bulged her eyes and cringed.

"He said he was locked out of his room and didn't want to wake the RA. He asked to stay for a while. He's such a dork. I thought he was harmless, and I had to study anyway. I threw him the TV remote and sat at the computer, studying. The next thing I knew, he was under my covers and fast asleep. It totally freaked me out. I've never had a random guy in my bed before. I tried to wake him, and he tried to kiss me."

The gaggle of girls snickered.

"Gross," Maxine said.

"I wonder if he remembers," Sharice added.

"He grabbed my arm and pulled me onto the bed. I didn't know what to do, so I ran out. But he had a shirt on when I left!" Bethany covered her face with her hands.

The girls erupted in laughter.

"Well, he was naked. In your bed. You need to burn those sheets," Claire said.

"Like yesterday," Maxine added.

"He's gone now," Amara said. "Our room smells like pot and beer. It needs a good cleaning."

"Can we crash here?" Bethany asked Ruby. "I don't want to go in there right now."

The girls crashed on Ruby's floor that night, sharing an air mattress in between the two extra-long twin beds.

Amara barely made it to her test on time the following day, and she knew she did poorly. Her father was going to kill her. He wanted her to go to a state college in Connecticut where the cost of tuition was a fraction of the cost of this private school in Rhode Island, but Amara begged, pleaded, and negotiated.

Her parents, George and Katerina, didn't have extra money, so they agreed if Amara paid tuition, room, and board, they would pay for whatever other necessities she needed. They transferred a few hundred dollars into her account every month and paid for her books. Amara didn't care that she was fifty thousand dollars in student loan debt, and she didn't understand how that sort of payment would follow her for the next thirty years.

Her mom always snuck extra money into Amara's account. "You should always have money that your husband doesn't know about," she advised Amara. "This is our little secret. When you're married, you'll understand." Amara didn't ask questions. She was grateful for the extra spending money to experience true college life.

"Remember, Amaryllis, if your grades slip, you'll be back here at the bakery," her father warned. Amara cringed at the idea of returning home to do-nothing Connecticut. She knew her parents believed her grades were the one thing that extrapolated to becoming a successful adult, and Ronnie almost ruined it.

Ronnie was always around, lurking in the corner of the dining hall or hiding behind his baseball hat in the common area. Amara knew Bethany was a grown-up who could handle her own life, but she didn't want Bethany to experience another compromising situation. Bethany needed to learn how to say no. She was too kind and should never have let him in their room alone.

Amara marched down to the RA's office and submitted an incident report. She explained she found a naked boy in her room when she returned home and it made her and Bethany uncomfortable because he lived close to them. As a result, they couldn't sleep in their room, and Amara's grades suffered because of him.

Two weeks later, Ronnie Mac had moved to a boys-only dorm. No one else ever knew why. Not even Bethany.

Amara scrunched her hair one last time, stood up, and grabbed her purse. "You ready?"

Bethany threw on her jean jacket and hooked her arm through Amara's. "Let's go, sis."

"All the frat boys better watch out! This twosome is a force to be reckoned with."

At the party, Amara, Bethany, and Ruby danced on the dance floor. Amara's heart pumped and beads of sweat formed along her hairline. For mid-June, the excessive humidity still hung in the air. Something hit Amara's shoulder and she lurched forward from the unexpected force.

She pushed her eyebrows together and spun around on one boot. He swayed to the music, and didn't appear to understand that he barreled into their circle. "Hey," she hollered over the music.

Bethany stood next to Amara. "You bumped into my friend," she yelled into his ear.

"Sorry." He swayed with the music. "My name's Ryan," he yelled back to Bethany. He ignored Amara. They danced as one group and Amara eyed Bethany and Ryan chatting and laughing.

A group of guys stumbled behind Ryan and clumsily danced into him. "Oof," Ryan said, not expecting the hit. His red solo cup tipped forward and warm beer splashed everywhere.

Wetness spread over and down Amara's top, coating her skin with a sticky film. She barely looked down and saw her nipples penetrating through the thin cloth.

"What did you do?" she shrieked, shaking the excess liquid off her hands.

Ryan leaned into her ear and she smelled a mix of hard liquor and beer. "Sorry. My friend pushed me." He shrugged as if to say it was no big deal.

Amara grabbed Bethany and Ruby's hand and stalked to the bathroom. "What do I do?" Amara asked. I'm covered."

Bethany ran upstairs and returned with a clean tank top. "It's my sister's. I'm sure she won't mind."

Grateful for her friend's loyalty and willingness to steal Mikayla's clothes for the night, Amara hugged Bethany. "Thank you, you're a lifesaver."

Bethany grinned and pushed her curly hair out of her eyes. "You would do it for me."

Amara swapped shirts and adjusted the white tank top. "It's too big."

"It's fine," Ruby said. "You're clean, you don't smell, and you look great, even if you wear a paper bag. Who cares? You only live once. Let's go out there and dance."

They exited the bathroom toward the lights and music.

"What do you guys think about Ryan? He's kind of cute," Bethany called to the girls as they pushed through the crowd.

Ruby smirked and bobbed with the music. *Is she nodding?* Amara rolled her eyes up to the sky.

Amara hesitated. "Ask me tomorrow." She was angry that she had spent so much time getting ready and within minutes, her outfit was ruined. Now she was stuck with a plain tank top that was tad too big and totally not her style.

Bethany winked and danced through the crowd holding her cup above her head.

Little did Amara know, her world tilted and teetered on the edge of collapse that night when a young, mousy man named Ryan Rainey met Bethany White. It took eight months for Hurricane Ryan to destroy Amara's home and everything that made her happy.

This is where Amara's story begins.

Chapter 2

Eight Months Later

Amara looked around the banquet room, eyes darting from corner to corner and top to bottom. All twenty-five pink and black balloons glided above the bistro chair at the head of the table. A balloon arch securely outlined the entrance. Twenty-five of Bethany's closest friends, plus family, milled around the open bar, sipping fancy drinks in fancy cups. The waitstaff roamed around carrying trays high above their heads. Tiny hot dogs, shrimp, and bacon-wrapped scallops danced around her, scissoring her line of vision.

Amara's body swayed to one side, pushed by a tall man she didn't recognize. "Oh," she exclaimed and stepped out of his way.

"Sorry. I wasn't paying attention." His lips pulled up into a welcoming smile and his blue eyes flashed under the fluorescent lights.

His smile was warm and bright, and his teeth could have illuminated the way in a power outage. Long blonde hair fell over his right eye, curving out at the end like a cresting wave.

She took a breath and rolled her eyes at his clumsiness. *How did he not see me?* "I'm Amara," she said, holding out her hand. "And you are?"

"Tyler. I'm Ryan's brother. Step-brother. I guess we're technically brothers," Tyler rambled.

Amara knew all of Bethany's friends and most of Ryan's family. "I didn't realize Ryan had a brother," she said, slowly sipping her drink. Her fuchsia lipstick rimmed the straw, forming two perfectly wrapped lips.

"Yeah, we aren't very close. I moved out when he was thirteen."

Amara did the math in her head quickly. If he moved out at eighteen, he was five years older than Ryan, making him a few years older than her. She glanced at his hand. No ring.

"I'm Bethany's best friend and roommate. Amara Leventis. I organized this party." She politely shook his hand, his grip wrapping around hers while her hand hung like a limp, wet rag. She rubbed her hands down her hips, smoothing out her black pencil skirt.

Ryan's mother approached Tyler from behind. "Tyler?" Her meek voice barely cut through the music. Amara saw him cringe and tighten his shoulders before he turned.

"Hi, Mona," he said with a wide grin.

"Can you help your father? He's trying to get the gifts out of the car, and we have quite a few."

"Oh," Amara interjected, "please put those on the table next to the bar. We don't want Bethany to see the gifts until after she walks in."

Amara planned the surprise birthday party down to the second and knew Bethany would be shocked. Amara imagined Bethany, hands up against her face, her mouth in an oval shape, which quickly transformed into a giddy laugh and grin. Bethany would grab Amara by the hands and swing her around in excitement. The music would kick on, and the entire room would dance.

Ryan's mother gave Amara a big hug, zapping her out of her fantasy. "Thanks for organizing this party. Everything looks beautiful."

Amara grinned, pride billowing out her ears, as she soaked up the compliment. "Thank you, Mrs. Rainey. I hope she's surprised." She watched Mrs. Rainey walk toward the open bar, probably to get a cocktail.

Amara checked her watch, wondering when Ryan and Bethany would arrive. They weren't officially late, but Amara started to feel jittery. Her heart rate quickened, her fingers found their way to her mouth, and she began pacing the room. Bethany was always late, and it made Amara's blood pressure rise. She scanned the room and took inventory of the guests. A handful of sorority sisters danced in the middle of the room on the small, perfectly square dance floor. A group of guys hovered at the bar, eating peanuts. A cluster of cousins sat along the edges of the dance floor among the round, metal bistro tables, and Bethany's fellow nurses mingled near the coatroom. It appeared that everyone was having a good time.

Amara pulled out her phone and texted Bethany. **Hi! The restaurant is filling fast. Will you be here soon or should I order without you?**

Within a few moments, Amara's phone buzzed. It was Ryan. **Outside. Be there in a minute.**

Amara dropped the phone and clapped her hands loudly. Her tall, five-foot-eight-inch frame commanded attention. She climbed up on a chair to rise above the crowd. Her heart pumped against her blouse. "Excuse me! Everyone! Everyone!" She fumbled through her phone, shutting off the music app to silence the room. "Quiet," she hissed, "they're here."

A chaotic hush fell over the room. Someone dimmed the lights, and everyone turned to look at her. "They're here." Amara whisper-screamed. "Shh!"

Amara hopped down from the chair and ran to the front of the group, her three-inch heels clicking on the wooden floor. She smoothed her jet-black hair, brushed her bangs back, and smiled in anticipation.

The door opened, and Bethany and Ryan entered, facing the crowd. A chorus of "Surprise!" echoed around the small room. Amara gave Bethany a giant hug, wrapped her skinny arms around Bethany's shoulders, and said, "Happy birthday."

Bethany looked at Ryan and then Amara. "I can't believe you did this," she exclaimed, hopping from foot to foot.

"It was all Amara," Ryan said.

Amara beamed. "You only turn twenty-five once." She pulled out her phone, snapped a selfie with Bethany, and turned up the music.

Bethany made her way into the room, greeting family and friends, barely having time to take her coat off or put her pocketbook down at the small table with the bouquet of balloons.

Amara smiled to herself for pulling off a surprise party of this magnitude. She meandered to the bar and ordered a martini. Something sophisticated and professional, but also fun. "Extra dirty martini," she said to the bartender, dropping a ten-dollar bill in the tip jar.

The rest of the night was easy. Dancing, drinks, and a light dinner made the evening fly by like a lightning flash. Amara's job was to make sure Bethany had a great time, but she didn't want to hang over her. She was her roommate, not her mother, and there were many people Bethany needed to see.

Before dinner, Ryan stood at the front of the room, tapping his champagne glass with a fork. The deafening sound silenced the crowd immediately. *Darn. Why didn't I think of that?* She grimaced at him, annoyed that she had to climb the walls to get everyone's attention, and he barely had to lift a finger.

"I have an announcement," he said to the group. Out of the corner of her eye, Amara caught his mother sitting forward, with her full attention on Ryan. Mrs. Rainey's leg shook and a massive smile spread across her face, reminding Amara of a circus clown. Amara tweaked her eyebrows and turned her head sideways. He never told her he was

12

going to make a speech. She returned her attention to the front of the room.

Ryan pulled Bethany up next to him and grabbed her hand. "Bethany White, you are the light of my life. I have loved you from the first day I saw you, and I never want to spend another moment without you."

It all happened in slow motion, but Amara knew what was happening, and she couldn't stop it. She yelled at herself for not seeing the signs. As much as she wanted to walk away, she couldn't. But it didn't matter anyway. She knew Bethany better than anyone. She knew her insecurities, fears, and what motivated her and made her happy. Truly happy. She and Ryan had been together less than a year. Amara couldn't imagine Bethany saying yes. Bethany was too spontaneous and independent to commit to a man at such a young age. She didn't want to be tied down to a man. At least, not yet.

Ryan dropped to one knee and reached into his shirt pocket. Amara saw the outline of a ring box and again wondered how she missed the signs. "Bethany, will you marry me?"

The room chattered with excitement, waiting for her response. Mikayla crept closer to the front where Ruby and Claire stood. The three girls watched in anticipation. Mikayla bounced on her toes, Claire's eyes sparkled, and Ruby pulled at her necklace. Amara crossed her arms and waited.

How did he afford an engagement ring? His salary as a real estate agent certainly couldn't afford such luxury. Amara loved the ring, even from this far, and knew Bethany would be dazzled by its extravagance. Bethany once told Amara she dreamed of an emerald cut engagement ring. From this view, she shared that info with Ryan and he got her exactly what she wanted.

Bethany stood frozen. *This is the moment*, Amara thought, smugly. *She's going to turn him down in front of all these people, and he's going to feel like an idiot.* Had he gone to Amara before the big moment, she would have talked some sense into him.

"YES!" Bethany's words flew out of her body and ricocheted off the walls. Her arms wrapped around him, and her lips smashed into his.

A giant rock, as massive as the sparkling ring, formed in Amara's throat as she watched this life-changing event unfold in real-time. Except it didn't feel like real-time, and it reminded her of a cheesy movie from her adolescence where everything was a cliché happy ending.

Everyone in the room clapped and cheered, and Amara stiffly followed suit. Her hands mechanically clapped at a slower speed and she busied herself with the refreshments. She smiled with excitement like the rest of them.

Bethany made her way around the group, accepting congratulations from those who desperately wanted to see her ring. By the time she got to Amara, Amara was already two drinks deep. The room started to get fuzzy, and she felt relaxed. "Congrats." Amara kissed Bethany on the cheek, hoping her voice carried enthusiasm and authenticity despite her growing disappointment.

Bethany flashed her rock to Amara, and upon closer look, Amara loved it even more. With tiny movements, the colored prism danced across the walls.

"You look radiant," Amara said. Bethany practically glowed, and Amara couldn't help but feel happiness for her friend.

"Thank you for throwing this party," Bethany gushed. "The people, the food, the balloons, the drinks…everything has been incredible. You always throw the best parties, Amara. This is your calling."

Amara raised her glass and didn't say a word. *My calling, huh?* She thought banking was her calling. Anything involving money was something Amara enjoyed. She got a thrill when she counted the till and all the numbers matched.

"Congrats again. I can't wait to hear about your night." She felt the drinks quiet her voice even though her brain kept moving like a freight train.

"Oh," Bethany said. "Speaking of the night. Ryan and I are going away for the rest of the weekend. Not far, just down to the beach for a romantic getaway. I'll see you Sunday, and we can catch up."

Amara's heart sank. She had been present for every other significant moment in Bethany's life since college. Amara slumped down in her chair, feeling forgotten and pushed aside. Amara realized Bethany needed to travel through this milestone without her. Despite the overhanging melancholy, Amara smiled and responded, "I can't wait to hear all about it."

Bethany hugged Amara one last time and moved around the room to say her good-byes. Amara settled at a table alone, sipping her martini. Gloom wrapped its lengthy, slender fingers around her. Bethany and Ryan disappeared, and the room eventually emptied. Amara was alone with Tyler and the waitstaff.

"You don't have to stay," she said to Tyler. "It's late." It was almost midnight, which wasn't late at all, but she didn't have the energy to talk to anyone, let alone a stranger.

"I don't mind. I'd like to make sure you get home safely."

Amara rolled her eyes. "I'm taking an Uber." She stumbled backward on her feet and grabbed the chair back to steady herself.

"I can drive you." Tyler's straw-colored hair brushed against his manicured eyebrows, and Amara wondered if they were natural.

"I'm good," Amara replied.

"Fine. But I will follow your Uber to make sure you get home safely."

Amara rolled her eyes at him. "Have you been drinking?" she joked.

"Nope. I don't drink. I would like to drive you home, if that's okay."

"Fine." Amara felt his judgment but didn't have the energy to fight with him or defend herself. "You can drive me home. But no monkey business." She wagged her finger at him, accidentally knocking the tip

15

of his nose. She giggled and walked away.

After sorting the balance with the restaurant, Amara and Tyler packed up the decorations, and filled a doggie bag with leftover food. She grabbed her purse and told Tyler she was ready to go. She climbed into his car and navigated him to her Providence apartment.

"Thank you for the ride," she said politely. "It was nice meeting you." Amara climbed out of the car, gathering all her energy, and slammed the door with a thud. The door sprung open from hitting the seat belt resting in the door frame. "Sorry," she said and tried again.

She dug through her bag, fumbling to find her keys, as Tyler waited and watched her. *Where are they?* Frustration grew, and Amara wondered how this night turned so sour. She threw her bag on the stoop, sat down, and emptied everything. She didn't care that she had an audience. Her eyes filled with tears, feeling hopeless because she couldn't even get into her apartment without help.

Tyler opened his car door, and Amara hollered, "I'm good," before he could offer his assistance. She stood up and waved her house keys at him. Even though she was unable to see him in the dark, she felt him watching her as she reloaded her purse, one item at a time.

A few minutes later, she found herself stumbling up the steps. The bright lights blinded her as she made her way up the two flights of stairs to their apartment. Amara kicked off her shoes, leaned against the door, and slowly stripped off her clothes.

The next thing she remembered, it was morning, and she woke up alone.

That night, Amara sat in front of the television eating Chinese food. She texted Bethany a handful of times to remind her that she was waiting for her return, but there was never any response. Amara didn't know where they were or when they'd come home, and she hated being alone. The cozy apartment was too quiet.

The girls lived on the third floor of an old three-family home in

Providence's College Hill neighborhood. Greek Revival, Colonial, and Victorian homes dotted their neighborhood, and they were a short walk to trendy restaurants and shops. The day they moved in, they found a variety of restaurant menus wedged under the door and confiscated them for their own eating pleasure. They had take-out every night that week, identifying their favorite restaurants.

The Chinese place Amara ordered from that night was in her phone book and the restaurant owners knew her by name. Amara devoured the General Tso Chicken and savored the pork fried rice. She grabbed the one and only fortune cookie and cracked it open. Usually, Amara gave her cookie shell to Bethany while Amara analyzed the fortunes and picked the best one for her current circumstances. This time, Amara didn't have a choice. Even the fast-food place knew she was alone. "Some men dream of fortunes, others dream of cookies," she read out loud.

Amara sighed, placed the cookie on the table, and tucked the fortune into her wallet. She had no idea what it meant. She checked her phone and pulled a crocheted blanket up over her exposed shoulders. If her mother were there, she would have told her to put some clothes on, but she liked her silky shorts and camisole because it made her feel like an adult. Paired with the bottle of wine chilling in the refrigerator, she was all about adulting tonight. Alone.

Amara couldn't believe Bethany was getting married. She and Ryan barely knew each other. Bethany could love him, but Amara was doubtful. Bethany and Amara had dreamed about their weddings, but they also dreamed about traveling the world together. Amara knew that Bethany would never explore Europe or vacation in the Caribbean with her. She would fall into the marriage trap. They'd buy a house, have kids, and Amara would never see her best friend again.

Amara looked around their apartment, shuddering at the thought of moving. Or worse. Getting a new roommate. She and Bethany were supposed to be best friends until the end. They were two girls, two musketeers, and two sisters. Not two girls and a husband, or two musketeers and a horse, or two sisters and a neighbor. Ryan had no place in their story.

Amara almost wondered if Bethany was breaking it off with Ryan that weekend. It made sense. Bethany didn't want to hurt his feelings at the party, with his entire family there. But now that they were alone, she could quietly break it off without making a scene.

Amara imagined Bethany removing her ring and gently placing it in the middle of the table in whatever fancy restaurant he took her to. The waiter would stand, watching them keenly, knowing all too well that breakups often happened in his restaurant. The ring would go down and Bethany would stand up and say dramatically, "I'm not in love with you." She would assertively exit the restaurant with everyone staring in awe. *How did she have that much confidence?* they would wonder. Awe would turn to sadness and compassion toward Ryan, and they would become angry at Bethany for breaking his heart.

Amara shook her head. No, they could never get mad at Bethany. Amara continued her fantasy. Bethany would rush home, throw open the door, and say, "Amara, my roommate. Thank you for all you do. I'll never forget how much time, effort, and money you threw into that beautiful party. Even though Ryan messed it up, I still loved it. Thank you," and they would clink glasses in celebration of things staying the same.

Amara took a sip of wine, snapped back to reality, and zoned out with the television. *What a boring night.*

The following day was Sunday, and the looming dread of Monday seeped into her skin like condensation on the bathroom mirror, making her bones feel heavy. For a moment, Amara forgot Bethany was gone. She made her usual six cups of coffee, and wondered if she could drink the entire pot. She refused to dwell on Bethany's weekend or Bethany's plans. Instead, she got dressed and went shopping.

The mall wasn't too crowded for a Sunday, and parking and traffic were easy. Amara found herself in Nordstrom, gliding through the racks searching for something, but she couldn't figure out what. She pulled fall coats, sweaters, and accessories off the racks and headed toward the dressing room to pass the time. Without thinking, she approached the register holding her wallet to pay.

By the time she got home, there was a light airiness to the apartment. All the curtains were open, and sunlight illuminated patchwork squares against the wooden floor. Amara smiled and briskly shed her shoes at the door. She quickened her pace to the kitchen until she heard soft chatter with occasional kiss smacks breaking up Bethany's sentences. Amara squished her eyebrows, realizing that she wasn't alone with her roommate. Ryan was here too.

She cleared her throat and gently slammed the door, trying not to make her agitation known.

"Hi," Amara exclaimed as she rounded the corner into the kitchen. "You're home." She gave Bethany and Ryan a welcoming hug. "How was your weekend?" *Probably late nights full of champagne, sex, and sleep.* Amara couldn't remember the last time she had that trio combination. Maybe never.

Bethany and Ryan's face glowed. They spoke over each other, giggling at the memories, but Amara couldn't follow. She studied them and pretended to listen.

Bethany's windswept hair gently pulled away from her face, accentuating her almond-shaped eyes and full, pouty lips. The angle of her lower jaw pronounced itself above the sheer infinity scarf. Ryan's cropped, tousled, hazelnut hair sat inches above his head, and Amara wondered if that style was intentional. He looked like a baby at just twenty-two years old, the angles of his face not yet fully developed. His blue eyes crinkled shut from smiling too hard.

"Amazing," Bethany said.

"So much fun," Ryan agreed.

"It was just what we needed."

They spoke to each other more than to Amara. Their eyes locked into each other, zoning out any background distractions. Amara nodded and walked through them to get to the sink. She filled a glass of water and flipped through the mail.

For a moment, the silent kitchen accentuated the hum of the running dishwasher. It created a rhythmic back-and-forth noise, like Amara's heartbeat. Amara waited for more. More excitement, stories, and laughter, but nothing came. Bethany and Ryan continued to gaze longingly at each other, communicating a foreign language with their facial expressions. Amara wasn't fluent in their language and she felt like a stranger in her own home.

"Great," Amara said, placing her glass in the sink. She cut through their trance on her way out of the kitchen and picked up her keys. "I'm running out," she called through the closed door. Pleasant chatter, laughter, and lip-smacking responded.

Amara didn't know where to go. She spent the day shopping, and had to work tomorrow. She drove without any clear destination and ended up at the state park overlooking the ocean. The lapping waves and never-ending water always calmed her when she felt out of control. She needed to erase the roller coaster of emotions she rode that weekend. She needed to get off the ride.

Amara sat on the rocks and stared out into the gentle lapping water. A wave of emotions crashed over her: anger, annoyance, sadness, and uncertainty. She didn't know what was going to happen. *What will I do if Bethany moves out?* She had never lived with anyone else and didn't want to at this point in her life. *Can I afford to stay in Providence without a roommate?*

Besides Bethany, she didn't have a lot of friends. Her parents always taught her that it was better to be strong and alone than weak and surrounded by people. Her father was especially strict and his expectations were high. If Amara's grades had slipped in school or with her activities, the first thing he would remove was access to her friends. He often used their bakery as punishment, forcing her to clean the shop. Those experiences taught her that if she stayed close to a few people who truly understood her, she wouldn't feel embarrassment or shame when things went wrong.

Amara thought she had it all together, and she did, as long as everyone else played their roles. Ryan interfered with her plan for the foreseeable future.

Looking out into the water, someone familiar walked on the beach. She squinted her eyes into the setting sun. She tried to place his build and walk but her mind drew a blank. His shaggy hair swayed in the wind, and his broad shoulders slightly hunched forward with his sight in the sand, like he was looking for something.

He was alone, as far as Amara could tell. She hopped off the rock and crept closer, trying to get a better look without being obvious. Too late. He turned in her direction as she approached, and she immediately recognized the wide, toothy grin.

"Amara?" His arm shot up and slowed down like he couldn't decide if he was going to salute or wave.

She smiled. "Tyler." She hopped through the sand, her flip-flops digging below the surface with every step.

Flashbacks from the party, the engagement, the alcohol, and the ride home zipped through her mind. She prayed she hadn't said anything stupid that night.

"How are you?" he asked.

"Good, good. Just killing time. I like to come here and clear my thoughts," Amara said.

"Same. I had to get away from my dad and Mona for a bit, so I left them to explore Providence alone."

"Where do you live again?" Amara didn't know if he had told her, but she pretended that she forgot.

"Boston area."

Amara chuckled, admiring his dimples. "Thanks for the ride home the other night," she said, digging her toe into the sand.

"Of course. I assume you got in safely?"

She nodded.

"Did Bethany and Ryan get back? I want to say goodbye to him before I go, but he hasn't returned my messages."

"Yeah," Amara said. "They got back a few hours ago. Do you want to come over tonight for dinner? I don't know what their plans are, but we can see if they're free."

He grinned and stroked his chin. "Yeah, that'd be great."

They walked the beach easily, skipping stones and talking, before Amara realized hours had flown by. She felt at ease with Tyler, but she didn't know why. It must have been that laid-back Boston vibe.

Tyler's lean, athletic build towered over most women, but Amara's tall frame challenged his authority. When she looked at him, her eyes rested against the bridge of his nose. His full lips and warm eyes invaded her periphery. Her belly tingled under his gaze.

"Where did you grow up?"

"California. That's where my mom is."

Amara didn't know where Ryan grew up. She found it strange that she knew so little about him but reminded herself she only knew him for eight months. An entire life story doesn't typically unfold for years.

"I'd love to go to California," Amara said.

"It's beautiful. I want to go back one day." Tyler smoothed his bangs, brushing them to the side.

"Even with all the fires and earthquakes?"

"Beauty overpowers tragedy, don't you think?"

So much meaning stood behind those six words. Amara stood silent, thinking about tragedies she had experienced in her life, and considered all the beautiful things that came because of it. Her best friend, Jada, died in a car crash when they were sixteen. It was a beautiful fall day but she took the turn quickly and lost control. Amara's heart shattered that day. She had considered Jada her soulmate and the reason she got through adolescence alive. After Jada died, Amara learned to only trust herself until she met Bethany. Bethany showed her how to love life again.

"What tragedies have you experienced?" Amara asked.

"Too many to count," Tyler vaguely responded. He looked out into the ocean, avoiding eye contact.

Amara let the silence simmer between them. She wanted to know more but her inner voice debated if he would open up to her this soon. She barely knew him, but she was intrigued.

A chill shook Amara's shoulders, reminding her she should have brought a coat. Tyler removed his sweatshirt and handed it to Amara. "Here. You need this more than I do. I run hot."

"Thank you." The sweatshirt smelled like sandalwood and shampoo and practically hung to her knees. The two of them sat on the beach in silence. Amara thought about Jada and now Bethany, and wondered if she was destined to be alone or if she would ever be able to open her heart again.

Chapter 3

꩜

S ummer transitioned to fall, and Amara and Bethany behaved
more like roommates and less like best friends. Amara patiently
waited for Bethany to share details about her engagement
because that's the information friends shared, but details never
emerged. Whenever Amara broached the subject, Bethany floated
around the apartment providing vague responses, such as, "I can't
wait," or "I can't believe I'm getting married."

Bethany and Amara saw each other less and less, but Amara figured it
was because of work. Amara had been promoted to loan officer at the
bank, which meant more hours and abundant training. Although her
workdays couldn't extend beyond eight hours, Amara found herself
playing catch up on the weekends.

Bethany worked in the emergency department at a local hospital,
and fall seemed to be when she picked up extra hours. The emergency
room flocked with college kids making stupid decisions. Bethany's
and Amara's paths barely crossed. When they did, Amara tried to make
the moments as pleasant as possible.

"Hey, Amara?" Bethany rummaged in the fridge. She emerged with
a chilled bottle of white wine and held it up. "Wine?"

Amara nodded, even though she had to get up early the following day.

"I have to talk to you," Bethany said.

Amara busied herself on her phone, scrolling up and down.

"It's important," Bethany said, placing a glass in front of Amara.

Amara put her phone face down on the table, signaling that Bethany had her full attention. "What's up?"

Bethany sat in front of Amara, her hands clasped and resting gingerly on the table. "I have news. Good news, and bad news."

Amara smiled nervously, not knowing where this was going. Images of Ryan and the ring popped into her head. Amara thought if they never talked about the wedding, it wouldn't happen, but now she was faced with mounting worry. She sat back in the armchair, dreading the words Bethany was about to spout.

"What do you want first?" Bethany asked, her pitch flying high in excitement. "Good or bad?"

Amara shrugged her shoulders, her long black hair swooshing to the side. "The good." She pretended to be interested but fear settled in her ears like a foggy summer morning.

"Well," Bethany started, twirling her engagement ring around her finger from the front to the back to the front again. "Ryan and I picked a date. We're getting married on June twentieth." Bethany clapped her hands and jumped in her seat, so Amara copied her movements.

"Awesome," Amara exclaimed. In her head, she counted the months. It was approximately nine months away. Amara gulped her wine.

"And we want you to be part of our wedding. You've been my best friend since we were eighteen. We've been through it all. Drunken nights, random hook-ups, bitchy girls, all-nighters, frat parties, finding our first jobs, graduating…through all the good and the bad, you've been there by my side. I can't imagine my wedding without you. Will you be my maid of honor?"

Amara pretended Bethany proposed. She smiled in delight, jumped up from the chair, and gave Bethany a tight hug. "Yes, I would love that." The metaphorical ring glistened on her finger.

Amara smiled, pride and enthusiasm bubbling up inside her. She knew she could make this wedding unforgettable. *Bethany's so lucky I'm her maid of honor. This wedding is going to be the party of a lifetime.*

"This is for you. For always being a friend." Bethany pushed forward a small gift box that sat on the coffee table. *When did that get there?*

Amara delicately opened the wrapping, pulling off the thin bow first, careful not to rip the paper at the creases. Inside was a beautiful starfish necklace. It shimmered in the light, the silver and crystals glistening. "This is gorgeous," Amara gushed.

"All the bling made me think of you. Thank you for being my maid of honor. Thank you for being a friend. I can't wait to celebrate with you."

Both girls squealed and hugged. Amara put on the delicate necklace and admired her tone physique in the full-length mirror. The starfish pendant rested above the notch of her collarbone, drawing attention to her firm, voluptuous breasts. "I love it. I can't wait. So, tell me about the wedding plans." Amara laughed and smiled with exhilaration, hoping Bethany couldn't see the jealousy creep behind her eyes.

"You won't believe this, but we're having a destination wedding."

"Really? Where?" *I could use a vacation. I hope it's somewhere warm.*

"We haven't decided yet, but are thinking about Jamaica. I've never been, and I've always wanted to go."

Amara's mouth dropped. She knew Bethany had always wanted to go there because they dreamed about going together.

"Is this a big wedding? I can't imagine it's going to be cheap." Dollar signs floated above Amara's head and her excitement turned to disappointment. She was broke, and as much as she would love a trip to Jamaica, she might have to work three jobs to afford it.

"Small wedding. We were thinking a total of twenty-five. I'm inviting my parents, sister, and you, of course. Those are the only people I care about being present. I'll tell others if they need an excuse to go on vacation, but I'm not paying for their stay or their meals or anything."

"Wait, you're paying? For everyone?"

"Yeah, Ryan's parents agreed to pay for the wedding party and immediate family if we kept it small."

Amara's head felt dizzy, and she took another sip of wine. She didn't know this Ryan character at all. *How are they paying for the wedding?* The numbers were astronomical. *If they have enough money to pay for a wedding in another country, why didn't Ryan have his own place?* It didn't make sense.

"That's great." Amara pictured herself lying on the beach, the hot sun beating down on her Greek body. Her long, slender legs would tan under the rays, and her feet would dig under the white, hot sand. Her polka-dot bikini would make her feel like a sexy vixen. A cabana boy would stroll over with a tray. His dark body would radiate warmth, and his blue eyes would penetrate Amara's soul. He would offer her a drink and slip a napkin with his phone number under her glass. They would meet up late at night and make out in the ocean.

A quick rap on the door pulled Amara out of her fantasy. "Come in," Bethany called.

The door opened, and Ryan appeared, holding two bouquets. He handed the larger one to Bethany and said, "This is for you, for being you." He gave the smaller one to Amara. "This is for you, for being a friend to my beautiful fiancée."

Sweetness coated him like a lollipop, and Amara cringed. Something about him caused a stop sign to flash in her mind, but she couldn't quite place why. "Thank you," she said, taking the flowers into the kitchen.

When she returned to the living room, Ryan and Bethany were

making out on the couch. Amara rolled her eyes and 'ahem'ed loudly. They separated like cockroaches when the lights flicked on.

"Ryan, Bethany told me about the wedding plans. Jamaica, huh? That sounds beautiful." She kept her tone even.

"Yeah, my family owns a timeshare down there and we can rent out additional suites for the guests."

Things started to click in place. Maybe he wasn't rich.

"Oh, and the bad news, for us." Bethany pointed to Amara and herself and then grabbed Ryan's hand. "I don't know how to say this because you're going to hate me." She looked at her feet.

"I would never hate you. What's up?" Concern rose in Amara's voice.

"Ryan and I are moving in together in January." Bethany's shoulders tightened and Ryan pulled her close into his chest.

Amara chuckled louder than she intended, and Bethany's cheeks flushed. *Ryan lives with his parents. He just graduated from college and is practically a baby. What is Bethany going to do? Move into his parent's basement?* "Sorry, I don't mean to laugh, but how are you going to move into Ryan's? He doesn't even have a place." She tried to keep her voice steady, but she felt like she was talking sense to a three-year-old.

"Right, but he will. Our lease is up on January first and I'm not renewing my portion."

Amara's heart stopped beating, and she sat frozen in her chair. The worst possible news floated between them, making breathing difficult for Amara. She never thought about this scenario, but why wouldn't Bethany and Ryan get a place before the wedding?

"You're really moving out?"

"I have to." Bethany's voice took on a song quality like she was lulling a fussy baby to sleep. "I'm getting married, and I can't live with you for the rest of my life."

"But what am I going to do?" Amara asked, tornado alarms sounding in her ears. "I can't afford this place on my own."

"Excuse us, Ryan," Bethany said, kissing her fiancé on the lips. She guided Amara into the kitchen and closed the door. Amara felt Bethany's eyes pore into her. Bethany lowered her voice to a whisper. "Amara, I asked you a few months ago if Ryan could move in, and you threw a hissy fit. You told me our place was too small for the three of us. What am I supposed to do? I can't afford two rents and I'm giving you three months to figure it out." Bethany paced around the small kitchen. Amara saw frustration grow in Bethany's heaving shoulders and balled up fists.

"I didn't want a stranger living in our house with access to all my personal belongings. Beth, you barely know him." Amara turned on the radio to drown out their conversation. "He could have stolen my credit cards or gone through my room when I wasn't looking. I'm sorry, but I don't know him at all. I don't trust him. There was no way I would say okay to having a strange man move in with us."

"A strange man? He's my fiancé." Bethany's voice rose above the rock music despite Ryan being on the other side of the wall.

"But he wasn't your fiancé five months ago when you asked if he could move in. And he's a fiancé I barely know. I don't even know his birthday." Amara tried to keep her cool but she was reeling from the announcement that her apartment was gone. Amara wanted to stay in Providence but there was no way she could afford this apartment alone. "What am I going to do?"

"Get another roommate? That's what I would do." The sarcasm was not lost on Amara. Bethany's superpower was making friends. She chatted with the cashier at the grocery store, complimenting her earrings, and the next thing Amara knew, the two of them were going out for coffee. Amara had a million friends on social media, but they were all connected through Bethany. Without Bethany to facilitate relationships, Amara wasn't sure she knew how to do it. *Where will I find another roommate?*

Amara scoffed. She was twenty-five years old, and she hadn't lived with anyone except Bethany since she was eighteen. The two girls knew how to live together without getting in each other's way. They had an understanding of the cleaning and cooking schedule. It was a well-oiled machine that never needed a tune-up. Amara couldn't imagine starting over with anyone else.

"I'm not getting another roommate."

"Okay, then don't, but I'm moving out by January first."

Tension rose between them, thick enough to suffocate Amara. Bethany stormed out of the kitchen. "Ryan? Let's go out to dinner tonight."

By the time Amara exited the kitchen, the apartment was empty. The wine in her glass suddenly looked like poison, and she placed the goblet on a coaster. Bethany must have hoped it would manipulate her mood before dropping a bomb on her perfectly planned life. Resentment toward Ryan, a nobody, flowed within Amara, and now she faced a steep mountain of animosity. She had so many opinions but didn't want to jeopardize her relationship with Bethany. Amara cracked her knuckles and rolled her shoulders. She tucked her anger deep inside and counted to five. Her practical side overpowered her emotional side and she recognized her muscles relaxing. *Think, Amara, think.*

Dollar signs danced around Amara's head, taunting her spending habits. Amara knew three months wasn't enough time to save enough money and move. If she renewed the lease alone, she would be evicted by May. It felt like a trap where either decision led Amara to failure. She could never tell her parents she was broke or needed help. Her father would scold her for being irresponsible and her mother would tell her to sell her clothes, shoes, and car, to make ends meet. Amara had just gotten a raise, but it wasn't enough.

If Amara stayed in Providence, she didn't have much time. It was already September, and all the college kids had moved back. January was when the transfers came, and they needed to secure a place by November, at the latest.

Amara doodled on a notebook weighing her options. She scrunched her nose and tilted her head from side to side, unable to see a clear path forward. Bethany breaking the lease was the worst possible scenario.

***

Amara tried to keep herself busy at work, picking up extra hours here and there. It was acceptable to move at a snail's pace because there was a lot of money on the line. Pressure to be precise was always looming over the employees. One mistake counting bills, either coming in or going out, could get you fired.

Amara believed that understanding how money worked would put her on the path of financial independence. She majored in finance and got a banking job to paint the picture of success, but too many designer shoes and lattes left Amara feeling like a fraud. After several years of banking, she still couldn't afford to live alone.

Amara took long strides to the bank's entrance. Her freshly-pressed black slacks creased perfectly down the middle of her leg and her heeled leather boots clicked on the pavement. She waved to the customer service representative standing at the door and dropped her bag in her office. The heavy tote hit the table with a thud, and Amara raced to the other side of her desk, flipping on her computer. Next to her monitor sat a fresh cup of coffee waiting for her to take the first sip.

"Thank you, Mallory," she hollered into the lobby. She saw Mallory through the glass wall separating herself from the tellers. Amara picked up the mug and Mallory waved.

The coffee was perfect, just how Amara loved it. The aroma of hazelnut and sweet cream permeated the air between her four walls. Amara basked in the smell for the next few minutes until the first customer walked in. Then, she was all business.

Amara entered Tania's office. "Hi," her boss said, looking abruptly at

Amara from her pile of papers.

"Hi, what's on the books for today?"

"Well, you have an appointment almost every hour. Summer's over, holidays are coming, and people need money. It's going to be a busy day."

Amara nodded, feeling nothing at the prospect of helping customers. She had worked at Bank of the Ocean State for three years now. The monotony killed her, but for the small amount of work she did daily, the pay was worth it. Consistent hours, consistent income, and a consistent pace allowed her to focus on other things without guilt.

"Oh, and you have new hires coming in at ten today. I left the orientation packets on the conference table. They're here for the day, but you have them for an hour. I need you to go through the human resources section. Valerie's out today, and I don't have time."

Amara wasn't sure she could fill an hour with demonstrating trivial tasks like how to fill out a timesheet, request time off, or set up email, but she nodded. *This is not part of my job description.* Amara walked back to her office and checked her email.

***

That night, Amara came home to an empty house. Long hours, varying pay, and organized chaos seemed to inspire Bethany to pick up extra shifts anytime she could. Somehow, Bethany thrived under those variables.

Amara breathed in the quiet and kicked on the radio, singing softly to herself. She tried not to think about the wedding or the apartment since she heard the big news a week ago. Amara plopped on the couch and grabbed her phone. She called her mother, hoping her peaceful voice would calm her anxiety.

Amara's paternal grandparents, Yia Yia and Papou, were born in Greece and the importance of family had been passed down from generation to generation. Amara recalled fond childhood memories spent at her grandparents' house with all twenty of her cousins. Laughter, music, and food were always present. When her grandparents died, all that family celebration stopped.

For most of Amara's life, she was an only child. She thrived in the spotlight, always yearning for more. When she was thirteen, her mother came home in a discombobulated mess. Her face had been puffy and pink and streaked with tears. She gave Amara cereal for dinner, and placed her in front of the TV. Amara hadn't known her mother was crying but felt the shift under her feet. Something was wrong.

Nothing came of it until Yia-Yia died, and her mother had to squeeze into a black dress for the funeral. Her rotund but firm belly pushed against the fabric until it buckled under the pressure and the button popped off, sailing across the room. Amara gasped, never seeing her mother this large.

Mama had shot Amara a look, silently telling her not to be rude. Her eyebrows arched and her lips created a straight, thin line.

"Mama," Amara cried. "What happened to your belly?"

Amara's father had worn a black suit and shiny loafers, and stood next to his wife. He hugged her close. "Amara, you're going to be a big sister."

Amara's entire world had imploded. Her classmates with baby siblings said it was awful. Their parents no longer had time for them, and they were on their own. Amara imagined dancing in her recital with no one in the audience because the baby was crying. She considered being forgotten at soccer practice because the baby was napping. Or being stuck at home because the baby was sick. It had never happened but being forgotten was always a fear.

The phone picked up on the third ring. "Hi, Amaryllis," Mama sang.

"Hi, Mama. How's it going?" She hoped she sounded happy, but Bethany's news still held Amara's head underwater.

"Good, we're busy. Your father's been at the bakery all day. Our oven broke, and Henry is sick. It's a mess."

Amara easily transitioned the topic to herself. "It's a mess here too. Bethany's moving out in January."

"That's great. Is she moving in with Ryan?" Amara rolled her eyes. Mama always saw the positive side of things. Well, except for that day when she found out she was pregnant.

"Mama, it's not great. What am I going to do?"

"Ah, you'll figure it out. Look at your budget and figure out what you need. A new roommate? Get a new apartment? Or you can move back home. We can use your help."

Amara rolled her eyes. Of course, they needed her help. "I don't know, Mama. I have a lot of figuring out to do." Amara noticed her dry cuticles. She chewed on the outer edge, a bad habit she started when her sister, Daphne, was born.

"Well, are you coming home any time soon?"

Amara thought about Bethany and Ryan, all snuggly on the couch, making her want to vomit or wash the blankets daily. She pictured them in Ryan's juvenile room, his baseball trophies displayed over his twin bed, playing house.

Amara needed to get away, clear her mind, and rid herself of the jealousy Ryan created. "Yeah, how about next weekend?"

A loud clapping sound echoed through the phone. Amara switched her phone to speaker and placed it on her lap. "Great! Daphne has a soccer game in the morning, and she would love to have you there."

Amara rolled her eyes again. At least it would be a change from the city. "Sure thing," she said. "See you then."

Chapter 4

The next weekend, Amara rolled her car through the windy roads of northeast Connecticut. The tiny town of Woodstock sat in the corner between Massachusetts and Rhode Island, a dot on the map, with too many trees and too few people. Amara hated living in Woodstock as a kid. She was the only girl in her school who celebrated Greek traditions, and had parents that didn't speak fluent English. Her background made her sick to her stomach, starting when she fell asleep at night and not stopping until she locked the front door behind her after school. Mixed in with so many blonde and brown-haired kids, she looked like an outcast and felt like an anomaly.

While driving, Amara thought about Jada. She imagined that Jada would tell Amara to rise above all the negativity life recently threw at her. The two girls had met at band camp before freshman year of high school when Amara's anxiety about entering a regional school kept her up at night. Jada had moved to Woodstock from New York City, and carried an urban coolness that no one else in Woodstock held. Her dark skin and braided hair automatically drew Amara toward her.

"Hi," Amara had said as she assembled her clarinet. "Are you new here?" Amara remembered blushing, wishing she could take back the assumption she spoke.

Jada had nodded, pushing together her saxophone. "Yeah, it's my first day. I just moved from New York to live with my aunt." Her deep brown eyes narrowed.

"You don't live with your parents?" Amara wondered what her life would be like if she lived with her mom's sister in Greece.

"I got into too much trouble and my parents thought a smaller town away from all the bad things would be better for me." She air-quoted *bad things* and Amara wondered if she was referring to drugs or boys, or both. Amara had zero experience with either.

"I'm not new here, but I feel like I am. Maybe we can stick together? I love your hair."

Jada smiled and touched the tips of her braids. "Thanks, and sure."

The girls had stuck together during camp, keeping to themselves and ignoring all the stares from their classmates.

Jada's life had run parallel to Amara's in many ways, which provided comfort and strength within their friendship. Jada didn't have a lot of money growing up. Her mother was a teacher and her father was a taxi driver. Jada didn't fit in with the Woodstock kids either, and Amara needed that camaraderie. Finally, Amara had a person she could share her celebrations and worries with, without judgment.

Growing up, Amara's parents barely had enough money to make ends meet. They gave her love and attention but not many material items. They lived in a small apartment in the center of town. Her father worked at a restaurant as a dishwasher. Her mother worked in the school cafeteria, serving Amara and her classmates' frozen pizza and sloppy joes. Amara ignored Mama whenever their eyes met, embarrassed if her classmates acknowledged their kinship.

When Amara's grandmother died, her parents received extra money that allowed them to open the bakery. Up until then, it wasn't unusual for the cable to stop working or a pile of napkins to appear in the bathroom masquerading as toilet paper. Then, Mama got pregnant, and they opened the bakery. It was more out of necessity than passion but it seemed to develop into a passion as Daphne got older.

When Daphne was born, the apartment walls closed in on the too-large family of four. Amara's parents took some of the money intended for the bakery and searched for a bigger apartment. The family now lived on the second floor of an old Victorian house. The house had character, which her parents loved. It had three bedrooms and one and a half bathrooms.

Her parents woke at three in the morning, arrived home by four in the afternoon, and fell asleep by eight in the evening. Now, Daphne was twelve, but behaved like a little grown-up. She figured out how to put herself to sleep and get herself to school on time years ago.

Amara lived too far to help and her parents understood. Now and then, she felt guilty for not being around to help with Daphne or the bakery, but she excused her absence with logistics.

On the familiar drive to Woodstock, warm wind whipped Amara's hair, partially blocking her eyes through the open windows. Amara pulled her hair back into a loose ponytail and appreciated the scenery. Muted orange oaks and vibrant red maples encapsulated the narrow roads.

Her immaculate BMW came to a rest next to her parents' clumsy Toyota, taunting the Corolla to get a bath and go for a spin. Her dad scoffed the first time he saw her new car because he couldn't understand why she needed an expensive BMW. He argued that there was no one to impress. Amara countered that first impressions could get you far in life.

Amara looked at the two cars. Her BMW was her surprise gift to herself on her twenty-third birthday. She woke up that day more depressed than usual. She saw her future flash before her eyes and she didn't love what she saw. Every day, she walked in and out of the bank, counted money, gave money to those who wanted it, and threw a monetary lifeline to desperate people. She felt like a fraud, crammed into her tiny apartment with frozen dinners piled in the freezer, while controlling the financial state of strangers.

Before her BMW, she drove a banged-up SUV from the early nineties. Its tape deck and six CD-changer was ancient technology that she didn't even know how to operate. Her SUV didn't fit the story's narrative she was writing for herself, so she stopped at the dealership on the way home from work and signed the papers. She fondly named her new car Bea, and referred to her as her sidekick.

It wasn't the most brilliant idea, her loan amount being almost as much as her share of the rent, but she had a good job and she deserved it. She could handle it. Bea may not fit a lot of stuff, but it carried her safely everywhere she wanted to go. She never regretted her decision, and her parents couldn't be mad at her take-life-by-the-balls-and-run-with-them kind of attitude.

Walking into the house, Amara found Daphne sitting at the table diligently doing her homework.

"Hey, Pip," Amara said. Daphne jumped at her nickname and rose from the table to give Amara a quick hug.

"Hi, Ame."

"Where's Mama and Baba?" Amara asked.

"Bakery. They'll be home soon."

Amara looked at the clock, forgetting how much time her parents spent at the bakery. She sat next to Daphne and watched her do her work.

Amara busied herself on her phone, checking fashion websites and celebrity sightings. She knew she should do something to please her parents while they were gone, but she barely remembered where anything was, let alone what they needed her to do.

As soon as Daphne closed her book, Amara asked, "Want to go for a drive?" In past visits, Daphne requested car rides so she could play with the gadgets and blast music as they cruised through town.

"Yeah." Daphne dashed from the table and grabbed her shoes. "Let's go."

Their straight, silky hair shined hues of blue-black in the sun. They both wore striking facial features, with elongated cheekbones and naturally arched eyebrows. Amara knew Daphne would be stunning once she made it through puberty.

The car zipped through town. Amara took turns a bit too fast and Daphne held up her hands like she was riding a roller coaster.

Daphne flipped through the music, settling on hip hop that brought Amara back to high school. Amara tapped her hand against the console with the beat of the bass, jerking her head in rhythm. Despite approaching dinner, the air was still warm and the sun sat high in the sky. Acorns littered the street, reminding everyone that winter was coming.

Loukoumades Bakery sat sandwiched between a pharmacy and a tobacco shop. The eatery's lights fell onto the sidewalk, but the sign said closed. Amara and Daphne knocked on the glass and waved to their dad, who was removing trays of muffins from the display case. Their mother stood at the register counting money, and a man about a decade older than Amara opened the door. He greeted them with crooked teeth and ruddy cheeks.

"Can I help you?" he asked, an English accent lingering behind his vowels. He stood tall, but Amara's stature exceeded him.

"Henry, it's me," Daphne said, taking off the cat-eye sunglasses she found in the door of Amara's car. She moved past him, proving her dominance. "Hi, Mama. Hi, Baba."

Henry's eyes followed her into the bakery. "Oh, Daphne, I didn't recognize you." His voice contained humor and lilt. He opened the door further. "Hello, Amaryllis," he said, holding out his hand for a firm handshake. "I'm Henry. I don't think we've met."

"Hi, Henry. It's nice to finally meet you. I've heard a lot about you. You can call me Amara," she said walking past him, her eyes locked on her mother and father.

"Amaryllis, what are you doing here?" Mama asked, embracing Amara in a warm hug.

Her parents were the only ones who could call her that. When she was a kid, she hated that no one shared her name. She knew it was a common name in Greece, but they didn't live in Greece. They lived in America, and Amara wanted an American name. When she was in kindergarten, her handwriting was so big, her real name never fit on the paper. She shortened it so she wouldn't have to move it down to the following line. At first, the other kids called her Amary. Eventually, her teachers morphed it into Amara, and her classmates followed suit.

She liked the name Amara. It felt unique but respectable. A name, especially in the banking world, needed to be unforgettable. It provided her job promotion opportunities because her customers remembered her name when they returned to complete the paperwork. Amara was short and distinctive enough to recall, while Amaryllis was weird and too long to remember.

"Daphne and I were hanging out at home. I told Baba I would come to the game tomorrow and thought I would surprise you tonight. Do you need any help with the shop?"

Mama glanced around the store. "Do you want to help Henry? He's finishing up the dishes and cleaning the front."

Amara preferred to plate the baked goods, but she didn't argue. "Sure." She smiled. "Henry, what do you need me to do?"

"Ah, you're here to help. Lovely." His British accent was back. He handed her a broom. "Sweep, and I'll pick up the chairs."

They worked together in silence. Daphne sat at a table drinking soda and snacking on another cookie.

40

When Amara finished sweeping, she asked, "Now what?"

Henry looked around. "Well, the windows could use a good rinse or you can take out the rubbish."

Amara silently trudged to the back room and pulled out the window cleaner. *Why did I come here? I should have stayed at the house and enjoyed the rest and relaxation.* The windows already looked clean, but she did as instructed.

She tried to make small talk with Henry while her parents finished up in the back, but he carried an aloofness and superiority that Amara couldn't shake. Every time he spoke, Amara felt smaller and smaller. He commented on her car, which sat directly outside the front door. Amara felt pride grow within her until he told her that BMWs are the worst car to have if you live in New England. The potholes. The snow. The hills. It was a money pit because repairs were so expensive. Amara's confidence deflated with every voiced criticism.

Eventually, she stopped responding hoping that her lack of participation in the conversation would make him stop. The judgment from his crooked teeth and round glasses shrank her down to nothing.

"Henry," Baba said. "Can you take this down to the shelter?"

Henry nodded.

"Shelter," Amara asked, but it came out as a statement.

"Yes, there's a shelter about twenty minutes away. We deliver bread to them every afternoon."

"Wow, I never knew," Amara said. Amara's heart warmed. "Can I come with you?"

Mama's face lit up. "That would be wonderful!"

Henry frowned. "Yes, that would be wonderful."

"Daphne, do you want to come?" Amara asked.

Daphne stiffened. "No thanks. I'll catch a ride home with Mama and Baba."

Amara and Henry climbed into his old SUV. He pressed down on the clutch and moved the stick into first gear. The vehicle jerked forward and smoothed out as they exited the parking lot.

"So, how long have you been working here?" she asked.

"About two years now," he responded vaguely. "It's nice to finally meet you." Amara heard a hint of animosity behind his voice but ignored it.

"It's nice to put a face to a name. My parents really appreciate all you do for the bakery."

"Yes, they needed someone to help in the mornings. I have baking experience, and I went to culinary school in London."

"What made you come to Connecticut?"

"A woman, believe it or not. We met in London when she ate at my restaurant. She was over there for six months for school. One thing led to another, and when it was time for her to leave, I couldn't quite say goodbye. Six months later, I was on a plane to Boston. We got married, and then divorced. I could've gone home, but I'm still here."

Amara imagined a younger Henry, who was handsome, determined, and madly in love enough to leave his family. "That must've been hard to pack up everything and move overseas."

"Oh, yes, my family thought I was crazy. I go back every year, but this place became my home."

Amara nodded.

They pulled up to a small house set back from the main road. The house looked like an ordinary home. No sign decorated the front yard, and Amara wondered how many times she passed this building without knowing.

"This is it?" she asked.

"This is it. We bring the food to the back. You might want to leave your purse in the car."

Amara balked at the thought of leaving her designer handbag in a beat-up jalopy at a shelter where anyone could steal it.

"I can't do that," she said. "My life is in this bag."

Henry shrugged. "Suit yourself."

Henry and Amara stumbled out of the old SUV and pulled out trays of food. Amara couldn't believe how much was donated. Her parents must have purposefully baked more, knowing it wouldn't get sold. She wondered how much money they lost every time they donated.

"Cheerio," Henry called into the back kitchen. It was empty, but Amara heard murmuring behind the closed door.

They placed the trays on the counter and entered a sitting area. A group of people lounged on the couches pressed against each wall. Henry waved, and Amara stiffened, unsure how to behave around the strangers. The people waved back, familiar with Henry. Nudges and head nods traveled through the group like the telephone game and they all stared at the unexpected guest. Amara felt her throat tighten and her shoulders slouch, trying to hide from the stares.

"Is Donna here?" he asked.

Someone pointed to the next room over. Henry cut through the center of the room, and Amara followed, hiding her leather handbag within her coat. She rushed through, hoping no one noticed her shoes, which probably cost more money than they made in a week.

"Hello, Donna! I left breakfast in the kitchen."

Donna's tired face nodded and she rubbed lotion onto her arthritic hands. She eyed Amara up and down.

"Ah, yes, this is Amaryllis, Katerina and George's daughter. She's visiting," Henry said.

Although Amara expected her to smile brightly at the connection between the baked goods, herself, and her parents, Donna's expression didn't change. Amara raised her hand to her hip and gave Donna a half-wave. *Should I have shaken her hand?*

"Thanks, Henry, you're the best." Donna glanced back to Henry. Amara wondered if Donna was a smoker based on the husky voice that exited her chapped lips.

Amara followed Henry past the people lounging in the den and pulled her coat tighter. She hid the gold belt buckle that screamed the fashion designer's initials behind her crossed forearms.

On the drive home, Amara questioned Henry about the shelter. She didn't know her parents generously donated, and she felt her heart warm with pride after the experience. Even if Donna didn't seem overly impressed or appreciative of the spread, Amara knew the people living there did.

"Do you donate to the same shelter every night?"

"Yes. Your parents like to keep their generosity quiet. They want to help our community and build relationships."

Amara dug through her bag for chapstick and rubbed it against her dry lips. "But, isn't it a lot of food?"

"Yeah, but there are so many people that need help."

Henry zipped through the curvy hills back to the bakery. The sun had set entirely, and the stars lit the way.

"Thanks, Henry," Amara said, climbing out of his vehicle. She hopped into Bea and drove back to her parents' home in silence. She thought about Bethany and work, home, and the shelter. She didn't know what to do about the wedding and dreadful January first.

Amara and her family sat around the table eating chicken gyros for dinner. Garlic and oregano aroma filled the tiny kitchen and emanated into the cluttered dining room. "How was your day, Baba?" Amara asked.

"Good. Same as every day. Busy." Her father was a man of few words.

"I liked bringing the food to the shelter. That was an experience I never had before."

Mama cleared her throat and took a sip of water. "You don't remember, but we went to the food bank often when you were young. We had to. We were forced to eat American food, which is how your love for macaroni and cheese happened."

Amara laughed. "I don't remember, but I do love cheesy maracroni."

"Yeah, when you were little, we drove to Hartford or Providence every month to get food assistance. We decided to give back to the community when Henry started working here. All the resources helped us get on our feet so we decided to repay the favor."

Amara took a bite of dinner. "I didn't know what to expect, but Henry put me at ease. I felt really proud being connected to the bakery."

Baba wiped his mouth and poured another glass of wine. "It's worth it."

"Are you coming to my game tomorrow?" Daphne interrupted.

"Of course, I am." Amara acted as if she went to all of Daphne's games, but she had only come home four times since Christmas of last year.

Daphne beamed at her sister. "It's going to be tough. We're playing the best team in the county."

Amara pretended to care. She nodded when she was supposed to and asked questions that didn't mean anything, like, "Oh, yeah?" Daphne seemed oblivious.

Her parents, on the other hand, recognized the disconnect. "Amara," her mother said. "What's the real reason you're home?"

"For the game." Amara winked at Daphne. "Also, I wanted to talk about Bethany's wedding."

Her parents loved Bethany as much as Amara did. Bethany was the spontaneous one who always pushed Amara out of her comfort zone. Bethany always suggested new adventures or experiences to explore. Bethany and Amara were complete opposites, which was why they worked.

When Amara moved for college, Mama and Baba met Bethany, who had already claimed her side of the room and unpacked her bags. Bethany's parents had dropped her off and then left so she could explore the dorm alone. When Amara and her family walked in and introduced themselves, Bethany shook everyone's hands wearing a bright, bubbly smile. Bethany's self-confidence and passion for others reminded Amara of Jada. Amara had loved her from that moment.

"I'm so happy for her," Mama said.

Amara took another bite, savoring her mother's home cooking. "I am too, but they've only been dating since October. Not nearly long enough to get married. I mean, marriage is forever. I thought she would say no." Amara did her best to remain neutral in the conversation and not speak badly of Ryan.

"A year isn't too short. Your father and I dated a year before we got married, and we're still happy. Time doesn't mean anything when you're in love." Mama touched Baba's hand and smiled at him.

"What's the boyfriend like?" her father asked.

"Young. Twenty-two. Just out of college. He works for a real estate office but I don't know if he's sold anything yet. He lives with his parents but drives a hybrid so he can help save the planet." Amara didn't know why she shared that last fact. She took a sip of water to force herself from sharing anything else.

Her mother furrowed her brows. "Hmmm. That doesn't sound promising. Isn't she a nurse?"

"Yes, she is usually very level-headed. For some reason, she's lost her mind. Maybe it's love. Or maybe she feels this weird need to take care of him."

"Okay, so she's getting married. What's the problem?" Baba asked.

"Well, she's moving out in January. That's the problem."

Her mom took another bite, her dad took a drink of wine, and Daphne left the table to study for a test.

"So?"

Amara grimaced, annoyed that they didn't see the problem. This was the issue Amara had with her parents. They didn't get it, and they didn't understand how other people's actions uprooted Amara's life. By Bethany moving out, Amara had to scramble.

"So that means I either have to get a new roommate or move out. Neither of which is fair to me."

Her father began again. "So, you came home because you were made aware that your roommate is getting married and moving out?"

Amara sighed loudly. "Yes." She sounded like a cry baby when he said it that way, but it was a big deal. "I needed to come home to clear my head away from her and Ryan for a few days."

"Stay as long as you need," her mother said. "Our door is always open."

That night, Amara slept in her old bedroom, which became her father's den after she left for college. Piles of lopsided newspapers overtook one corner, and a desk overflowing with documents, pens, and files, sat where her bed used to be. Her closet, which at one time contained her shoe collection, was now the makeshift linen closet for the only full bathroom in the apartment.

Her dad pulled out an air mattress from the linen closet and instructed her to inflate it.

Amara huffed and puffed. She forgot how little room was left for her. She imagined sleeping on the couch, but her parents woke so early, even on their days off, it would be disruptive. She imagined sharing a room with Daphne, but Daphne's room was smaller than the den. It fit a twin bed comfortably if you could squeeze through the narrow walkway between the wall and the edge of the bed. It reminded Amara of a prison cell.

Sleeping that night was tough. The air mattress deflated in the middle of the night, so when Amara woke, her butt pressed against the floor, and her body was slightly u-shaped. "Ugh," Amara groaned, trying to roll over, but her muscles were stiff and tight. She deserved better than this. She left her options open and kept her bag packed. It might be better to go home to Providence and think. At least there, she had a bedroom with a door that closed.

Amara climbed off the floor and stretched, her shoulders cracking with every movement. Her parents had left for the bakery, the click of the door waking her. They worked every day, only closing for two weeks in the year. Once for summer vacation, but they never actually went anywhere. Instead, they sat around the house catching up on chores, yard work, and home repairs. They also closed for a week during Christmas break so Daphne could have some happy memories with her parents. Amara never came home for either week.

The coffee pot was a quarter of the way full and cooling, but Amara didn't care. Iced coffee on this late summer day was enough to get her moving. A note on the table said, **Amaryllis, please bring Daphne to the field by two. Her game is at three. We'll meet you there.**

Amara knew where the field was because it was the only field in town.

What am I going to do today? She knew her little sister would follow her like her shadow. Amara stuck her head into Daphne's room and found her reading in bed.

"Hey, Pipsqueak," Amara whispered. "Your game's at three. Do you want to go shopping today?"

"At the mall?"

"Sure. We can go when they open, walk the mall, do some shopping, and then head to your game. Do you need new clothes?"

Daphne nodded. "Yeah, Mama and Baba haven't taken me yet. I need new jeans. All of mine are way too short."

The mall was a perfect distraction from Amara's current situation. Maybe she could find a new bag or wallet that was winter-themed. Her parents would also be pleased that Amara got Daphne's shopping out of the way.

"Let's go. We'll head out in an hour," Amara said, checking her watch.

They found a parking spot right at the entrance. Amara ran down the plan. "We have two hours to shop. Then we'll grab lunch. Then run home, change, and get to your game." It sounded easy enough.

The girls raced into the mall like they were on a timed game show. The clock ticked down.

Amara hadn't spent time alone with her sister since Amara's college graduation three years ago. When she graduated, her real life started, and she didn't have any reason to come home, except for the occasional visit or obligatory holidays.

After she graduated, her parents begged her to move back to rinky-dink Connecticut, to work at the bakery. Amara had been flabbergasted that she'd spent so much money learning how to run a business and manage money, and her parents wanted her to return home to the starting line of her adult life. She deserved to be far away from her family's influence and wanted to make a name for herself.

Yes, her degree and education would have benefited the bakery, but the bakery was her parents' dream, not hers. She didn't want to be a slave to their business. She wanted to be a slave to whatever kind of work she chose.

The two sisters weaved in and out of the specialty shops looking for clothes that fit Daphne. Amara couldn't help but divert from the path and sneak into a few designer stores. Handbags were her kryptonite. They gave her the confidence to face all situations and helped her get ahead when first impressions were necessary. They worked the same way as her BMW.

Daphne smiled as they sat down in the food court, eating cheap pizza and guzzling fountain soda. "Thanks, Ame."

Amara smiled. "Of course. That was fun."

They carried bags in both hands and piled them in the backseat of Bea.

"Hurry up! We only have twenty minutes." Daphne tapped her

fingers on the console and gripped the seatbelt strap. Her eyes fluttered between the clock on the dashboard and the speedometer.

Amara zoomed home. Shopping took longer than she planned.

While Daphne changed for her game, Amara sat in the car, feeling the sun beat down against her skin. She pulled her sunglasses over her eyes and applied a fresh coat of lipstick. She looked good. No, she looked great. And maybe, while zoning out pretending to watch the game, she would come up with a great idea to keep her apartment and make her life even better.

Daphne climbed into the car sporting purple and gold, the same colors of Amara's cheerleading uniform ten years before. "Buckle up," Amara said as Daphne's door slammed closed. They flew out of the driveway onto the main road.

They pulled into the parking lot, and it was empty. No cars and no kids. Nothing. Just two large husky puppies dragging their dog walker.

"Where is everyone?" Daphne asked, her pitch rising.

"I don't know." Amara dug through her purse searching for her phone. "Mama and Baba said at the field, right? Isn't this the only field?"

Daphne leaned back, her face paling. She checked her watch. "We're going to be late. I don't know. I don't know where everyone is. What do we do?"

Amara quickly texted her mom: **Where are you? Where's the game?**

The field.

Amara looked at the field expecting to see her parents waving on the other side but there was nothing. **We're at the field but it's empty. ??**

The field. Near the school.

"Hey, Pip, is there a field near your school?" Amara asked. "Do you have practice or games there sometimes?"

Her phone dinged repeatedly with clarification and demands to get there ASAP. Amara silenced her phone to focus on Daphne, whose eyes bulged and tears covered her blue irises. "Daphne? Don't panic." She took Daphne's hand to ground her. "Is there a field near the school?" she asked again.

Daphne nodded, unable to speak.

"The high school?"

Daphne nodded again.

Amara checked the one-sided conversation with her mom and clicked on the address. "Let's go."

She peeled out of the parking lot, gravel flying behind. "We'll get there. The game doesn't start for another forty-five minutes. You'll be fine."

Somehow Amara held it all together, because crying made her uncomfortable. It didn't matter who it was. It could be a random woman crying at the movie theater, a child crying at a playground, or herself. Crying brought back all the uncomfortable memories of when she was a kid, and her father told her crying was for the weak. It was something she couldn't do, and she hated to see others do it.

They pulled into the packed parking lot, and found an isolated spot in the far corner. Daphne exited the car before Amara turned off the ignition. Daphne ran like lightning, her black ponytail flapping in the wind.

Amara slowly approached the bleachers. She didn't know anyone or what the unwritten rules were about where you were allowed to sit. Her parents promised to be there by the time the game started, but she was alone in a crowd of strangers for the next thirty minutes. Amara lowered her sunglasses over her eyes, hoping to avoid any contact with people from her graduating class who happened to be at the game. She assumed some of them still lived in town.

To pass the time, she scrolled through social media. She texted back and forth with Bethany, who wanted to know when she was coming home. Amara rolled her eyes. *She's never home and now she wants me to check in with her?*

Amara shut her phone down and thought about January. She was too old to get a new roommate, and she couldn't afford a two-bedroom, nor did she need one. That left one option. Downsize, but she didn't have enough money for first, last, and security. She would never ask her parents. They would kill her. She was supposed to be self-sufficient by now.

Amara scrolled through the apartment listings, wondering how much a one-bedroom or studio would cost. She balked at the prices compared to the neighborhood and condition. Would she prefer a dumpy kitchen or just a kitchenette? A bathroom straight out of the seventies with an olive-green toilet or the fifties with a faucet that had two knobs you had to turn to get the temperature right? And here was one of the worst neighborhoods in the city.

She sighed, hoping that maybe, just maybe, Ryan and Bethany would break up. She might be a terrible friend, but it would certainly make her life a whole lot easier.

Amara's parents came bustling through the crowd wearing jeans and Loukoumades Bakery polo shirts. Mama's black hair was tinted white with flour, and Baba's rotund belly pulled his shirt taut.

"Hello, Amaryllis." Baba's face remained stern. Amara anticipated a lecture on punctuality. The people next to Amara shifted and scooted to accommodate her parents.

"Just in time," Amara said, keeping the conversation light.

Her mother smiled. "Did the game start?"

Amara shook her head. "Daphne was upset we were late. We were late anyway, and when I went to the wrong field, we were really late." Amara tried to guilt and blame her parents without actually saying, *it's your fault if she does poorly today.*

"We're glad you finally found the place." Her father stared ahead at the field.

They watched the game in silence. Cheering and hooting erupted in the bleachers as Woodstock took the lead. Daphne made the goal, which put their team on the board. After three unanswered goals, it was a runaway win. Daphne couldn't stop smiling once the game ended.

Big hugs enveloped her and held Daphne tight. Congratulations and compliments showered her.

"Thanks for being here, Amara," Daphne said. "And thanks for taking me shopping."

"Anytime."

"Are you coming back to the house?" Mama asked.

Amara shook her head, checking her watch. It was already after five. She had to get home to check in with Bethany and catch up on her television shows. "Sorry, Mama, but I have to get back." Bethany was the reason she came and the perfect reason to go.

Chapter 5

The return trip to Providence was uneventful and long enough for Amara to get lost in her thoughts about the wedding. She tried to picture the big day, but nothing solidified in her mind. Getting ready for a trip to Jamaica was expensive…and if she had to move, she might not have enough money to pull off both expenses.

When she got home, eerie quiet filled the apartment. Bethany had texted her asking if she wanted dinner, and they decided on pizza. Amara breathed in deeply, anticipating the garlicky aroma, and her belly grumbled. Instead, she didn't smell a thing. She heard soft giggles coming from the living room. Amara rolled her eyes and took long strides and deep stomps, hoping the click-clack of her boots on the hardwood floors disrupted whatever was happening.

"I'm home," she hollered from the coat closet. Amara stood still for about twenty seconds, fumbling with her keys and pocketbook, giving them enough time to button up if needed. Amara imagined Ryan's puny, pale body hidden under the blankets, and she shivered in disgust. *Are they in the living room or Bethany's bedroom?* The two rooms stood side by side, and from the front hallway, there was no way to guess.

"Hi, Amara," Bethany called down the short corridor. "We're in here."

Amara smiled and made her way down the hall, through the living room, and into the kitchen.

"We made pizza instead," Bethany said while opening the oven door and gliding the uncooked pizza in. "It'll be ready in ten minutes."

"Hi Beth, Hi Ryan. What kind did you make?" Amara greeted them individually but directed her question at Bethany, ignoring Ryan's cold stare.

"For you, I made spanakopita because it's your favorite. I knew you wouldn't eat pepperoni, so we made you your own. Ryan had never heard of spanakopita pizza, so I had to show him. I used feta, spinach, balsamic, and diced tomatoes. We're out of onions but I think you'll like it just the same," Bethany rambled.

"That's so kind of you. Thanks."

"How was your trip home?" Bethany asked.

"It was fine. My parents are my parents. I spent some time with Daphne, which was nice. I took her shopping and watched her win her soccer game. She was excited to see me."

Ryan interrupted Amara, turning to Bethany. "Dear, did you set the timer?"

Dear? What in the world? Ryan is twenty-two years old. He shouldn't have a dear in his life. He should have a babe. Amara narrowed her eyebrows at him, questioning his choice of vocabulary. *What kind of man is he?* Her shoulders shuddered. *He looks like a boy.*

Bethany nodded at him and kept her eyes on Amara. "That sounds great," she replied.

"Yeah, I went to a homeless shelter. That was interesting."

Bethany raised her eyebrows. "Oh yeah? How come?"

Amara explained how her parents bake extra every night to feed the homeless and felt worried her parents were being taken advantage of somehow. Memories of cereal for dinner and free lunch at school flashed through her mind, reminding her of how far she'd come since childhood.

"That's amazing," Bethany said. "I love your parents. They have huge hearts."

Amara let the comment roll off her back. "They do, but I hope they know what they're doing. How was your weekend?" Amara changed the subject, not wanting to think too hard about the bakery.

Bethany grabbed Ryan's hand. "So fun. We went ring shopping. I found so many beautiful rings. The pave and curved bands were my favorite. I'm not ready to pick one out yet, but it sure is fun to shop around. I told Ryan I need to think about it because a wedding ring is sacred and forever." Bethany touched her ring finger and stroked the brilliant diamond set in white gold.

Amara nodded, hoping that her friendship with Bethany wouldn't falter, even though it felt like Ryan was always around, slowly taking her place. "I know you'll find the perfect ring." Amara stared out the kitchen window overlooking the dumpsters.

They ate pizza and continued to talk about the wedding. They moved to the living room to watch a romantic comedy about a couple falling in love and continued to talk about the wedding.

"Ryan, what do you think of those flowers?" Bethany pointed to a bouquet on the DVD cover.

"Those are pretty, but didn't we decide on a blue color scheme? To match the ocean?"

"Those are pretty, Beth," Amara added. "Have you guys seen this movie before?"

"I know we talked about blue, but purple is close to blue. Maybe it's close enough?" Bethany responded to Ryan.

Every time Amara tried to change the subject to something neutral, Bethany found a way to circle back to the wedding. Amara questioned if they knew she was there. She stifled a mock yawn and said, "I have to work tomorrow. It's time for me to hit the hay."

She excused herself from the couch and went to her favorite room in the house. Her king-sized bed looked like a giant marshmallow and invited Amara to tumble into it. Even though it was fall, Amara loved to be chilled from the ceiling fan but buried under piles of blankets. The sound of the fan lulled her to sleep and the pillows over her head kept her warm.

As she lay in bed, she could faintly hear Bethany and Ryan kissing through the wall, and she prayed they fell asleep in Bethany's room. Amara hated waking up and having to stumble through her apartment in the dark because people were asleep on the couch. At first, it didn't bother her, but as the instances happened more frequently, she started to feel like a guest in her own home. Amara never told Bethany because she didn't want to rock the boat, but the resentment toward Bethany's new man continued to fester.

The next morning, Amara rolled out of bed, stumbled to the kitchen for a cup of coffee, and hopped in the shower. She practically fell into the toilet because Ryan forgot to put the seat down again. "Ugh," Amara cried in disgust. *Why is he still here?* He was getting too comfortable in their cozy apartment, interfering with her and Bethany's friendship.

Amara climbed into her car and turned the key. Nothing happened. The engine didn't turn over, no matter how many times she tried. None of the lights turned on, and the radio was dead. "Why? Why? Why?" She banged the steering wheel.

She looked around, wondering if she had left the door cracked open overnight. She specifically recalled hearing the beep of the lock because she listened for that sound every night. As she retraced her steps, her younger sister's face zipped through her mind. *Daphne.* When Daphne and Amara left the mall, Daphne put on her oversized sweatshirt because it "looked so comfy." She must have hit the middle light with her hand when she reached to pull her arm through, and the battery drained overnight. Amara fumbled with the light, unsure if she turned it off or turned it back on again.

Amara closed her door, slammed her hand on the roof of her car, and ran into the apartment. "Bethany," she hollered. "Bethany, I need a ride to work."

Shirtless Ryan stepped out of the bedroom, his inadequate chest accentuating his sternum and ribs. "She's in the bathroom."

Amara listened and heard the water running. "Put some pants on. I need a ride to work," she commanded. As much as she didn't want Ryan's help, she couldn't be late again.

Ryan didn't ask questions. He disappeared into Bethany's bedroom, emerging less than two minutes later fully dressed.

"What happened?"

"My car won't start. Thank you, Ryan. I really appreciate it."

Ryan nodded and grabbed his wallet off the kitchen counter. "Bethany, I'll be right back," he called through the bathroom door.

They drove through the city, hitting every light. "Ryan, don't go that way. There's construction."

"I can't get over." He gestured toward the traffic ahead. "Big truck."

Amara rolled her eyes. She saw the semi speeding down the lane, her eyes frantically hopping from lane to lane, looking for an opening. "Shit. I'm going to be late. This is the third time I've been late since the start of the month. First I overslept, then I forgot I needed gas. If Tania finds out, she's going to kill me."

Ryan looked over his shoulder as he changed lanes. "I'm going as fast as I can."

They rode in the exit-only lane toward the bridge construction. The highway exit went from two lanes to one, and eventually merged into the shoulder. Cars crawled, trying to squeeze between the edge of the bridge and the Jersey barriers.

"What time do you have to be there?" Ryan asked.

"Uh, ten minutes ago. If we got into the left lane earlier, I would've been there by now." She tapped her fingers on the middle console, glancing at her watch. *How does he not know how to get around Providence?*

"Do you want to call and let them know you'll be late?"

"No, hopefully they won't even notice I'm not there." Amara knew they would notice. She had her own office, and the bank wasn't exactly milling with people when the doors opened. She hoped Tania was in a meeting.

"I'm going as fast as I can, but this traffic is brutal," Ryan spoke calmly, as if he were reading Amara a bedtime story. He paid no attention to the cars and trucks jamming into him, trying to get into his lane.

Amara slammed her head against the headrest and closed her eyes.

Of all days, her car had to break down, and she had to get a ride with this kid.

"It's a nice day today," Ryan deflected.

Amara didn't want to talk. "Mm-hmm," she responded. "Sorry if this makes you late for work."

"I took the day off. Bethany and I are going to research how to plan a destination wedding."

The wedding again. "Sounds fun. Good luck."

The car ride lasted forever. Amara didn't want to talk about the wedding for another second. She busied herself on her phone, looking for an alternate route.

Traffic stopped completely. Amara watched an officer methodically wave to get the cars through the construction and back onto the highway. She glanced at her watch, and her heart rate quickened. They were twenty minutes late, and she needed to be in the conference room briefing her managers.

The tension in the car rose as Amara thought of consequences related to frequent tardiness. *Fired? Probably not. Written up? Sure, depending on what time I arrive.* She knew she should call. Traffic wasn't a reasonable offense to get fired, but missing a presentation in a meeting could be.

Amara imagined everyone sitting in the conference room, staring at each other, wondering if they got the date or time wrong.

Finally, forty-five minutes after Amara's intended arrival at work, Ryan stopped the car.

"Thank you for the ride!" Amara opened the door and jumped onto the sidewalk. She stepped in a crack and stumbled. *Snap!* Her high heel broke at the base and she struggled to regain her footing. "Ugh," she screamed, shoving the heel into her pocketbook.

The door slammed before Ryan could respond. Amara brushed down her skirt and dug out the extra pair of flats from her oversized handbag before confidently walking into the bank.

The car slowly pulled away, and Ryan waved. Amara ignored him as she scurried through the heavy lobby doors.

Tania stood in Amara's office, her nails tapping the desk.

"Where were you?"

"Construction," Amara said, rushing to the chair to drop off her bag.

"Where are last week's loans?" Tania busied herself in Amara's cabinet drawers.

"Right here." Amara pulled out a folder from her workbag. "I brought them home to work on them."

"You know that's not allowed." Tania narrowed her eyes and glared.

Amara shrugged. "It needed to get done." *It didn't get done, but it would have if I didn't have to go home to Connecticut.* She imagined Tania's reaction when the numbers weren't ready for today's meeting. Amara had intended to do it, but other things came up. Like an eviction date. She handed the folder to Tania.

Tania galloped out of the room, her knee buckling as she stepped wrong. Amara stifled a giggle, and Tania turned. Her eyes squinted, her lips scrunched up, and her eyebrows narrowed. "You have two minutes," she barked.

Amara stood at her desk, staring out the window. She didn't like people telling her what to do. She stood defiantly, her body erect, and poured a cup of coffee, savoring the hazelnut flavor.

The phone on her desk rang, and Amara knew it was Tania, demanding that she join the meeting. Instead of answering, she took her coffee and trudged to the conference room. She had raced through her morning to get to work on time, and Tania didn't seem to appreciate her effort, so Amara leisurely moved to the already in-progress meeting.

Everyone turned to stare, their eyes boring into Amara's. No one smiled, and everyone looked tense.

"Sorry I'm late," Amara apologized. "Car trouble."

She sat in an empty chair and pulled out her files. "Excuse me," she whispered Mallory. "Do you have a pen?"

Mallory shook her head and smiled an apology. Tania's eyes widened like a bullfrog. Amara slowly roamed around the table. Tania rapped the table with her pen, gaining everyone's attention. "Here. Have mine." She threw the pen at Amara.

Amara raised the pen and smiled in thanks. She opened her folder and cleared her throat. She vaguely reviewed the number of opened and processed accounts from the week before, and left the meeting when no one had questions.

A few hours later, Tania called Amara to her office. The large phone rang, startling Amara from her in-depth analysis of the most recent celebrity magazine. "Come to my office. Pronto."

Amara rolled her eyes. Tania sounded so authoritative.

Amara and Tania joined the bank family in the same year. They had the same seniority even though Tania was technically Amara's superior. Historically, Tania needed more help learning her job, and Amara was the one who answered all her questions. Now, Amara couldn't take her seriously.

"I'm removing you from loans." Amara had barely sat down and crossed her legs before the words exited Tania's mouth. Her voice floated over Amara's head like bubbles.

"What?" Amara interrupted; her voice louder than she intended. All the bubbles popped, leaving a slippery film over Amara.

"I'm removing you from loans. You're not reliable." Tania kept it concise.

"You can't do that."

"I can. And I did. I spoke to Pam this morning, and we reviewed your history. You've lost files, you miss deadlines, and you don't care. You also have a history of tardiness. As a loan officer, you have too many appointments that you can't be late for. We decided to move you to a different department. You're on thin ice, so please don't screw up again."

Amara opened and closed her mouth. So many words ran through her head, but she knew when it was best to shut up.

"You can go home now. Tomorrow you'll be at the teller counter, and your hours are seven thirty to four with a thirty-minute lunch." Tania motioned toward the door, her lips tight and body stiff.

Amara sat there, stunned. Her legs stuck to the chair, and her mouth formed an "o." She had never been fired before, and this felt like a firing. Shame and incompetence battled with indignation inside her brain.

"Wait." Her voice crackled, sounding like a log being thrown into a blaze. "Am I being demoted?"

"It depends. Do you consider tellers to be below the loan department?" *Kind of.* "If you're referring to pay, your hourly wage will remain the same."

Amara nodded blankly. "What about my projects?"

"You can give them to me. I'll take over."

Amara's blood festered and boiled. *Of course, you want to take over. You love to get credit for work you didn't do.* Amara's mouth twisted into a sneer, and she bit her lip until the pain radiated through her face. *Keep it together. You cannot get fired.*

"Thank you." She stood up and exited the office. For a moment, she felt relief for still having a job. Then she felt anger at Tania for being such a jerk. And finally, she felt defeated for failing herself.

She packed up her bag and slinked out of the office, choosing a time when all the loan officers were busy, and a line of customers snaked through the lobby. Everyone would know what happened when she showed up for work tomorrow morning.

Amara stood in the middle of downtown Providence stranded without a car. She was so busy stressing about work that she never coordinated with Ryan for a ride home, and she didn't want to disturb their happy wedding planning. She considered a taxi, but couldn't spend the money now that she lost an entire day of work.

Instead, she walked around downtown, meandering in and out of the shops. Amara always went shopping when she felt stuck. Finding new clothes to reinvent herself was a great solution to help sort her thoughts and figure out what direction she wanted to move. She tried to enjoy her free time, but melancholy nagged at her whenever she entered a dressing room. It taunted her, reminding her she was probably broke. Finally, after four excruciating hours of being alone with her thoughts and trying desperately not to feel like a failure, Amara called a taxi.

She still didn't have a car and didn't know what she would do about work tomorrow. She had the entire afternoon to call the dealership and schedule an appointment to get a new battery. The thought had crossed her mind a few times, but she couldn't muster up enough energy to make the call. Now it was evening, and her car wouldn't be looked at until tomorrow.

Amara slammed the front door, praying Bethany was out. She didn't want to explain how her day went from bad to worse. First the car, then the construction, then the missed meeting. Her stomach grumbled.

She forgot her lunch and was too busy putting out fires to notice.

Just as she hoped, the apartment was silent. Amara imagined Bethany out to dinner with Ryan, laughing and smiling about how amazing they were and how much they loved each other. Amara plopped down on the sofa with a pint of birthday cake ice cream. There was no way ice cream wouldn't bolster her mood.

She felt like a loser, sitting alone in her apartment with a half-melted tub of ice cream on her lap. Her feet throbbed from walking, her black ballerina flats coated with dirt and grime. She thought about her day and all the things that went wrong. No car, no way to get to work, practically fired, practically homeless, and involved in a wedding that she didn't think should happen. Amara's life was crumbling piece by piece.

She showered before going to bed, hoping that her problems would resolve themselves if she slept the entire night. She heard the door open around ten, but the apartment remained silent. Bethany probably didn't even realize Amara was home. Amara kept quiet and fell back asleep when the last light darkened.

The next morning, Amara woke to her phone ringing. It was eight thirty, and Amara felt like a new woman. "Hello?" she rasped.

"Amara, where are you? You're an hour late." Tania's shrill voice pierced through Amara's brain like a hot fireplace poker, and her head throbbed with every word.

"Shit. I can't. I forgot to tell you yesterday."

"What do you mean you can't?" Tania croaked, her voice mocking Amara.

"My car. The battery died, and I don't have a ride. That's why I was late yesterday. I didn't tell you because you were so mad, but my car isn't ready yet."

Tania took a deep breath and sighed audibly, the rustling from her breath tickling Amara's eardrum through the receiver. "Fine. I'll document your absence. This is strike two. Do not screw up again or you'll be fired."

Amara hung up and rolled to her side, snuggling with her covers. *I have to call the dealership*, she reminded herself before falling back asleep.

***

"The car's ready. It's $275, plus towing charges. Your total's $375," the mechanic said.

Amara pulled out her credit card and cringed as she watched him swipe. She regretted turning down Roadside Assistance when she bought the car. At the time she justified that she would never need it, but here she was. That $375 could have gotten her far, especially since she didn't know if she had a place to live after the new year.

Amara got home right before dinner and saw Bethany at the table. Bridal magazines in clustered piles with sticky tabs highlighting important pages decorated their kitchen.

"Hi." Amara frowned.

Bethany turned. "I'm so glad you're home." She didn't know Amara hadn't worked, and Amara didn't plan to tell her. She couldn't handle Bethany's critiquing eyes. "What do you think of these?" She showed Amara a variety of wedding dresses. "Which one screams beach wedding to you?"

"That one." Amara pointed to a woman with a flowing white mermaid silhouette dress and a wreath of flowers in her hair. "I love the flowers and the hair. Your hair is so curly and would look beautiful down. If you keep growing it out, it will probably be down to your shoulder blades by the time the wedding rolls around."

"Yeah," Bethany said noncommittally. She tilted her head to get a better view of the pictures. "I don't like how casual it feels."

"It's a wedding on the beach. I don't think a Cinderella dress would make sense. It would be heavy and hot and sandy." Amara grabbed a few magazines and flipped through the pages. "Have you thought about the bridesmaid dresses?"

Amara imagined a chiffon dress cut above the knee with a tight bodice and spaghetti straps.

"I won't know until I have my dress picked out, but I was thinking something fun and flirty. I want something beachy that's easy to dance in. I was thinking we should walk down the aisle barefoot. What do you think?"

Amara's head perked up. "Barefoot could be fun. We could get pedicures the day before and wear matching polish."

"Yeah. Imagine walking in the hot sand with turquoise water just a few steps away. It's going to be the best weekend ever!"

Amara had been part of two weddings before and neither were the best weekend ever. First, she was a flower girl and remembered the day based on pictures. The second was for her cousin, and she was only included to make the bridal party equal. Amara was in college and wished she had turned down the offer. It was an expensive weekend to be a placeholder, but she did it for her parents, who wanted her to get more involved with the family. After the wedding, she spoke to her cousin only at funerals and holidays.

"Awesome. I can't wait to go shopping."

"We need to coordinate with Mikayla and Ruby. I want all of us together when we try on dresses."

"Oh, totally." Amara flipped through the magazines with a new sense of energy, looking for inspiration. She should have shown the same attention and focus at work, but lost interest long ago.

The two women ate chips and dip for dinner and ripped out potential ideas. As much as Amara hated hearing about the wedding, she needed to distract herself from work. She crossed her fingers and toes that she had a job, but it was wedding time for now.

***

The next few weeks, work rolled by with intentionality. Amara kept her comments to herself, trying her best to remain neutral. Most days, she bit her tongue whenever work or the wedding came up in conversation. Bethany spent all her time with Ryan, and Amara was on the outside looking in. Ryan was over most nights, eating their food and claiming space on the vanity counter in the bathroom. The seriousness of their relationship sunk in when Amara had to move her extra hair products out of the bathroom and back into her bedroom. She felt like a fool for thinking things would remain the same.

The bank now considered her a worker bee, after so many years of service. She no longer had the authority to tell others what to do. Tania made Mallory her trainer, and she had only been at their branch for three months. Mallory stood next to Amara, eyeing her as she opened her till.

"What?" Amara asked, not even saying hello.

"You forgot to check your slips."

"I know. I will. I've done this job before, you know. Tania thought this was a better fit for me, but it's only temporary." Amara didn't know if it was temporary, but the thought of being a teller long term was enough to make her want to poke her eyes out with a stick.

"Oh," Mallory mumbled in surprise. Amara saw her roll her eyes and ignored her rudeness. She focused on the paper before her, reacquainting herself with the deposit and withdrawal slips.

She probably needed a refresher, but she wasn't about to ask Tania or Mallory for help. She'd rather muddle through, learning as things came up.

Amara stayed busy that first week, processing transactions at breakneck speed. She was better than this and she deserved to be back in her own office with the window facing the courtyard, but she had to pay her dues and prove that Tania made a mistake. She needed to impress the other managers, whom she had no real interaction with before. Getting to know them professionally and personally was a delicate balancing act. She wanted to give them their space, but didn't want to be forgotten.

Every night she'd come home exhausted from the constant flow of people and the forced smile she plastered across her face. Her feet throbbed from the heels. Although Amara knew no one could see her shoes, she also knew she had to dress the part. She noticed her co-workers discreetly analyzing her clothing choices, and Amara assumed they were jealous. Even though she couldn't afford to shop at the specialty stores, she did anyway, and Mastercard became her new best friend.

She became the Queen Bee quickly. Customers liked her because she was pleasant and efficient. Tania smugly stood in the corner, arms crossed against her red blazer, watching Amara interact with the customers. Soon, Amara was processing three times as many transactions a day as her colleagues.

Her co-workers started asking her for fashion advice. What would look good with a pear-shaped body? Where can you get a good deal on boots, and is the Outlet store a big discount? Amara loved the attention. She shared all her tips, and eventually, never ate lunch alone.

Back at home, Bethany flitted in and out of the house like a moth searching for light. Most nights, Ryan stayed at the apartment and was there a few times without Bethany when Amara came home from work. Amara spent most of her time in her bedroom, wishing her best friend was more present in her life. She hadn't even told Bethany about the job change because Bethany stopped showing an interest in her life.

Amara didn't understand what Bethany saw in Ryan, but she could never ask. One time, right after Amara first met Ryan, they had an honest conversation that didn't end well.

"Don't you think he's a little young?" Amara had asked, swirling her spaghetti around her fork tines.

"Not really. He's three years younger than us. That's practically nothing." Bethany commented.

Amara shrugged in agreement. "But he lives with his parents. That makes him seem young. Like he doesn't have his life together."

Bethany laughed. "Amara, you meet random guys at the club, and I bet most of them live at home. They're out there with their cropped hair, earrings, and necklaces, looking the part. I bet they all drive clunkers because they're so broke. You never question them."

Amara rolled her eyes. "Yeah, because I'm not taking them home and introducing them to my family."

Bethany stopped chewing and held up her pointer finger to communicate that she had a response, but was too polite to speak with her mouth full. "Not true. My family hasn't met him yet. Just you."

Amara nodded, eyeing her meal but no longer hungry. "Okay, so where does he work?"

"He's trying to get into real estate. He got his license and is looking for an agency. He wants to sell beach cottages."

"Will anyone take him seriously? How can he sell a home when he doesn't have one? I want you to end up with someone who will make you rich and happy."

Bethany brushed her bangs out of her eyes. "I don't need rich. I need happy, but not rich."

"Suit yourself," Amara replied. "I've learned from watching my parents that money may not make you happier, but it sure makes life less stressful."

They had eaten in silence for the rest of the meal. Amara knew she crossed an invisible line that put Bethany on the defense. Amara had done her best to support the relationship, but something didn't feel right. Now that they were getting married, Amara needed to be there for her best friend, despite her poor choices in a partner.

***

Another Monday morning rolled around, and Amara threw a few bridal magazines into her leather tote bag. She had been spending her lunch breaks searching through magazines for the perfect bridesmaid dress.

At work, she perused the announcements posted in the break room. It had been almost a month, and her old job was up for grabs again. She needed it back. She missed the privacy, the slower pace, the authority to decline or accept an application, the control, and the power. Now, she was a minion working for the man.

She and Tania spoke little since the demotion. Amara focused on Gail, her new supervisor, and asked her about the job position.

"Gail, do you think I should apply?"

"I don't know, Amara. You don't have an impressive track record. You can apply, but I don't think you'll get it."

How can Gail be so cutthroat? What does she know, anyway? I know how to do that job in my sleep.

"But Gail, I was so good at my job, and I made lots of money for the bank."

Gail pushed her glasses up the bridge of her nose, sending daggers at Amara for interrupting her counting. She placed the money on the counter and turned to Amara. "Sorry, you asked for my opinion, and I don't know if Tania would take you back. But what do I know? Give it a go. The worst they can say is no."

Gail's words lingered in between Amara's ears, ricocheting inside her head like a ping-pong ball. Throughout the day, the phrase *I don't think you'll get it*, popped in and out of her mind like lightning bugs in the night sky. Amara knew she had to apply to prove everyone wrong.

She also had to make herself look average in her current position. If Gail fought for her to stay behind the counter, she would never get a second chance. She needed Gail to dislike her, so she would be okay if

Amara left her department.

Amara needed to screw up purposefully. Not enough to get fired, but enough to convince Gail that it would be better if she weren't under her supervision. She needed to be a thorn in Gail's side.

Amara could do that.

Chapter 6

B y the time Thanksgiving rolled around, Amara was in the second stage of the interview process. She had met with Tania and pleaded her case, begging her to believe that Amara learned her lesson and would be a more conscientious employee. Her second interview with the Branch Manager was scheduled for the Monday after Thanksgiving. Amara practiced answering interview questions and prepared a portfolio to summarize her strengths. If her work didn't speak for itself, she needed to find another job.

"Mama, what do you put in the stuffing again?"

"Pine nuts, prunes, raisins, dates, chestnuts, rice, meat, and cloves," Mama replied, counting on her lanky fingers.

Amara pulled out all the ingredients. "Do you have a recipe?"

"Mix it all together, then stuff it in the bird." She smiled. "Cooking doesn't need to be exact. It needs to come from the heart. If it comes from the heart, it'll be delicious."

Amara propped her head up with her fist and leaned on the counter, searching for a recipe on the internet. "Where's Baba?"

"At the shop. He's preparing rolls for the shelter. Your father has become quite generous. He and Henry'll deliver the food and then

Henry'll come over for dinner since his family lives in England." Mama placed a box of instant stuffing on the counter. "This is for Henry. He's allergic to pine nuts."

Amara laughed. "Will Henry eat traditional Greek food?"

"Let's just say he's more of a meat and potatoes kind of guy, so I made sure to have food he enjoys too."

"Why isn't he with his friends for Thanksgiving?" Amara flattened her lips and crossed her arms in front of her chest.

Her mother placed her hands on Amara's cheeks and Amara looked into Mama's gentle eyes. "Amara, dear, we are his friends and your father and I think of him as family. Ever since he started at the bakery, he's been the one we rely on when we need help." Mama turned away, retrieving more ingredients from the cabinets.

Daphne stood at the counter preparing spanakopita, quietly singing to the radio. Happy beats of traditional Christmas carols softened the insult that her mom threw at Amara. "Geez, Mama, you make it sound like I never come home."

"You don't. We only see you when you need us. Whenever we need you, you always have some excuse. Eventually, we stopped asking."

Amara froze at the sink, staring out the window. Her shoulders tensed and her breathing slowed, trying to remember back to the last time her parents called on her for help.

"What are you going to do about your apartment?" Mama asked.

Amara shrugged. "Not sure yet." She didn't want to tell her parents she had no money saved and no plan. She imagined living in her BMW. She pictured curtains against the windows, blocking the moonlight while she slept across the seats, scrunched up like a newborn.

"Can I store my stuff in the basement?"

Her mother hesitated. "It's not only our basement, and there isn't a lot of room. You might need to rent a storage unit."

Amara nodded, but panicked inside. She didn't know how much

that would cost.

"What time's dinner?" Amara changed the subject, her heart fluttering against her chest, and her face feeling warm and prickly.

"After two. The bakery is closing early, and your father is due to deliver the bread around noon." She hummed with the Christmas carols, throwing the stuffed turkey in the oven.

As the turkey cooked in the oven, Henry and Baba entered the kitchen carrying a tray of extra baklava. Amara leaned down and inhaled the cinnamon-orange syrup and a hint of pistachios. "Did you make this today?" Amara asked.

Baba tipped his head up with a small grin pulling at the corners of his mouth. "I pulled it out of the oven about an hour ago."

Amara roamed around the kitchen helping Mama and Daphne prepare the side dishes while Henry and Baba talked shop in the living room. Amara found herself dancing to the music and singing to herself as the three women worked together to provide a delicious, filling meal for the family.

Amara watched her parents interact with Henry during Thanksgiving dinner and noticed small differences in the way they behaved. He appeared comfortable in their home and carried a politeness that could charm anyone. He reached across the table without asking to get seconds and retrieved a bottle of wine for her parents, hidden in the back of the refrigerator. They talked mostly amongst themselves, pre-planning the upcoming holiday rush, changing the bakery menu, and creating a loose outline of the homeless shelter's schedule for food drop-off.

Amara half-listened, more interested in the confidence and ease her parents displayed through their leaning posture and consistent eye contact when communicating with Henry. Her parents were right. They treated him like family. *And they show more interest in him than they do their own two children.*

Amara ate quietly, making small talk with Daphne. She couldn't handle listening to more conversation about baklava, loukoumades, or kourabedies.

"This baklava is delicious," Henry said to Baba.

"Yes. We're going to have extra. The trick is to never refrigerate it. Believe it or not, if you refrigerate it, it'll get tough. If you store it in an airtight container, it should be fresh for two weeks."

"Baba," Amara interjected, "I tried to make baklava for Bethany but it came out soggy. Do you know what I did wrong?"

Her father gazed directly at Henry and away from Amara, like he didn't hear her. He continued to engage Henry talking about the different flavor combination of traditional baklava. Amara took another bite of stuffing, pretending she didn't ask. She tried to add to the conversation now and then, but her words were ignored or brushed aside. Amara clearly had no place in the discussion of the bakery.

***

Amara packed her car and drove back to Providence the next day. The wedding shower and bachelorette party were a few months away, but Amara knew their success was in her hands. If Amara waited too long before securing reservations, Bethany's party wouldn't happen. Bethany had commented that she wanted a big party for both occasions because most people couldn't afford to go to the wedding. It was Amara's job to make it happen.

Back in the apartment, Amara pulled out a piece of paper and jotted down questions about the bachelorette party. **Location? Things to do? Fun gag gifts? Invites?**

Amara considered reaching out to Ruby to get the contact info for Bethany's work friends. When Bethany and Amara moved in together, Bethany started her first job, which she learned about from Ruby. Ruby had interned in the emergency department and knew of a few openings before they had graduated. Bethany and a few nurses from her graduating class applied and they all were hired.

For Bethany's twenty-second birthday, she, Amara, and ten of Bethany's nursing friends went club hopping in Providence. Amara didn't feel any connection to the nurses and struggled to make small talk amongst words like bradycardia, contusion, and angina.

Around midnight, Amara couldn't hear another story about the resident doctor or the patient with congestive heart failure. She tried to convince Bethany to go home with her, but Bethany stayed out and didn't return until the next day. Amara didn't ask how the rest of the night went, because she didn't want to know. All she knew was that Bethany preferred the company of her work friends over her.

Amara knew that reaching out to Bethany's nurse friends to plan the party would guarantee Bethany's satisfaction, but she didn't want to share the limelight. Amara hadn't relied on them for Bethany's surprise birthday party and despite the consequences, Bethany considered that party a success.

Amara sighed and made some calls. The party planning was all on her, and she was going to prove to Bethany that she was the best friend Bethany could have.

Amara spent the rest of the weekend alone, waiting for Bethany to return from a weekend away with Ryan and his family. She looked around her cluttered bedroom and scanned all the clothes in her closet. If she had to move out in a month, she needed to get started. She and Bethany had lived together for seven years, and the amount of stuff they accumulated overwhelmed her. Amara didn't know where to begin, but she knew she had to do something. She grabbed cardboard boxes from the recycling bin and dug through her room, tossing things that she no longer needed.

Amara loaded four large boxes into her car and dumped a few more boxes at the donation drop-off center. She also had boxes and bags of trash to toss but the dumpster behind their apartment was full.

She texted her dad. **Hi, Baba. Can I come over for dinner tonight?** Within moments, her phone dinged with a simple response. **Yes.**

Amara had seen them, not forty-eight hours earlier, but she was alone and bored and needed the dumpster behind the shop. She didn't want to use her parents for their trash receptacle so she planned on stopping by for dinner before preparing for her interview.

The forty-minute ride to Woodstock was peaceful, with few people on the road. Chilly air zipped through her slightly open window, and Christmas carols sang through her radio. Two oversized bags of trash sat in the backseat like passengers.

The bell above the bakery door dinged.

"Hi, Mama. Hi, Baba." Amara pulled off her sunglasses and found Henry standing with his back to her, wrapping pastries.

"Hi, Amaryllis," Henry said.

"It's Amara," she reminded him again.

"Oh, sorry. Your parents call you Amaryllis. I'm accustomed to hearing that name." His deep British accent carried through the empty store.

"Yeah, they call me that, but no one else does."

"Of course." Henry threw her a smile over his shoulder. "Are you coming to the shelter with me? I have another batch for them."

Amara hesitated. She wasn't planning on it, but why not. "Sure. But first, I have to run in the back. I'm moving, and I have a few bags of trash to toss. Are my parents here?" she called as she stepped into the back room.

"No. They left about an hour ago."

Amara heaved the bags over her shoulder into the tall dumpster before climbing into Henry's beat-up car. He piled trays of food onto the back seat, and Amara tucked her purse under the front seat so it remained safe.

"Do you do this every day?" she asked.

"Yes, every day. I think I have been delivering food since January. The person who runs the shelter is a friend of your parents, and I guess they wanted to give back." Amara nodded, surprised to hear about this piece of their past. She didn't recall any family friends, let alone family friends that ran a homeless shelter.

As much as she found Henry to be stuffy and boring, he seemed to have good intentions. They pulled up to the shelter, and Amara grabbed a tray of bagels. She immediately put the tray back and took off her leather coat. There was no reason to rub her good fortune in the noses of those who weren't so blessed.

They carried the trays into the kitchen, taking the same route as last time. Amara recognized some men and women from her last drop-off, and a small level of sadness filled her. She wondered what they did to get stuck in a place like this. Amara turned to Henry. "Any more in the car?" she asked.

He nodded, and Amara hurried out the door to ease the discomfort settling in her body.

On the way back into town, Henry turned to her. "I saw you back there, and you looked uncomfortable."

"Me?" Amara scoffed. "Not at all." She didn't know why she denied it. She barely knew Henry.

"Your shoulders got tense. You didn't smile at anyone, and you conveniently spent more time outside than you did in."

Amara felt her shoulders tense again at the accusation of his words. "I was trying to be helpful," she replied with staccato biting off the end of her words.

"Why does it feel so weird to you? To be in a place like that?" he asked.

"I don't know." Amara searched for the right words, but it was too late. She had already admitted her weakness, so she had to finish her thought. "I just…I don't belong there. I've never been around homeless people before."

"You have. You just didn't know it. Could you pick out the homeless shelter on that street? Simply by looking at it?"

Amara shook her head. "It's a beautiful house."

"Exactly. You didn't know. Just like you have no idea who's homeless or sick or down on their luck just by a glance. I'm going to tell you something, and I bet you had no idea."

Amara gazed at him, but his eyes remained straight ahead, navigating the narrow road. She waited for him to continue.

"I was homeless once."

Amara pulled back and pressed her shoulder against the door to get a better look at Henry's face.

"Relax. You don't have to get all weird on me. My parents kicked me out of the house when I was seventeen, and I lived in my car on the outskirts of London for at least six months. Maybe more. It was the lowest time of my life. I bet you didn't know that by looking at me, did you?"

Amara wasn't sure how to respond to a personal confession from someone she barely knew. "I had no idea."

"Exactly. That's what I mean. I'm a person, and they are people too. Sometimes shitty things happen, but the result isn't forever. For me? It felt like forever, but I got help. They can do it too, and they can pull themselves out of the trenches. You need to stop judging them because you don't know their story. You need to put yourself in their shoes and show some compassion."

Amara opened and closed her mouth numerous times. *How could Henry speak to me like that? He doesn't even know me!* Every response she concocted in her brain felt amateurish and self-centered. Instead, she kept her lips sealed and seethed on the inside.

"Thank you for the ride," Amara politely said when they pulled up to the shop. She grabbed her purse and climbed out of his car. She didn't want to see her family anymore. Her jovial mood had deteriorated with Henry's lecture.

Sorry, Baba. Something came up, and I won't make it tonight.
Amara weaved her way through the tree-lined roads and got on the highway. When she pulled up to her apartment, Amara stared at her home. Like Henry, she found herself homeless, and things were not looking up.

***

Amara pulled into the empty bank parking lot thirty minutes before the bank opened. She pulled out her notes and ran through potential interview questions, hoping that the coffee kicked in enough to put her brain into hyper-gear. She spoke aloud to herself, emphasizing words, raising her pitch, and practicing catchy tag lines. She needed this promotion. She didn't deserve to be a teller. She was better than that.

Amara closed her eyes and pictured herself in the conference room surrounded by her superiors. She imagined Tania, smug lips and narrowed eyes, waiting to squash every positive thing Amara had to say about herself. A pit the size of a baseball settled at the bottom of her stomach.

At eight twenty-five, she quietly snuck into the bank. Now that she didn't have an office, she didn't have anywhere to hide. Instead, she sat in a lobby chair as if she were a customer waiting for help to open a loan. Amara picked at her nails, took a sip of lukewarm coffee, and reviewed her notes again.

Today, she dressed extra smartly, wearing a black pencil skirt, low-heeled pumps, and a black blazer over a white button-down shirt. She applied enough makeup to appear confident, but approachable. The problem was, they all knew her. First impressions happened years ago, and now she fought against the judgment they created when working with her.

"Amara," Gail said. Amara stood, confused as to why Gail was part of the interview committee.

"Hi," Amara voiced with confusion. She cleared her throat to reset herself. Her fingers turned numb, and her coffee cup threatened to crash to the floor. She imagined the carpet soaking up the hot liquid, her black pumps sticky with coffee. She tightened her grip and followed Gail.

"I need you to sit down," Gail said. No one else was in the office. Unease settled in Amara's throat. Her chest tightened and her face grew hot.

"What's up?" she asked.

"We have a slight problem. Over the weekend, we had a number of calls explaining that deposits never transferred into the proper accounts. The common factor in all the discrepancies was that you handled the deposit."

Amara sat quietly. The words entered her brain, but she didn't quite comprehend. She bit her lip, concentrating on Gail's lips moving.

"We investigated every claim, and the numbers were off by one digit. Obviously, you weren't paying attention. You didn't check the ID or facial recognition to make sure you were in the right account, and you didn't print the balance on the deposit slip, which would have been another clue to the customer that you screwed up."

Amara cringed. *You screwed up. You screwed up. You screwed up.* The words echoed in her mind. Over the past week, she put less effort and attention into her job. She needed Gail to want to give her up. She never intended to screw up to the point of being reprimanded. Amara looked at her watch and cringed again. She was ten minutes late for her interview!

"Gail, I'm sorry. I promise it will never happen again. If you'll excuse me, I have a meeting that I should have joined ten minutes ago." Amara flashed Gail her white teeth, hoping to escape the main office.

Gail's eyes widened. "Amara, you are not late. I canceled your meeting. You can pack whatever stuff you have and go. Your services are no longer needed at this bank." Gail stood, hovering over Amara, speaking to her like a child.

Amara continued to sit. She couldn't believe they canceled her interview.

"Go, Amara. You have been terminated." Gail swung open the door and stomped out of the room.

Amara's heart beat through her skin and her knees shook. Her face flushed and tears splashed against her face. *I will not cry. I will not cry.* Amara brushed her cheeks, smearing the wetness against her hairline, and raised her face high. *This will not define me.* Amara gathered her belongings and exited the bank, staring straight ahead, refusing to make eye contact or focus on the hushed whispers behind her.

Amara furiously sped home. Her day had gone from bad to worse within seconds. The concept of no job settled into Amara's brain. How had her life so quickly crumbled when she least expected it? *No job, no money. No money, no apartment.* It didn't matter if she found another roommate or figured out a way to live alone. It wasn't happening.

Amara flew through the front door of their apartment and heaved a loud, frustrated sigh. She dropped her keys on the side table and sped into the kitchen, not sure what to do, but her body was dripping with negative energy.

Bethany sat at the table, sipping her coffee. She wore a purple bathrobe, her curly hair tied up in a messy bun. She stared at Amara silently. Amara's tight lips pulled across her face, and her shoulders stood tall. She felt like a caged animal desperate to break free. She kicked off her shoes into the corner and loudly pulled out a chair.

"What are you doing home?" Bethany asked.

Amara stood and filled a mug with black coffee. She sat next to

Bethany, coffee splashing over the rim when the mug's base hit the table. "Fired," Amara frothed.

Bethany raised her eyebrows. "Fired?"

Amara stuck out her bottom lip and squinted her eyes. "Yep, fired." She didn't want to talk about it.

"What happened?" Suddenly Bethany's voice was smooth and soothing, like she was comforting a child who dropped his ice cream cone on the hot pavement.

Amara rolled her eyes. "I don't know. I had an interview for a promotion but apparently made some mistakes last Wednesday at the till. They didn't even ask me what had happened, and told me I was no longer welcome."

Bethany balked. "How can they do that?"

Anger slipped away, and despair seeped in. "What am I going to do?"

Bethany didn't answer. She sat back in the kitchen chair, her feet kicked up and rested on the chair beside her. *She looks rather comfortable,* Amara thought. *Why wouldn't she? She wasn't fired. And she's getting married. Her life is great right now.*

Amara hopped up and went to her room. "I need some space. I need to think."

Her emotions traveled throughout her body like a wooden, rickety roller coaster. One minute she was up, hopeful for the future, and the next, she was down, convinced her life was over. Amara lay in her bed for hours, considering her future after this devastating turn.

She heard a gentle knock on the door. "Yeah?" She kept the covers tucked under her chin.

"Can I come in?" Bethany's syrupy, muffled voice pushed through the door.

"Sure."

The door opened, and Bethany stood in her scrubs. She wore a stethoscope around her neck and held a water bottle in her hand. "I'm heading out to work. Is there anything you need?"

Amara laughed out loud. "A million dollars?"

"Sorry, Amara. I'm all out of those. I'll be home around midnight. Text me if you need me."

Amara nodded and pulled the blankets up over her head. It was early afternoon, and she should be at the bank, but instead remained huddled under her warm, wishing for night. "Thanks, I'll be fine," she called from under her comforter.

***

The next morning, Amara climbed out of bed with a resurgence of motivation but also a jackhammering headache. She couldn't repeat yesterday, all mopey and crying into her wine glass alone. It was a mistake to open that bottle, and Amara knew it, but her body had moved without her brain's consent. Amara didn't remember finishing the bottle, but it lay empty, next to her bed filled with hidden secrets.

Amara slightly recalled stumbling to bed, hoping she could sleep her emotions away. Her reflection in the mirror revealed blotchy skin and wild hair. Amara made a face at herself, convinced she could smell the alcohol seeping out of her pores. She brushed her teeth, rinsed out her dry, sticky mouth, and showered.

She walked through their Providence neighborhood alone. The cold air woke her up much quicker than her shower did. She remembered her hat but forgot her gloves, and her fingers numbed almost instantly. Amara stuffed her hands into her sherpa-lined pockets and shuffled around the block. She shivered from the top of her head to the bottom of her feet and violently readjusted her hat. The cold air wouldn't kill her but she kind of wished it would.

Amara stumbled into a coffee shop to grab a hot drink. Not only would coffee warm her body, but the cup would warm her hands. A young man with blond hair and a black beanie held open the door for her, and Amara locked eyes with him. She hurried past him to the counter, mumbling her thanks.

He followed her in. Amara felt his eyes on her, and her confidence slightly swelled. She looked like death today. She held her body a little taller, her breasts popping out a little further forward, and she shook her head to loosen her hair.

"Large black coffee and a blueberry muffin, please."

The man came up next to her to give his order to the second employee. "Large black coffee and blueberry muffin, please."

Amara turned when her words echoed. A small smile crept along her face. He looked so familiar, but she couldn't place him. She stared at his blue eyes and glistening teeth a moment too long. She looked away and hid her smile.

"Amara, right?" he asked.

Amara's head shot to the right, still unsure how she knew him.

"Hi, do I know you?" Stupidity sat on her shoulders. Of course, she knew him if he knew her. She blushed and dropped her gaze, realizing that she may have insulted him by not remembering.

The cashier handed them both their coffee and change.

"It's Tyler," he reminded her.

Amara smiled and looked at her coffee, trying to place him.

"Are you in a hurry? Do you mind if I sit with you?" Amara flinched, remembering that she looked like death, and probably like she didn't have a job. *Oh wait, I don't.*

"Sure." She pulled her hat further down her forehead, hoping the shadow would hide the bags under her eyes.

They settled at a table near the window. Frost decorated the bottom of the pane, with each tiny snowflake fully formed and glistening.

Tyler removed his hat and his long hair fell into place. Bethany's birthday party flashed through her mind.

Tyler! "I didn't recognize you with your hat on." Her voice revealed surprise and enjoyment. "The last time I saw you, it was summer, and you were barely wearing anything." She flushed at the thought of him being naked. *Amara, stop!* "You know, at the beach," she clarified.

"How are things going?"

"Doing great. What are you doing here? Aren't you up in Boston?" Her rate of speech quickened as the butterflies in her chest took flight.

"Yeah, well, Thanksgiving. And I stayed a few extra days to spend with my dad and Mona."

Of course. Thanksgiving. God, that felt like a lifetime ago. "How was your Thanksgiving?" Amara asked.

"Not bad. I saw Ryan and Bethany, and they seemed like they're doing well. All they did was talk about the wedding. Are you in it?"

"I'm the maid of honor. I haven't done much yet. I have so much going on right now." The stress of being responsible for planning the events leading up to the big day hung over her like a rain cloud.

"Yeah, I'm in it too. I don't know why, since Ryan and I aren't close, but I think it has something to do with our parents." Tyler laughed. Dimples pulled at his cheeks, and his eyes disappeared into small crescent moons.

"I'm supposed to be planning the bridal shower. Bethany wants Ryan to be there too. Maybe we could work together? I don't have any of his family's contact info."

"Sure," Tyler agreed.

"Bethany and Ryan don't have to know. If it goes great, we both get credit, and if it goes wrong, no one will know who to blame." Under the table, she crossed and uncrossed her legs, trying to get the jitters out.

Tyler chuckled at her plan. "Sounds good to me. I've never been involved in planning a wedding." He looked at her with hypnotizing blue eyes.

"Let's do it." Amara smiled and stuck out her chin to accentuate her cheek bones. She tried to shake his hand and he clumsily gave her a high five. Amara laughed at his awkwardness, finally feeling like she could be herself. "When are you heading home?"

"Tonight, after dinner. Let me get your number. That way, we can stay in touch about the wedding."

He held out his hand and she gave him her phone. His cell buzzed on the table next to his coffee. "There, now you'll always have it."

Amara looked at her recent calls and saw the word **Ty** on the top line of her history.

"Thanks," she said.

"Give me a call sometime." He stood from the table and adjusted his hat. "I have to run. I told my dad and Mona I was grabbing milk for breakfast, and I've been gone a while. I'm surprised they haven't called a million times by now."

"It was great running into you," Amara said.

"Yeah, we'll be in touch. See you later." Tyler stood from the table and waved, picking up their trash on the way out.

Amara sat in the warm coffee house for a while, watching the frost melt on the opaque window. She dreaded wedding planning, but was thrilled to spend time with Tyler, the handsome man from Boston. Amara imagined staying up late with Tyler, planning the shower and parties without worrying about work. She could even drive to Boston and see him at his house, possibly spending the night if it got too late.

Amara continued to fantasize, reminding herself that this was Ryan's brother. But not his actual brother, so there were no shared genes. Amara considered telling Bethany about her run-in with Tyler, but wanted to keep their moment private. She wasn't sure where Bethany stood on Tyler, and she didn't want any opinions on the matter.

Amara's life was falling apart. She needed a little sunshine, and if that sunshine came in the form of a handsome man, then Amara was ready to open the dusty windows and let in the light.

Chapter 7

mara sat on her oversized couch with a hot tea steaming beside her, and a pile of Oreos resting on a napkin. She stuffed a cookie in her mouth, whipped open her laptop, and searched for jobs online. There were so many banks in the city; there must be something that would fit Amara's strengths. Nothing seemed good enough. Either the pay was too low, the responsibilities too menial, or the commute too far. None of the listings motivated her to revise her resume or hit the apply button.

Amara closed the laptop and shut her eyes. This was going to be harder than she expected.

Amara pulled out the wedding magazines and scoured for bridal shower décor ideas to distract herself from her bleak future. Bethany wanted a large group so those who couldn't afford the wedding could still celebrate. *The wedding is during the summer, so the shower should probably be in the spring.*

Amara ripped out pictures of table vases, flower bouquets, buffet menus, and party games. She arranged the photos on construction paper, gluing them down to create a clear-cut vision for how everything would fit together. Amara called all the clubs in the city that could accommodate one hundred guests and made appointments to tour and taste the food.

She texted Tyler: **Are you free on Saturday? I made appointments to check out venues for the bridal shower. Do you want to come?**

Moments later, her phone dinged. **Sure.**

Sure. Amara's heart pumped loudly against her chest. Goosebumps emerged on her forearms like miniature mountainous terrain. She wiped her hands on her pants and typed back. **Great, I'll send you the times later. Setting up additional appointments now.**

Any uncomfortable feelings blew away like confetti after a pinata busted open at a five-year-old girl's birthday party. Amara felt lighter, her footsteps not making any noise or creaking the floor boards in the old, dusty apartment. Her headache subsided, and she found herself smiling at all the beautiful wedding images.

It was early December, and time was ticking away. She needed to get moving, or Bethany would be disappointed in her wedding party planning skills. But the thought of having Tyler at her side made Amara's heart flutter and pound. Maybe getting fired wasn't the worst thing in the world after all.

***

That Saturday, Amara took extra care to get ready for her day with Tyler. She had to remind herself that it wasn't a date but a completely platonic planning event. She pulled out her black slacks that hugged her butt and accentuated the strong muscles that developed with regular squats. She pulled a red v-neck sweater over her head, the top of her cleavage poking through the neckline. Amara prided herself in her perky c-cup breasts that peeked out of her shirt with the help of a push-up bra. Her long onyx braid rested between her shoulder blades. A little mascara and a neutral lip stain completed the look. She checked herself out one more time in the mirror and admired her body. Tyler should be thrilled to join her today.

Amara grabbed her bag off the couch and strolled out the door, her heeled boots clicking on the old wooden slats. Tyler sat in his black SUV looking like a model. His blonde hair hung loosely over one eye, and his blue irises peeked through the strands. Amara climbed in the front seat, unable to believe her luck. She would've been working had she not been fired.

"Hi," she breathed, fastening her seatbelt.

He smiled, his straight white teeth glistening in the sun. "Hi. Where to?" he asked

"Believe it or not, we're going to the same place where we held Bethany's twenty-fifth. I thought it might be cute, right? The place he proposed is the same place we celebrate their future." Amara blushed, associating the word wedding with date, and then to Tyler. She turned her head to look out the window until her skin returned to its normal peachy undertone.

Tyler weaved through old established neighborhoods, moving away from the highway and closer to the ocean. His GPS spat out directions even though Amara could navigate. She pressed her body against the leather seat and enjoyed the view from her passenger window.

When they walked in, the hospitality manager greeted them, immediately recognizing Amara. "Hi! Good seeing you again." She shook both their hands.

"Hi, Ana," Amara said. "We're planning a wedding shower for about a hundred people and wanted to see if the Oceanside would be a good fit. It's for Bethany and Ryan, the couple that got engaged during the party I organized a few months ago. I don't know if you remember."

Ana nodded vaguely.

The three of them sat down to discuss ideas for the bridal shower. "Since you're a repeat customer, we will give you a ten percent discount on the rental fee and catering fee if you use our caterer."

Dollar signs saved practically floated above Amara's head. She smiled widely at Tyler.

"Sold. Where do I sign?" Amara giggled, not quite believing her luck. The first place they went, and it all worked out. This wedding planning thing was less complicated than she imagined.

"You sure?" Tyler asked after Ana rose from the table to grab the contract. "We have a few other appointments today." He spoke carefully and diplomatically.

"Yes, This is perfect," Amara said.

Tyler raised his shoulders and smiled. "Sure, if you think so." He looked around the banquet hall and strolled over to the windows overlooking the beach. "What do you want to do now? I have all day."

Amara's stomach leapt to her heart like a kid at a trampoline park. *Pull it together, Amara. He isn't asking you out on a date or anything.*

"Let's go to the party store. We can buy some decorations."

Amara signed the contract, gave a small deposit, and pushed the balance from her mind. She would figure out how to pay for it later.

"When do I come back to meet with the caterer?" she asked Ana.

"I'll have her call you with her next appointment," Ana assured.

Amara jumped up from the table and shook Ana's hand. "Thank you for everything!"

She and Tyler walked back to the car, Amara chattering about their incredible luck. She turned abruptly to Tyler and grabbed his solid lower arm, below the elbow. Her fingers barely wrapped around the circumference. She gave it a squeeze and then dropped her arms to her side.

Tyler turned and Amara saw a sparkle in his eyes that encouraged her to share her thoughts. "Maybe I can do this for a living. I'll be a wedding planner." She didn't hear his response. She was pleased with her success at planning the party, and her brain moved on to the next item on her bridal shower to-do list.

Amara's elation continued at the party store. The abundance of holiday décor distracted from her goal. Shiny sequins and Christmas cheer called her to gaily play. They tried on Christmas attire, Santa suits, and elf accessories.

"I can't believe Christmas is three weeks away." Amara wrapped garland around her neck like a layered necklace.

"Me either. I have so much work to do before the long weekend." Tyler approached Amara wearing a fuzzy red hat with a giant white ball on top and a long, white, curly beard hanging against his face. "How do I look?"

His goofiness made her grin and she admired his spontaneity. Amara pulled on a green sequined elf hat to distract herself from the strong urge to touch him. Heat radiated up her body, spreading throughout her abdomen, chest, and face. There was no one else in the aisle, and she couldn't see the store employees.

"Hey, Santa," she called out, her voice throaty and raspy. She cleared her throat, feeling silly but pushing through. "I've been a good elf." She sashaying her hips as she stepped toward him.

Tyler turned, and Amara stood inches from his face. "Hey," he whispered.

Amara felt a magnetic tug toward him. She knew he felt it too. She could see it in the awkward way his Adam's apple bobbed when he swallowed. His gaze traveled around her face, avoiding her eyes. He looked nervous, which Amara found endearing.

"I've been a good elf. Do I get anything special?" She was used to men swooning at her feet. This role-playing activity in a store wasn't something she'd done in the past, but they were practically alone. Nothing would happen except a bit of teasing, so Amara continued, hoping she didn't scare him away.

"Yeah." His voice cracked, and Amara giggled. He looked like he wanted to say more. His tense body stood tall; his feet firmly planted.

Amara traced her finger from his temple down to his chin, feeling the fuzzy beard under her fingernail. "I want a big, red candy cane for Christmas," she whispered.

His neck muscles protruded, and he loudly swallowed, his eyes darting over her shoulders.

Amara turned around, strutted to the end of the aisle, and grabbed a candy cane before disappearing behind the endcap. She ripped the hat off her head and put her hand against her beating heart. *What am I doing? This is crazy. I barely know the guy.* First, she felt fearless, but now that she just threw herself at the enemy's brother, she felt foolish.

She turned the corner with her head down. She fumbled with the Christmas stock, straightening the shelves. Her shoulders slumped forward and she pulled into herself. When she raised her eyes, Tyler remained frozen. The Santa hat hung loosely against his stubbly face.

"Okay, you ready to go?" she asked casually. "I asked the clerk, and they won't get spring stuff until February. We'll have to come back then."

Tyler quickly stripped himself from the costume and followed her out the door.

In the car, he turned to her. "What was that?" The question accused her of doing something wrong. If she was honest with herself, she didn't know what came over her. Usually, she wouldn't approach an attractive man with such aggression unless she had two or three Rum and Coke's running through her veins. Perhaps it was the safety of being in public or the high she felt from booking the party, but Tyler made her feel safe and adventurous, all at the same time.

"What was what?" She tilted her head down and looked at him through her eyelashes.

"That. That thing. The elf, the candy cane, all of that." He looked at her, but his eyes rested on the crest of her lips.

"That was me going a little too far," she replied. Amara bit back a smile, wondering if she had scared him away.

Tyler looked forward, frowning.

"Are you okay? Was it too much?"

"No, it wasn't too much. It was ballsy, and it surprised me, but I kind of liked it. How do you know I'm not seeing anyone?"

"Tyler, I assumed if you were seeing someone, you wouldn't have volunteered to help me with all this wedding planning. You would know better. I'm not looking for a boyfriend, but I do like to have fun every now and then."

"You're lucky I'm single," he grinned. "I'd like to get to know you better, too."

Amara turned toward him, analyzing his profile. No matter where she looked, she was drawn to his electric blue eyes. "Tyler, why are you single? You're young, successful, handsome, and kind. My mother would call you a catch."

Tyler grinned and shrugged. "Relationships are too complicated. I like to go slow before diving in."

Amara looked at his lips and wondered what they would taste like against hers. She turned her head forward and felt her fingertips numb. She pulled out her ponytail and put it up again, hoping continuous movement would distract her brain from focusing on what was happening to her body. "I completely agree. Relationships are way too complicated."

Amara reached across and brushed her hand against Tyler's. A zap of electricity coursed through her veins and Amara pulled away. Tyler's rosy cheeks told Amara he felt it too, and her stomach tumbled.

They grabbed a late lunch at an Italian deli in Federal Hill before Tyler dropped off Amara at her apartment. The mood shifted as soon as they sat at the counter in the deli. Instead of talking about the feelings attached to the Santa-elf escapade, they safely returned to the wedding planning.

"So, tell me about you," he said, taking a bite of his sandwich. "Who are you?"

"What do you know?"

"You're best friends with Bethany. That's it. I'm not especially close to Ryan, but I hear things through my parents when I sporadically call them. Besides that, nothing."

"I'm from Connecticut." Amara took a large bite of her Italian sub and chewed loudly, the pickles crunching between her teeth. "Bethany was my roommate freshman year of college, and we hit it off. We did everything together. We pledged to the same sorority, hung out in the same crowd, and have lived together ever since. We got our current apartment three years ago."

"What do you do for work?"

Amara cringed, hoping he couldn't see the frustration in her eyes.

"Long story short, nothing. The Monday after Thanksgiving they terminated me." Amara air-quoted the word terminated because she still didn't believe her actions required termination.

Tyler's eyes widened. "I'm sorry. What happened?" Compassion and concern coated his words.

"Ah, I don't want to talk about it. I was in banking and loans. I graduated with a finance degree and have worked for banks ever since. Actually, for *that* bank ever since. I'm sure I'll find something." She changed the subject. "What about you?"

"I work outside of Boston for a tech company. I've been there about five years or so."

Amara placed her napkin over her mouth and ran her tongue over her teeth to clear any stuck lettuce. "Do you like Boston?"

"I've been living there for the past few years. I like it. I was never too far from my dad and Mona. I used to go home every weekend to do laundry, but now I don't have to. My place is pretty nice. It has a washer and dryer in the apartment."

Amara laughed. "Those little things are so important." She bit down on her straw and sipped her water.

The rest of the meal was easy. They chatted like old friends, not once mentioning the Santa and Elf experience earlier that day. Whenever the image of him dressed as Santa flashed through her mind, she felt her stomach drop and her chest tighten. *I'm such an idiot. Why did I do that? Thank you, Tyler, for not making me feel like a bigger idiot than I already feel.* Amara busied herself with the sugar packets on the table and pushed her inner thoughts out of her mind.

"Tell me about Ryan," Amara said. "I know little about him. Bethany keeps their relationship to herself and I don't want to pry."

"He seems happy," Tyler said.

"Sure, but don't you think it's too soon? I was shocked when she said yes." Shame wrapped around Amara for talking negatively about her best friend's boyfriend to his brother. Well, step-brother.

Tyler shrugged. "He's young and has no direction, but it's his life. We all make choices without thinking. Sometimes they work out, and sometimes they don't. He's not a bad guy; he doesn't know who he is, I don't think. He comes off as this super-successful, put-together guy, but he's still living at home."

"Right?" Amara leaned her body over the table and rested her head in her hand. "That's what I thought! Isn't that a huge red flag about maturity and responsibility and accountability and all that?"

Tyler nodded. "He's always been a mama's boy. He told me he's living at home to save up for their life after the wedding. If that's the case, doesn't that make him smart and responsible?"

Amara shifted in her seat, her head tilting side to side as she contemplated his point of view. "Maybe."

"Who knows. But it's his life. If they love each other, then that's all that matters, right?"

"Sure, but can you know in six months? They had been dating six months when he proposed."

"Sure. You might know in three days. There is no timeline for love." Confidence and certainty bounced off his words so much that Amara believed him.

After lunch, they pulled up to the front of Amara's building.

She grabbed her purse and held out her keys. "Thanks for hanging out. I had a great time."

Tyler nodded. "Me too. Let me know if you need me for anything else."

Amara's legs quivered and her heart jittered as she thought of what she might need from him. "I will. Drive safely. And really, I'm sorry about before." She bit the inside of her lip feeling the fleshiness between her teeth.

"No problem. It was fun."

She walked toward the door, her hips rocking rhythmically with every step. She felt his eyes on her backside. When the door closed behind her, she ran in place, giddy with excitement. Her arms jerked over her head like she had won the lottery. The next few months were going to be fun if it meant hanging out with Tyler.

Chapter 8

"**M**ama? Baba?" Amara called into the bakery kitchen from in front of the display cases. She knocked on the swinging door as she entered the back room.

"Amaryllis, hello," her dad bellowed, glancing up while kneading dough beneath his calloused, stubby fingers. From what Amara could see, he was making loukoumades. She bounced over to him and kissed him on the cheek.

Henry waved and Amara smiled.

"Loukoumades, Baba?" she asked, glancing at the fryolator.

"Yes, Amaryllis. You must make loukoumades at Loukomades Bakery, right? It's our trademark."

Amara inhaled deeply, the confectioner sugar tickling her nostrils. She walked over to the display tray and popped a cooled donut hole into her mouth. "These are my favorites, Baba. Great job. They remind me of eating homemade loukoumades at Yia Yia's house."

Baba grinned. "I learned from the best. So, what are you doing here?" He glanced at the clock. It was still morning on a Wednesday. "Shouldn't you be working?"

Amara sighed. It had been three weeks, and she hadn't told her parents yet. Bethany expected her to move out in a week and a half, and she didn't have a place to go. "I have the day off," she lied. There was no point in upsetting her father, at his place of employment, when it could wait.

"What brings you here?" he eyed her suspiciously. "What do you need?"

Amara pulled her eyebrows up, surprised at his assumption. "Nothing. I wanted to see you and Mama. I have some news." His eyebrows popped up again, the creases in his forehead deepening.

"I'm going home for lunch in one hour. We can talk then."

Amara exited the kitchen and sat at the counter facing the floor-to-ceiling windows. She pulled out her phone and searched for bridesmaid dresses. Bethany, Amara, Ruby, and Mikayla were dress shopping after Christmas.

Henry stood behind the counter, plating kataifi bites. The syrup-soaked shredded phyllo dough stuck to his fingers as he arranged them with precision on the platter. He smiled at Amara and adjusted his hat, pushing the top of his wrist against the stiff brim.

"Hi Henry, do you need any help?"

"Hi, Amaryllis. I'm all set, thank you."

Her body stiffened, hearing her real name on the lips of a stranger. She debated telling him again not to call her that, but let it slide. Amara returned to her phone, waiting for her dad to take his lunch break.

Amara drove her dad back to the house. He had never been in her fancy car and commented on the low profile, leather seats, and electronic dash. "How do you even know how this works?" he asked.

"I don't," Amara admitted. "I know the basics, but that's it."

"Why have this car if you don't know how to use it?" He was too logical sometimes.

Amara rolled her eyes. "Because it sends a statement."

"What statement is that?" he asked, his voice booming.

"I don't know. That I know what I'm doing with my life?"

"A car?" Her father guffawed and leaned in closer to touch the buttons on the stereo. His stubby fingertips smashed into the flat screen and the audio switched between radio and Bluetooth. "No, no, a car tells me if someone is foolish with their money. This is not practical. This is foolishness."

Amara shifted away from Baba and rolled her lips back and forth. She pulled her body into her core like an octopus squeezing itself into a fishbowl and ignored his disappointed stare. They continued the rest of the drive in silence.

Back at the house, Mama sat at the table, papers surrounding her in short stacks.

"Amaryllis." Her mother did a double take and pulled her glasses off, placing them on the table. "What brings you here?"

Amara's shoulders slumped and she regretted coming home. *Why was an unexpected visit such a surprise?*

"Hi, Mama. I had the day off today."

Her mother cleared the table and motioned for Amara to sit. She sat next to her mother, the pile of papers dividing them in one tall stack on the floor. Baba sat on the other side and faced both women.

"George, what would you like for lunch?" Mama jumped up from the table, knowing Baba only had a short time before returning to the bakery. She pulled out a variety of deli meat and condiments and placed them on the table.

"I'll have a turkey sandwich," Amara interjected. Her father glared at her and Amara dropped her eyes to her hands. "I'll make it Mama. You can get Baba's."

"I'll have ham and cheese, please," he said.

Amara stood next to her mother as they made sandwiches. Once eating, the tension dissipated and Amara cleared her throat. Her parents looked up and Amara cleared her throat again and took a quick sip of water. "I have some bad news."

Amara stopped and waited for a reaction. Both parents appeared to be listening. Mama's arms froze in midair, holding her sandwich above the plate. "I got fired." Still no response. "From my job. And my lease is up in January, and I have nowhere to go." Amara looked down and scraped her dry, cracked cuticles. As the moment of silence increased in length, her shame increased in weight.

"What do you want us to do about that?" Her father could be tough as nails. Amara knew that he thought that with enough effort, anyone could better their lives. Just like he and Mama did.

Amara shrugged. She didn't want to move back home, but she didn't have a choice without a job. She didn't want to beg for something she would do anything to avoid. "I need help."

"What do you need? What do you want?" Baba repeated. Mama finished her sandwich and rested back in her chair.

"I either need to borrow money, or I need to move home." Amara looked around, knowing that there was nowhere for her to claim as her own space in the apartment. "I could bunk with Daphne until I get on my feet."

Baba cackled. "You and Daphne? What about all your stuff? There's no room. You're twenty-five. You're an adult."

"Why can't you stay in your apartment? Can't you get a new roommate?" Mama asked.

Amara balled her hands at her side. "Bethany kicked me out."

"What?" Baba boomed.

"Bethany told me I had to move out because she and Ryan were staying. I have no choice." Amara looked down, remembering the fight that followed Bethany's announcement. She couldn't tell her parents that she ran her mouth while intoxicated. She had told Bethany she was making the biggest mistake of her life and that Ryan was a loser who was using her.

Amara shuddered, remembering the words, "I hope you get divorced and regret the mistake you made," flying out of her mouth. In response, Bethany picked up the almost-full wine glass on the table and threw it at Amara's head. Amara raised her hands to protect her face and the shattered pieces of glass settled around Amara's feet. Red wine splashed on her white sweater, resembling gunshot wounds. "Get. Out." Bethany seethed. "I want you gone this weekend."

"Yeah, it's probably for the best." Amara looked at her parents, hoping she wasn't wearing her shame like a coat.

Mama leaned forward. "And what about your job?"

"I messed up. I wasn't paying attention, and I made a rather expensive mistake." There was no point in explaining further.

"How many jobs have you applied to since you got fired?"

Amara opted for the truth. "Two jobs in three weeks."

Baba cleared his throat. "Two jobs?" His voice echoed off the walls.

"There isn't much out there," she defended.

"Your father and I have to talk about it. We don't have any extra money for you to borrow. The only option is moving home, but I don't know how that could work. Your bedroom is Baba's office, and we don't have time between the bakery and the holidays to rearrange the house." Mama was direct and to the point. "Give us forty-eight hours, and we'll let you know if you can come back. Understand, though, that it would be temporary."

Amara appreciated her mother's kindness. Amara placed her head in her hand and glanced around the table. "I'm sorry," she mumbled. Her father ignored her eyes, and her mother busied herself with the empty plates.

"Amara, dishes," Mama said.

***

Amara picked up the last box and transferred it to the moving truck. Christmas was in two days, and the year was officially over. She stood in her empty room, her eyes traveling from one blank wall to the next, and cried. It wasn't fair.

She blamed Bethany for kicking her out and blamed herself for losing her job. Amara typically loved Christmas, but this year, a heaviness sat on her chest like a sleeping cow that was nearly impossible to wake.

Her father and Henry stood in the kitchen, waiting for her. Amara felt tremendous guilt for having her dad help. He needed to be at work, setting up for the Christmas platters or the shelter donation. Amara continued to feel like a teenager who didn't have her life together.

"Ready," she said, nodding toward the door.

Bethany stood in the living room, sitting on the couch, looking like she wanted to get up, but was afraid. "Bye Amara," she said with a meek wave.

Amara threw her a glance, narrowed her eyes, and said nothing. She ignored her former best friend as she exited into the hallway, pulling the door closed.

The drive over to the storage unit was quiet. Baba and Henry drove the U-Haul while Amara followed in her BMW. The only sound was the rev of the engine. One more Christmas carol, and she dared herself to drive off a cliff, crashing into the ocean.

The storage unit was the right size to hold her old bedroom. All the furniture to transfer into the bare, sterile block, was her bed, dresser, and the kitchen table that she snidely removed while Bethany watched. Everything else in the apartment was Bethany's. It had only taken a few hours to load, navigating the stairwells and multiple entrance doors and sidestepping the slush-covered sidewalk. Emptying the truck was a clear shot from the vehicle's tail to the storage room door.

The three of them worked silently. Amara's hands tingled and burned from exposure to the frigid air while manipulating the lock and carrying the boxes. She shivered, knowing she deserved whatever level of discomfort she was experiencing. Now and then, she glanced at her father's grimace that seemed permanently etched across his face.

Amara pulled out a box of clothes and personal items she couldn't live without and placed them in her car. She pretended she was going to sleep-away camp and needed to pack enough to survive until she could return home.

Baba and Henry climbed into the truck. "Amaryllis, we're taking the truck back, then going to the bakery. See you at dinner."

"Thank you so much for your help." The pitch of her voice traveled up and down like a yo-yo. "Honestly, I couldn't have done it without you. Thank you." She almost felt like she should tip them for their services, but knew it would never be appropriate to pay her father.

"Bye, Amaryllis," Henry said. "Welcome home."

Amara cringed. Hearing her name from him forced confidence to retreat into her insecure childhood psyche.

Alone in the packed storage room, big, ugly tears rolled down her cheeks. *What am I doing? This is insane.* She didn't know how long her life would be in limbo like this. She didn't want to go back to the house in Connecticut. It was too small and too personal. She didn't want to work at the bakery, but she was homeless if she disagreed. That was the deal. Move home rent-free, work at the bakery, and sell the car.

Anger surged throughout Amara's body like an explosion, and she kicked the box closest to her feet. "Ah!" Pain seared up her foot to her ankle, and she hopped up and down, embracing the discomfort. She was an idiot for thinking she was in control of her life. She knew she should have tried harder.

The ride back to the house was challenging. Her beautiful car was going back to the dealership the day after Christmas, and was less than two years old. Although she would get hit with the early termination fee, she would save herself seven hundred dollars a month. She didn't want to do it, but it was part of the deal.

Amara ran her hand over the chilly, clean leather seats, pressing her fingers and her palm against the comfy chair. She admired the circle emblem wedged into her steering wheel and traced her finger along the circle, remembering the good times. She appreciated the stereo and turned up hip hop songs that reminded her of high school until her ears bled. She went for a final joyride, emptying the tank.

She drove back into Providence and sat at the beach one last time. Violent waves crashed against the jetty, the storm surge rising from the nor'easter out at sea. White flakes covered the sandy beach, and the gray sky encouraged Amara's dismal mood. She sat alone until the sky turned dark, then she reluctantly returned to her childhood home.

The drive to Connecticut took forever. As she drove away from Providence, her hands perspired against the steering wheel. Her chest tightened, and she fought back more tears. This drive home symbolized a dramatic change in Amara's life, and she didn't like it.

She walked into the kitchen, carrying one suitcase and one box. At the moment, she had nothing else.

"Ame." Daphne jumped out of the wooden chair and ran over to take Amara's suitcase. "Let me bring this to our room." She disappeared around the corner, and Amara set the heavy box on the floor next to her feet.

"Welcome home," Mama said, stirring the pot on the stove. "Where have you been? Your father has been home for hours."

It began. The badgering and nagging and having to check in all the time.

"I went to the beach to clear my head." Amara walked past her mom, their hips knocking together, as the kitchen wasn't quite large enough for them both.

She knocked on Daphne's door, which was now her door as well.

Daphne turned, her long straight black hair whipping around her shoulders. "Come in! I've been busy making room for you." Her bright smile, cheerful voice, and welcoming demeanor warmed Amara's heart.

On the floor next to Daphne's bed sat an old twin mattress covered in a blue blanket. One dresser drawer was open and empty. "Is this for me?" Amara asked, pointing at the bed on the floor.

"Yes. Or me. I don't mind sleeping on the floor. You can have my bed."

Amara couldn't stop herself from smiling. Daphne's naïvity regarding the harshness of life reminded Amara that maybe it wouldn't be so bad. Amara pretended they were having an extended sleepover.

"Thanks, Pip. I'll take the floor."

Daphne kicked the mattress away from her bed to create a walkway just wide enough for the width of her foot. "There, now if I get up before you, I won't step on you."

Amara sat on the old mattress, the lumps and springs pressing through the pile of blankets heaped on top. "Thanks, Daphne. This is nice." Amara didn't know how long she could live like this. *One day? Okay. One week? It's pushing it. Into the foreseeable future? It'll be unbearable.* She smiled warmly at Daphne, wishing she were more like her. Her little sister had a kind heart and good intentions.

"What else do you need?" asked Daphne, looking around the cramped, cluttered room.

"Nothing. Just a corner to drop my purse and maybe half of a shelf somewhere to put out my deodorant and perfume." This setup had disaster written all over it. Amara abruptly stood up, walking on the mattress, her feet practically sinking to the floor. "I have to talk to Mama."

Amara tripped over Daphne's shoes and stumbled out the door. "Hey, Mama? Do you need help cooking?"

Her mother hummed softly to herself, stirring the pot on the stove. She wore a floral apron over her blue jeans and black sweater. "Sure, would you mind making the salad?"

Amara retrieved all the ingredients and started chopping. "Thanks for having me home."

"Yes, well, we could use the help at the bakery. Your father and I are getting old, so we need to think about the future."

Amara rolled her eyes. She had no intention of running a bakery in boring Woodstock. "Daphne's done a great job welcoming me."

Mama tasted the sauce. "She's a good kid."

"Yes, she is. Do you know if I'll share a room with her the entire time I'm here? I need more space. It's a small room for one person, let alone two."

"Your old room is tied up right now. We told you that. We don't have time to clean it out."

Amara looked up. "Can I?"

Mama tilted her head to the side and flattened her lips. "I don't see why not, but no asking for help. We've already done plenty and your father has enough to worry about with the bakery."

Amara's mood lifted as the light at the end of the tunnel got brighter. "Thanks, Mama. I'll get on it."

That night, tension built around the dinner table. Baba groaned and huffed about how exhausted he was. Amara shrank into her seat, afraid to make eye contact. Daphne chattered to no one in particular about Christmas break, as Mama spooned dinner on everyone's plate.

"So, what's the plan for Christmas?" Amara asked. Her eyes darted around the table.

"Church, presents, and the shelter. Henry is coming over for dinner on Saint Basil Day." Her father ticked off the items like a shopping list.

"Do you donate food to the shelter on Christmas too?" Amara felt like an intruder, not knowing anything about the bakery. "I don't remember dropping off food last year."

"Yes, we donate all the bread products."

"Daphne, do you help too?" Amara asked, looking at her sister.

Baba responded for Daphne. "She will this year."

Daphne stabbed her salad and glanced at Amara. "I'll be there."

Amara wondered what Bethany was doing for Christmas. She wanted to text Bethany to tell her she made it home safely, but didn't want to apologize first. *She may not like it, but what I said was true.*

"What do you need me to do tomorrow, Baba?" Amara asked. It was her first day at work.

"We leave the house at four-thirty for the bakery. We come home at twelve for lunch, and we come home for the day at three."

Her stomach clenched thinking about her alarm ringing in the dead of night. "Sounds great," she lied, mustering up whatever enthusiasm she had in the pit of her stomach. Amara hadn't been up for a four-thirty start time ever. She didn't help with the bakery when she was a kid because she had school, sports, and band.

When Amara was in middle school, she took home economics and her final grade was determined by the success of cooking her family a three-course meal. Amara made salad, spaghetti, and cake because it was easy. All she had to do was chop lettuce, throw pasta in boiling water, and mix an egg into the cake mix.

Her father had balked at the outcome. The salad was wilted because it sat out too long, the pasta was mushy because she overcooked it, and the cake was dry because she forgot to set the timer on the stove. For an easy assignment, Amara's father gave her a C+, which pulled her final grade down to a B-. Then, she got in trouble for not having an A.

Amara sought out every extracurricular activity she could squeeze into her schedule so she wouldn't have to work side by side with Baba after school. He had never apologized for that night and Amara had never forgotten how small he made her feel.

"You'll work for me until you can afford to move out," he reiterated.

Amara nodded, remembering why she moved out of her apartment. She was broke. But being back home meant she no longer had control of her life. There was no flexibility, and her father ruled with an iron fist. He would never hurt them, but his words were sharp daggers, and his disappointment often sliced her heart open.

"Great."

***

The following day, Amara's alarm buzzed at three-thirty. In her dream, she was driving in her car, music transitioning into a repetitive beat. Her car flew over the highway, growing wings. She flew into the clouds, where she saw Bethany and Tyler. As she got closer, a bang sounded, and the cloud disappeared. Amara's car started falling. The rhythmic explosions got louder.

"Amara." Her father's deep voice penetrated through the door. Amara opened her eyes, unable to see in the dark. "Time to get up."

She fumbled for her phone and hit the snooze button. She maneuvered her way out of the room, tripping on a pile of books, and stumbled into the dresser. "I'm up. I'm up."

Unable to turn on a light, Amara dressed through the sense of touch. She threw on her jeans from yesterday and a t-shirt sitting at the top of her bag. She pulled her black hair, still silky-smooth despite being slept on, into a high ponytail.

She remembered to pull out her toothbrush the night before and flipped the light switch on in the bathroom, shutting the old door with a loud creak. Her dark, puffy eyes stared back at her in the outdated vanity mirror. Amara wished she had concealer nearby, but she threw everything haphazardly into who knows where. Her makeup was probably sitting in storage. Amara splashed water on her face and exited the room. Unease settled in her stomach, but she knew she would feel better when the sun rose.

"Time to go," her father said, throwing her a white polo shirt with the bakery's name embroidered into the right breast corner.

"Thanks."

They didn't pass one car on the drive to the bakery. The roads eerily illuminated the shadows from the overhanging trees.

"What do you do when it snows?" Amara asked.

"I leave a half-hour earlier. There is no excuse for being late."

The storefronts next to the bakery stood in silent blackness. Amara looked around erratically, imagining a mugger lurking in the shadows. She pulled her handbag closer to her body.

Her father fumbled with the keys and flipped on the interior and exterior lights.

Amara rushed inside, looking behind to ensure no one followed. She shook her shoulders and her unease dissipated in the recessed lighting.

"Amara, your shoes," her father said, pointing down. "Those won't work."

Amara compared her leather boots with the chunky heel to her father's sensible sneakers. "I'll be fine," she said.

"No, no. What size are you? Your mother keeps a change of shoes here."

Amara rolled her eyes, hoping her father didn't pick up on her borderline disrespect. "I'm an eight, but really Baba, I'll be fine."

Her father fished out a pair of beat-up black sneakers and handed them to her. "These are eight and a half. They'll work for today. I can't have you slipping."

"They're too big."

"I don't care. Stuff toilet paper in the toe I can't have you slipping," he repeated.

Amara eyed the walking shoes with the woven top. She imagined foot fungus and odor penetrating through her socks and into her pores. But she couldn't argue with her dad. *Just for today.* "Thanks, Baba." She carefully slipped them on, only touching the edge of the tongue, and shuddered. It was too late to worry. Her foot was already sitting in bakery sweat.

They got to work. Baba barked orders, and Amara obliged without saying a word. She knew better than to make small talk. The doors unlocked at six and they had to be ready. The scent of fresh bread, bagels, and Greek pastries wafted through the small room. Baba baked while Amara continued to set up. They had a good routine, and Amara was well-versed in following his directions without needing clarification.

Henry came in at seven, carrying a cup of coffee from their competitor.

"Hey," Amara exclaimed. "Is that allowed? You shouldn't be drinking their stuff."

"Well, I need coffee to wake myself up so I can be productive at work," he replied matter-of-factly.

"I hope you hide the cup from customers," Amara laughed.

"It's usually gone before I get here." Henry took one long swig before tossing the cup into the trash. "Fancy meeting you here. Are you working?"

Amara sighed. "Yes, I'm a slave to this place now." Amara didn't want to rehash her parents' demands. "Thanks for your help yesterday."

Henry waved her off. "No problem. I had nothing better to do."

"I heard you're coming over for dinner on Christmas?"

"No, not Christmas. New Year's," he replied.

"New Year's is our Christmas," Amara explained. "Saint Basil Day is January first and we celebrate with an enormous meal and Greek traditions. December twenty-fifth is a day for church and clothing. Usually, we get new shoes or an extra coat or something. Something practical."

"A celebration on New Year's day sounds grand. Your parents graciously offered, and I have no plans. I think of them as my American family. Well, my Greek family in America."

Amara squinted her eyes and tilted her head. *How is it that Henry feels like family, yet I don't know him?* The three of them worked, and

111

Amara watched Henry and Baba together. They worked seamlessly, understanding what each needed without verbalizing.

Amara felt remorse for not staying closer to her family, especially since Henry seemed to have taken her spot. Maybe Henry really was the son her father always wanted, and Henry would inherit the bakery. Amara's thoughts spiraled out of control, the what-ifs floating out of reach above her head.

The three of them worked while listening to faint Greek music fill the room. Amara snuck bites of baklava, loukoumades, and galaktoboureko when the rush of customers died down. She savored each bite, thankful for being surrounded by the food that created her past. She wondered how much money she made that day, considering it would be close to a ten-hour shift. Her disheveled hair hung around the frame of her face, her feet ached, and she was starving for a filling meal.

"Amaryllis."

Amara snapped to attention. "Yes, Baba?"

"First, you will call me George, just like everyone else when we are here. Second, you and Henry will deliver the pastries and rolls tonight, and he will drive you home." It was a done deal, and there was no use in arguing. By the time Amara would get home, it would be dinner time.

"Yes, George." Her voice dropped as she questioned how she ended up here and how long she would make it.

***

On the morning of December twenty-fifth, Amara, Daphne, Mama, and Baba went to the bakery to load up the car with all the pastries and bread they baked the night before and drove to the shelter. The shelter brimmed with festivities, although Amara couldn't find the tree.

"Where's the tree?" she asked.

"There is no tree because not everyone celebrates Christmas," Mama explained. "The shelter program encourages Christmas to be like Thanksgiving, where the purpose is to give thanks for all they have."

The shelter's lobby overflowed with people. Amara had never seen it so busy, and she couldn't tell who lived and who worked there. No one wore their Sunday best, probably because they owned nothing fancy. Amara smiled, made eye contact with the residents, and happily carried the food. A few children played with toys on the floor, some adults sat on computers, and a few women chatted on the couches.

She noticed a young woman about her age, sipping tea on the couch. Trepidation stopped her in her tracks. If her parents hadn't been there for her, she could very well be that woman. Her parents were the reason she wasn't homeless. Nausea bubbled up, and the room tilted slightly. She smiled harder and passed through the living room into the kitchen. Her noodle arms weakened, and she dropped the tray on the counter with a clang.

"You okay?" Mama asked. "You look flushed. Are you hot?"

Amara nodded, pulling at the collar of her sweater. "Yeah."

"Why don't you go outside and get some air?"

Amara didn't want to walk through the lobby again. She felt their eyes on her, probably wondering how she got so lucky. She stared at the exit and made her way without making eye contact with anyone. Cold air rushed at her, and Amara breathed a sigh of relief. She filled her lungs with frigid air and held it, feeling the ice move through her veins and throughout her body.

She'd rather stay outside, her toes going numb, than go back in there. She waited for what felt like an hour. Eventually, her family came out, the car beeping to let her in. It was no warmer, but at least she could sit.

"Are you feeling better?" her mother asked.

"Yes."

"When we get home, you should have a bite to eat. You are too

skinny." Her father meant it with love, but the bluntness stung.
***

"It's Christmas! Wake up." Daphne jumped on Amara's bed, her weight causing Amara to bounce up and down.

Amara moaned and rolled over; her face pressed against the wall. "It's New Year's Day," she grumbled.

Daphne's voice chirped with excitement. "New Year's Day to everyone else but Christmas to us. Come on Amara. You can't tell me that getting a new coat and socks is better than celebrating Santa."

Amara tried to roll to the center of the mattress, but her body folded like the letter u, and her hips and butt rested on the floor while her shoulders sat three inches higher. "Merry Christmas," she said, pulling a pillow over her face. "I'll be right down."

Amara made the mistake of staying up late the night before to watch the ball drop. New Year's Eve was never a fun night when she was growing up because she and Daphne needed to be sleeping before Saint Vasilios could deliver the gifts.

Freshman year of college, Bethany and Amara had joined a sorority, and the sorority hosted a party with another frat house. It was a night of tequila, whiskey, and beer and had ended with Amara puking in the shared dormitory bathroom. She sat on the floor of the stall, her legs curled up under her as Bethany held her hair and rubbed her back. That was the worst New Year's Eve she experienced, and she had promised herself never to get that drunk again in celebration of any holiday.

Last night, she sat on the couch with Daphne until a minute past twelve, when it officially turned a new year. They cheered in hushed tones to prevent her parents from waking up. Amara tucked Daphne into bed and told her to get a good night's sleep.

Daphne woke up with enough energy for both of them. "Wake up," Daphne shouted again, shaking Amara's shoulders. She yanked the pillow out from under Amara's head.

"Ugh. Fine. How are you not tired?" Her irritated voice carried throughout the room. Amara stumbled up, grabbed a sweater, and trudged behind Daphne to the living room.

Under the small tree lay four stockings full of gifts.

"I'm getting Mama and Baba." Daphne skipped down the hall.

The three of them emerged, her parents rubbing their eyes, and they settled around the tree with mugs of hot coffee.

Dark sky peeked through the windows and heavy shadows fell upon the gifts, which glowed hues of red, blue, and green. The festive colors darted from the tall tree and highlighted the cross hanging next to the door.

"A new basketball," Daphne hollered, pulling off the wrapping paper and tossing it on the floor. She immersed herself in her gift, gently tapping it on the floor before their father grabbed it and tucked it under his arm.

"The neighbors."

Daphne bit her lip and smiled in apology. She returned to her stocking and removed another gift.

Amara opened a new watch, her favorite chocolate candy, and gift cards, which were squished in her stocking like an overflowing Halloween bucket. She smiled at her parents in thanks and proudly showed the watch to Daphne. "Look what Saint Vasilios gave me."

Daphne smiled with glee. "I got one too." Daphne thrust her wrist in front of Amara's nose. "We can be twins."

"We can," Amara replied.

The four of them sat together in the living room, playing with their new toys. Santa even brought Mama and Baba cookie sheets and measuring cups. "We needed these," Mama said, winking at Baba.

A few hours later, the aroma of lamb, potatoes, and tzatziki wafted out of the kitchen. A sudden knock on the door and a cheerful "Ho ho ho," greeted them. Henry carried a small bag of gifts in one hand and a bottle of wine in the other.

"Perfect timing," Baba said, grinning. Amara wished he smiled at her like that.

Henry entered the house, gossiping and chatting with Baba about nothing in particular. Mama turned on Christmas carols and lit a sizable red candle on the kitchen table. The house smelled decadent, and Amara's belly rumbled.

Amara placed Christopsomo on the table; the butter glistened against the beige bread.

"Wow, did you make that?" Henry admired the artistic woven cross on top of the crusty bread.

"I did," Amara said. "It's called Christopsomo or Christ's Bread, and it symbolizes prosperity and productivity for the rest of the year. It's a tradition we always do on Christmas Eve, but I baked it last night, so I guess that counts."

"It looks beautiful. You certainly have talent."

Amara smiled, pleased with herself. "Have you had it before?"

"Never. But it smells great." He leaned down and sniffed above the bread. "What's for dinner?" He glanced toward the kitchen. "I offered to help, but your mom shooed me away."

"She's making lahanodolmades, which are cabbage rolls stuffed with pork. It's another tradition. Do you like cabbage?"

Henry nodded. "Cabbage brings me back to Britain, but I don't think I have ever had it prepared that way. It smells lemony. I'm excited to try it."

"We also made vasilopita. Have you had that before?" She raised her eyebrows, challenging him to say yes.

Henry shook his head, grinning. "I can't even guess what that is."

"It's similar to cake in taste and texture. It's baked with a design on top that symbolizes our culture. Traditionally, we cut around the icon, which is what we call the design, and serve people based on head of home and then birth order. There's a coin baked in the batter and whoever gets the coin gets good luck for a year."

Henry lips pulled up in one corner. "Well, Amaryllis. I'm happy to be here and part of your traditions."

Amara cringed at the sound of her name but hugged him for his gratitude. "It's Amara," she reminded him. "It's nice to have someone to share our traditions with. I know my parents love you and it's important to them."

Baba thundered into the living room. "Your mother and Daphne are finishing up dinner. Amara, please set the table. Henry, help me with the extra table."

Baba commanded order and control, like he did at work. Everyone scattered to their responsibilities, not wanting to be the one who delayed the event. As Amara placed the last cup on the table, Daphne emerged carrying the vasilopita on a large, round platter.

"Amara, we have to do this first."

"Tradition," Amara said to Henry, giving him a lopsided smile. "Usually, we eat it at midnight to celebrate Saint Basil, but Mama and Baba are always sleeping at midnight. We adjust."

"Not because we want to, but because we have to," Mama said, carrying the desserts for later. "If George and I don't get our sleep, we are a mess the next day. And I would hate to have this meal messed up because I stayed up too late."

"Daphne, did you make it?" Henry asked.

"I helped Mama. I put the coin in. If you find it, you'll have good luck for a year. I think I put it right...here." She pointed to a spot underneath the boat.

"Why do you have a boat on the cake?" Henry asked.

"Because that is what you do in Greece," her dad answered. "Instead of decorating your tree, you decorate your boat. My father was a fisherman in Greece before coming to America and every year when I was a boy, we decorated the boat with bright white lights. It was my favorite."

Amara cut around the boat and then cut slices into the cake. They ate carefully, eager to find the coin, but not biting so hard they broke a tooth. The mixture of orange, yogurt, vanilla, and butter, exploded Amara's taste buds. "Mama. Daphne. This tastes so good." The moist cake sat on her tongue and seeped into every cell. She held the cake there and savored the sweetness.

Midway through, she bit down on something solid. "Oh!" she pulled the coin out of her mouth. "I found it!"

Her family erupted in cheers before devouring the rest of their cake without a worry.

"Amara, may this year bring you the best of luck." Mama licked her fork clean and served herself another slice.

"To good luck," Henry seconded.

"To prosperity," said Baba.

"And happiness," finished Daphne.

As much as Amara hated her situation, pride for the Greek traditions her parents instilled in her, joy at finding the coin, and hope for the future replaced her bitterness, frustration, and annoyance.

Maybe she wasn't different from anyone else, and living at home wouldn't be that bad. Perhaps it would bring her closer to her family, and they could make up for lost time.

Amara looked around the table and saw Henry admiring them. *I wonder if he's missing his family right now.* Amara tapped him on the arm. "We're happy to have you here," she said. She raised her glass one last time. "Cheers!"

The family and Henry sat around the table waiting for Baba to serve the hot food.

Amara thought back to her childhood when her Yia Yia and Papou were alive and dinner was at their house. Her aunts and uncles and cousins saturated the house with boisterous conversations reverberating off the walls. After Yia Yia and Papou died, the entire family segregated into their own clans.

Amara missed the loud, animated family, but was happy to have Henry, the man from Britain, joining them.

Chapter 9

Amara pulled out her phone and shifted her weight from one leg to the other. Her hips jutted back and forth and her knees popped rhythmically. It was a nervous habit she developed in high school. If she had a test to study for or a public speaking assignment, she resorted to singing in her head and dancing to the beat without actually dancing.

"Do you need to go to the loo?" Henry asked, interrupting her thoughts.

"No, I'm good." Amara continued scrolling through her phone and singing to herself.

"What are you doing?"

The bakery was empty except for Amara and Henry, and all the pastries were out on display. Amara looked around. "Nothing." Her phone slipped through her sweaty fingers and crashed to the floor. "Oh, no."

A large crack ran across her and Bethany's faces on the screen. Amara analyzed the damage and continued scrolling. "Just checking to make sure it still works," she said, distracted by the buttons.

It had been two weeks since she moved home, and Amara had not heard a thing from Bethany. Or Tyler, now that she thought about it. It was like she lived in an alternate reality with no wedding to plan. Amara felt unsettled, like Bethany and Ryan purposefully eliminated her from their lives.

"Henry, what do I do?" Amara asked, still fiddling with her phone. "I'm in this wedding for my best friend, but we got into a fight, and I haven't heard from her in almost a month."

"Have you tried to contact her?"

"No." She was waiting for an apology from Bethany for kicking her out.

"I need the story to know how to answer." Henry sat on the large stool in the doorway.

Amara hesitated, considering how to sum up her situation. "Basically, she's getting married in six months and told me she was moving out of our apartment to live with her boyfriend. Everything was fine until she told me I had to move out of our apartment because they decided to keep the lease. I told her I didn't like her boyfriend and she was making a mistake. We got into a fight and she kicked me out that weekend. That was a few days before you and Baba moved me out. And here we are." Amara motioned around her.

Henry winced.

Amara continued. "My bedroom is probably his office right now."

"Let me get this straight. You're upset with her because she told you she was breaking the lease, and she didn't. She's probably mad at you because you don't like her boyfriend."

Amara shrugged. "Should I call her?"

Henry lifted his hands and raised his shoulders. "I'm not a woman, so I don't know how you work. I would call casually to say hello and check in. But if it all goes south, it wasn't my fault."

Amara drummed her pink fingernails on the counter.

Henry shook his head for emphasis. "You asked my opinion." He was straight and to the point, the opposite of any female friend Amara had.

Amara adjusted her ponytail behind her visor and straightened her posture. "Thank you, Henry." She pulled up Bethany's number and stared at it. "What do I say?"

Henry kept busy restocking the utensils. "You say, 'Hi. I was hoping we could talk.' Keep it simple. No point in making a big deal if she ignores you."

Amara bit her lip, her heart beating rapidly as she typed the words Henry dictated at a snail's speed and hit send. She stared at the phone, waiting for a response. After a few moments of silence, she texted Tyler the same message.

Amara threw her phone in her bag, wedged it under the counter, and sighed. "I tried." She barely tried, but at least she put some effort into reconciling their friendship.

After a few moments, Henry broke the silence of the empty store. "You're doing a good job here."

Amara ran her hands down her face, her skin pulling tight with gravity and pressure. She didn't want to believe this was her life. She deserved so much better than this dumpy bakery, living in her old bedroom on a mattress on the floor, and driving a used Toyota. Her life from six weeks ago was full of promise. Now, she bumped into people she hated in high school at the grocery store.

"Thanks. I need to save money to move back to the city. I'm just buying my time, but don't tell my parents." The words flowed out of her mouth as if they were automatic, like breathing or digesting.

"I don't know if your parents need you forever. Your dad told me it was just temporary," Henry replied.

"Right, but things happen. What if I move out and they decide that they need me to help full time? Or what if we get comfortable in the apartment and it feels easier for me to stay?" Amara rubbed her hand against her forehead.

"Well, I believe you're putting in effort here. You know the menu, the gist of the business, and you help with the shelter. Your parents are proud of you and your performance at the bakery, but when it's time for you to go I know they'll understand."

Amara scrunched her nose. *My performance? What is this? A band concert?*

"You're so young, and you're living life, making mistakes, and dealing with the consequences. This time of your life is all about learning. Don't worry, Amaryllis."

Amara dropped the tip jar and stared at Henry, her mouth curling into a sneer. "Henry, for the love of God, please call me Amara." Irritation in her voice matched her pursed lips and tightened brows.

"I'm sorry. I keep forgetting."

"Only my parents call me Amaryllis." She spoke to him like she would a child. "I would appreciate it if you called me Amara. I know you've called me Amaryllis in the past, but please don't." She sounded harsher than she expected, but it had been weeks of tolerating the wrong name.

He stepped back, standing tall, his glasses pushed up on his nose. "My apologies. I didn't realize it was a big problem." He left the front showroom and entered the kitchen. "I'm taking my lunch. I'll be back in thirty minutes."

Amara stood alone, checking her watch continuously to see how much longer until she clocked out for the day. She had two hours before closing, and then the shelter run with Henry. Amara's feet throbbed against her new black sneakers. She felt a blister rub against her heel and removed her shoe.

The bell above the door rang, and Amara looked up. Bethany entered with confidence, long strides, and arms swinging. "Amara," she said. Bethany stopped in the middle of the bakery. "I didn't expect to see you here."

"Hi, Bethany. Did you get my text?" Amara knew she sounded rude, but her patience had worn to a thin thread.

"No, I didn't. Is everything okay?" Bethany's gaze dropped to the display case filled with syrup-soaked pistachio treats.

"What are you doing here?" Amara smoothed back her hair, embarrassed to be seen in this food service uniform. *Maybe she came to apologize.* Amara took a deep breath and rolled her neck hoping her earlier frustration rolled away with it.

Bethany's eyes shot up and Amara detected a flash of apprehension before weariness glazed over. "I've been in contact with your parents about my shower." Bethany's voice cracked and quivered.

Amara's blood turned to ice. "The shower? What do you mean?"

Bethany shifted her bag from one shoulder to the other. "I decided I wanted to be involved in the planning of it."

Amara crossed her arms over her chest, not blinking. "So, what… am I out of it? Do all my ideas and planning not even matter?"

Bethany sighed and pulled out her wallet. "I thought it would be better. I should have told you, but I didn't think you wanted to hear from me. I canceled your reservation at Oceanside. Here." She shoved a piece of paper toward Amara. "Your deposit. I was going to mail it, but since you're here, here it is."

Amara took the check, and folded it into fourths before putting it under the register. The vein in her forehead throbbed and her neck turned hot. "Thanks," she seethed with a forced smile.

The shower was her job, and Bethany snatched it away without even telling her. Amara stared at Bethany until she shifted her weight, pulled at her jacket, and sat in a chair a few feet back.

"Your parents should be here in a few minutes with a menu and some samples for me to try." Bethany glanced at her watch, avoiding Amara's eyes. "I didn't expect to see you here."

Amara's face dropped. Her parents never told her they were communicating with Bethany. She pulled back and mustered up as much professionalism as possible. "You're welcome to wait for them at any table." Amara pressed her foot into her shoe and winced. She turned and pretended to organize the showcase.

Tension in the room escalated, despite the savory aroma and upbeat music playing in the background. Amara couldn't help but feel betrayed by Bethany and her parents blindsiding her like this. She needed Henry to return so she could leave.

Bethany sat at the table and drank coffee from a disposable coffee cup, which she must have purchased somewhere else. Amara scowled at her rudeness, staring at the back of Bethany's head. Bethany's shoulders occasionally tightened. Whenever she turned back, Amara smiled sweetly, rolling her eyes the moment Bethany returned to facing the street.

The storm door slammed at the back entrance. Amara jumped. She grabbed her coat and her purse, ready to break out of that hell-hole. George entered instead of Henry, and Amara froze. "George, Bethany's here for you. When Henry gets back, I'm taking my break." She slinked into the wooden chair behind the display case and stared at the clock, listening for the bell to ding above the door.

"Bethany, hello." Ignoring Amara, he sat next to Bethany, laying out a spread of Greek desserts. He had a box for her to take samples of their most popular items home, trying to sell her on the kourabedies and baklava. His English wasn't perfect, but his enthusiasm was admirable, and Amara knew Bethany would say yes.

This was not the dad Amara knew. The father she knew spoke in concise phrases and sentences, and he never elaborated or showed emotion. Amara watched George laugh, smile and lure Bethany with the butter cookies and pistachio phyllo dough. It was enough to make Amara's skin crawl. He never showed interest in Amara, yet he conversed with Bethany like they were best friends. Nausea bubbled inside Amara as she watched Bethany pretend it was perfectly normal to ask her ex-best friend's father to cater the bridal shower she was no longer invited to attend.

Bethany exited the bakery carrying a large box of pastries, a menu, and a business card. "Bye, Amara."

The corners of Amara's mouth barely turned up as she waved and watched her ex-best friend walk away.

***

"Amaryllis." Her father's deep voice echoed off the walls. Amara grabbed her flattened pillow and covered her ears. She didn't make a sound. Amara's new bedroom contained her bed and dresser from the old apartment. In the far corner of the room sat Baba's desk, covered in piles of paper. When Amara moved out of Daphne's bedroom, Baba told her that the room was not hers, only a temporary sleeping space. He still needed his office.

Bang-bang-bang. The door shuddered. "Amaryllis."

Amara groaned and rolled over. "What?"

"You're late. You need to be at the shop in less than ten minutes. Up and out."

"Give me the day off," she yelled through the closed door. It was still dark.

Her door swung open, and her father's presence towered over her. A blinding light flashed across Amara's eyelids. When she tried to open them, the bright overhead light prevented anything from coming into focus.

"Baba!" Amara couldn't remember her father ever entering her room unannounced. He grabbed the blankets across the foot of her bed and yanked.

"What are you doing?" She grabbed the sheet and wrestled it up over her torso.

"Get up. You're living here for free and you must earn your stay. And this room is a mess." His arms flapped around like he was a wizard willing the cleaning fairies to come out and help.

"It's my room, Baba."

"Oh yeah? It's my house. You're late for work. That reflects on me." Baba stomped to her closet and threw her uniform at her.

Amara rolled her eyes. It wasn't even five in the morning. Who were they rushing for? "Relax, Baba. We don't open until seven."

Baba's eyes bulged out of his head and he bared his teeth. Amara knew she'd gone too far. She had forgotten the art of arguing with her father. Disagreeing was okay as long as the line of respect was never crossed.

"You have ten minutes to get out of this house. If you're late, there will be consequences." Spittle flung across the room. Baba stormed out of her room and gently closed the door to prevent waking Daphne down the hall, but it was probably too late unless Daphne wore noise-canceling headphones to bed. When he was angry, the entire house shook.

Amara sat up in bed and rolled her neck and shoulders. Melancholy grew around her like a weed and wrapped itself around her chest. She didn't want to get out of bed, but she also didn't want to upset her dad further. Amara forced herself to her feet and threw her polo shirt over her tank top. She was already wearing yoga pants and socks, and retrieved her boring, black sneakers before stumbling to the kitchen.

Mama sat at the table, sipping her tea in silence.

"Where's Baba?" Amara asked.

"He left a few minutes ago."

Tears climbed behind Amara's eyes until her vision was a sea of wavy lines. She had gone too far.

Mama watched Amara search for her car keys. "Amaryllis, are you okay?"

Amara blinked a few times and her vision regained focus. She didn't want to talk, even though she knew Mama had heard the whole thing. There was no way she hadn't. Plus, she didn't have time to talk. "Yeah, fine." She grabbed her keys and walked toward the door before spinning to face her mom. "Why did you agree to bake for Bethany's shower?"

Mama took a sip of her coffee before responding. "Because she asked."

"Mama, you knew I was planning her shower. Isn't it weird that she came to you with that request when she shouldn't have known any of the details?"

Her mother's bony shoulders lifted. "We didn't realize she wasn't involved in the planning. You haven't talked about the shower since before you moved in, so how were we supposed to know?"

Amara threw her hands up in the air. "You guys shouldn't have done that. You should have asked me." She heaved a long, breathy sigh.

"Amara, we're business owners. When someone wants our business, we don't ask questions as to why. We smile, say thank you, and deliver what they want. I'm sorry if you're upset, but it was a business decision and had nothing to do with you."

Amara stormed out, slamming the door on her way. The house shuddered and then fell silent.

Amara talked to herself during the drive to work. She was disappointed in her parents, angry at Bethany, and frustrated with herself. To top it off, she was stuck working with her father at a job she hated.

The locked shop lit up the black sky and goaded her to enter. Henry was due to arrive in thirty minutes. Amara fumbled through her purse, searching for the shop keys. She couldn't find them and knocked loudly on the door. There was no movement inside.

She returned to her car and checked every nook and cranny but came up keyless. "Where are they?"

She didn't want to do it, but she had to call her dad. His phone rang four times before his gruff voice answered. "You're late."

"Hi, George, nice to talk to you too," she said, dripping with sarcasm. "I'm outside. I misplaced my keys." She was careful not to say lost. "Can you let me in?"

"You'll have to wait. I am elbow-deep in phyllo dough." He hung up before she could protest.

Amara stood in the cold, feeling the wind blow through her sweater. She left her mittens in the car but didn't dare exit her post at the front door. Her watch sat on the bathroom sink, so she didn't know how long she was outside or what time it was.

"Come on, Baba," Amara muttered. She gazed out at the horizon, where the sky peeked out through holes in the forest and tinted the ground. The colors turned from pewter to slate to watermelon. She watched the sun rise, wishing she had grabbed a coffee before she left the house.

"Cheerio." Henry hurried across the empty street toward the front entrance. "Aren't you cold?" he asked. Amara pulled her hands into her sleeves, rubbing her fingers back and forth against the soft knitted yarn.

"Yes, waiting for my dad. He's inside. I left my key at home."

"Here, let's go in." Henry pulled out his keys and maneuvered the dead bolt. "All set." The door swung open, and a wave of warmth hit Amara like a brick wall.

"Thank you, Henry," she exclaimed with glee. She rubbed her hands together, encouraging the warm air combined with friction to speed up the defrosting process.

"Amaryllis," George called from the kitchen doorway. "You're an hour late."

Amara's mouth dropped open. *Is he for real?* "What? No, I was thirty minutes late. You knew I was here. I was waiting for you to open the door."

"No excuse," he said, shaking his bald head. "You're late. Do it again, and you're fired."

Henry threw her a sympathetic glance from the corner of his eye and squeezed between her and the counter, where Amara stood frozen. She wanted to respond, but knew her father wouldn't tolerate a response. He was a no-nonsense guy with inflexible expectations. Amara did what she always did. "Yes, George."

The rest of the day, Amara thought about the last two months. The fight with Bethany, the move out of Providence, being back in her old bedroom, and working at the bakery had smothered her confidence. Amara wouldn't have believed it if a psychic had predicted this sequence of events. She deserved better. Now, she had a job that wasn't worth sharing with others, a crappy car that wasn't even MP3 compatible, no best friend, and no boyfriend. Her life was traveling in the fast lane down the highway in the wrong direction.

When she and Henry went to the shelter that afternoon, she was in more of a funk than when she had woken up.

"Amaryllis, did you grab the croissants?"

Amara stiffened at the sound of her name. "Yes."

"Did you bring one tray of bread or two?"

"One. There was only one."

Amara kept her eyes low and turned her body away from Henry. She didn't feel like talking.

Henry tried making small talk. Amara continued to look out the window, watching the trees fly by.

"Are you okay? You seem quiet."

Amara spoke to the street. "Yep. I'm peachy."

She stopped smiling days ago, and people were noticing. It all began when Bethany showed up and uninvited her from the shower. *What did I do? All I did look out for her and give her advice. Bethany needs to apologize to me. She's the one who kicked me out of the apartment. She lied to me when she told me she was terminating her part of the lease.*

"Amaryllis, are you sure you're okay?"

Amara's head whipped around. "Why do you insist on calling me that?"

"My apologies but I called your name three times. I've listened to your parents call you Amaryllis for years. It's difficult habit to break." Henry pulled his chin into his neck and readjusted his glasses. "Nevermind, my mistake." He walked to the other wall and refilled the coffee cups.

"Amaryllis was my name when I was a little girl. Amara is my name now." Her voice softened, realizing Henry didn't deserve the brunt of her frustration. "I'm sorry. I'm having a rough week and I miss my old life."

Henry nodded but didn't respond. Just when Amara thought the conversation was over, he said, "I felt that way when I left London. Coming here backfired. It was ghastly. I was in culinary school, paying for an education I didn't even know I wanted. I only applied so I could get into the country. Then she divorced me. I was stuck in school, fighting with lawyers, and up to my ears in debt."

Amara crossed her arms over her chest and rolled down the window. The frigid air rushing through the window drowned out Henry's voice.

"Your father is a good man," he hollered.

Air audibly traveled through her nose, and she exhaled deeply. She rolled up her window and turned to him.

"No, really. He's a good bloke. He's rough around the edges, but you must consider his life and everything that made him hardened. His parents were foreigners and had no money. I've heard many stories about his early life."

Amara bit her lower lip and scrunched her lips to one side. *How does Henry know so much about Baba's past and I don't know anything?* She forced a smile and nodded, pretending that she knew what Henry was talking about.

Maybe her father's life was tough, but so was hers. Amara wanted to argue with Henry, to explain that he knew nothing about who she was or what she endured as a child. *Why does no one acknowledge my hardships?* Amara practically raised herself because her parents worked three jobs combined. They only prioritized their livelihood when Daphne came around.

Amara sat quietly, her muscles tense, her legs pressed together, facing the passenger door. Her hands wrung together in her lap. "Yes, I know," she eventually muttered.

After dropping off the food, they drove back to the bakery in silence. Amara's breathing slowed, and her muscles relaxed. By the time she got home, dinner was on the table. Amara excused herself from the meal and crawled into her bed. She pulled the covers up to her chin and placed the pillow over her head again. If she was going to get to work on time the next day, she needed her sleep.

Amara lay in bed and thought about the mess that she and Bethany created. She learned at an early age that it was better to be alone than to invest in others when the balance could so easily be disrupted.

***

Every day was the same. Amara woke up before the sun, worked a full day on her feet in the bakery, delivered the baked goods to the shelter, and then ate dinner and went to sleep. She couldn't remember the last time she hung out with other young, single people looking to enjoy life.

Amara and Henry worked together almost every day, with her parents popping in and out to bake. She had been there a little over a month now, and no one batted an eye when she said she'd like to learn the family recipes. George told her that all recipes contained a secret ingredient. When Amara could identify the difference, he would share the recipe with her. Even Henry didn't know how to make their famous loukoumades batter, and he was George's right-hand-man. She craved more responsibility than only cashing people out and sweeping the floor.

"Henry, how often do you bake for the shop?" Amara asked one day as they drove up to the shelter. His beat-up SUV struggled with the steep hills and strong wind. The engine rattled, and the heat cranked, blowing stale air across her torso.

"Never. Your dad is particular, and he doesn't like to share. I think he believes that if he tells me, I'll open up my own bakery and steal his desserts. I also think it has to do with me being English. How can an Englishman make a Greek dessert correctly?"

"But doesn't that bother you? You went to school for this, and here you are, hanging around, working well below your pay grade."

"Not really. The thing I like most about this job is the ability to pay it forward and give back to less fortunate people. Donating my time on holidays to ensure people get a good meal carries me much further than just working in the shop. This place isn't just a job. It's making a difference."

Amara eyed him up and down, wondering how he became so compassionate. "Why does this act, this donation, fill you up so much?"

Henry laughed. "You don't feel the same?"

Amara nervously chuckled. "I never said that."

Henry threw Amara a glance with eyebrows raised. "You don't have to. You look like you're better than them, that you feel sorry for them, or that they are an inconvenience in your hectic life." His shocking words rippled across her extremities.

"Who? My parents?"

"No, the people who live at the shelter."

"That's not true."

"No? That's the impression I got, and I'm sure they did, too. Why don't you try talking to them, getting to know them? You might find that their life experiences can help guide you with yours."

Amara narrowed her eyes and pulled her head back against the headrest. "What does that mean?"

"What I mean," Henry cleared his throat and sat up taller as he navigated the snowy road, "is that they're people who probably lived a lifestyle like yours. Good job, nice car, lovely home, and somehow, like you, it all disappeared. They're people. You should treat them like that." He spoke to her like he was her school teacher, explaining the importance of not bullying others. Amara didn't dare say another word.

She sat in stunned silence. *Do people view me that way? How could they judge me like that?* Flashbacks from her childhood, college, and high school dotted her periphery. Jada once told her that the kids at camp didn't think she liked them because she never smiled when they talked to her. When she pledged her sorority, her big sister, Maxine, told her that the best way to get a boyfriend was to ignore them and play hard to get. Amara tried and she heard through the grapevine that she was a bitch and a tease.

She thought about the shelter and how uncomfortable she felt. It must have been written all over her face. As if Henry read her mind, he said, "Don't judge them. You know nothing about them."

They arrived at the shelter, and Amara helped Henry empty the trays. She painted on a bright smile as she walked in and paid close attention to Henry's movements. When he laughed, she laughed. When he smiled, she smiled. She didn't want to make anyone feel uncomfortable, and if Henry was certain he was better than her, she was going to make sure she copied every move.

Henry eyed Amara curiously with every giggle and smile she emitted. Amara ignored his questioning look. She wanted to prove that she cared, and if this was how Henry did it, then this was how she would do it, too.

The engine's hum was the only sound on the ride back to the shop.

It revved up to four thousand, fighting to switch into second gear. The car lurched forward as it trudged up the hills. She thought about the shelter and how her parents' selflessness made a difference in other people's lives. She didn't always understand her parents, but their past experiences taught valuable lessons. Amara decided during that drive home that she would stop feeling sorry for herself and recognize her blessings.

"Thanks for the ride back. I'll see you on Wednesday," Amara said.

"Not tomorrow?" Henry asked.

"No, I'm off for a few days. I don't know what I'm doing, but I'm getting out of Woodstock to think." The isolation was killing her.

That night, Amara texted Bethany to apologize for her behavior at the bakery. Amara knew she should have shown more interest when she saw her best friend at the shop. She typed and reread the message three times before hitting send. She hoped the tone was kind and couldn't be misinterpreted. **Hi Beth! I have the day off tomorrow and was hoping to see you. Are you free?**

She threw her phone on her bed, refusing to get sucked up into the waiting game, and found Daphne at the kitchen table. "Hey, Pipsqueak," Amara said, plopping into the hard wooden chair next to her.

"Hey, Ame." Daphne looked so grown up. Amara admired Daphne's straight black hair, glistening against the light. Her thin frame seemed to shoot up overnight. Her lanky arms rested across the table and her pants were three inches too short.

"I have the next few days off. Do you want to do something? I feel like we haven't hung out lately."

Daphne smiled, her crooked teeth lighting up her face. "I have a test to study for, and I have to do well on it."

"What about Tuesday? We can go bowling or to the movies or something. It won't take too long. I can pick you up at school early."

Daphne shook her head. "I have basketball practice every day after school. I really can't miss it."

Amara's shoulders slumped. Her two days off were going to be wasted alone. "Okay, Pip, if you change your mind, I'm up for whatever."

Amara retreated to her room, stuck with her thoughts. She picked up her phone, and still nothing. She texted Tyler hoping he was free. It had been nearly two months since they last saw each other, and the hypothetical shower was three months away. Despite not having any direction, time was still flying by.

Hi Tyler! It's Amara. I wanted to check in and talk about the wedding.

She waited again, unsure if she was approaching this subject from the right angle. Her heart fluttered, and her hands sweat.

Amara settled on her bed and watched television, waiting for her phone to ding. Eventually, it did.

Can I call you?

Amara's face hurt from smiling. She counted to sixty and then replied. **Sure.**

Her phone rang, and Amara jumped at the sound. She opened the call and her phone fell through her fingers. "Wait a minute," she yelled toward the upside-down phone. She righted the phone and changed her voice to calm, cool and collected. "Hi, Tyler."

"Hey, Amara. I talked to Ryan, and the wedding is in July now. Did you get an invitation?"

Amara leaned back against the wall. Her head hit harder than she intended and she rubbed the bump on her skull gingerly. "No. Wait, does that mean I'm out of the wedding?"

Tyler hesitated. "I don't know. You'll have to ask Bethany. They put me in contact with some of her nursing friends, and they're in the middle of planning the shower and the bachelorette party. I thought you knew."

"No, I had no idea."

Amara couldn't believe Bethany had kicked her out of the wedding and didn't tell her. She squeezed her hands, digging her fingernails into her palms. *Bethany has some nerve.*

"Why would she do that to you?" Tyler asked.

Amara sighed. She didn't want to get into this. "Because one night, I got drunk and told her she was making the biggest mistake of her life marrying Ryan. I don't remember what I said, but it was something like 'he's a child,' 'he's a loser who lives with his parents,' and 'you're going to regret it.' She kicked me out of the apartment."

"Ouch. I didn't hear any of that, so she may not have shared it with Ryan. Who knows what she told him?"

"I meant what I said, but I feel bad saying it to her face." Amara blushed with embarrassment for insulting Ryan to his step-brother.

"You don't like Ryan?"

Amara heard the humor behind his words. She considered her options when responding.

"I don't know him," Amara admitted. "But I don't get a good vibe. He's not right for her."

Tyler said nothing at first and then agreed. "I can see it. He's a good guy, though. He wouldn't hurt a fly."

Amara settled into her bed, relieved that Tyler knew her side of the story. "Hey, what are you doing tomorrow or Tuesday? I know it's a long shot, but I have the days off, and I need to get out of the boondocks."

"The boondocks?" Tyler asked.

"Yeah, like the middle of nowhere Connecticut. I need some excitement, some shopping, and real restaurants. Are you free?"

Amara's heart drummed in her ears, and she wondered if the sound carried through the phone.

"I can leave work early tomorrow. Do you want me to meet you somewhere? Does two work?"

Amara checked the forecast, which predicted sunny skies for the rest of the week. "Sure, how about Providence? Do you want to hang out at the mall with me?" With the temperature in the twenties, she needed some place warm and entertaining

"Sounds great. Two o'clock."

Finally, Amara had something to do and a friend to hang out with. Her chest thudded and her throat constricted. She remembered feeling this way when she sneaked out of her house to meet a cute boy from science class in tenth grade.

That night, Amara wondered if Bethany really had kicked her out of the wedding without saying a word. She needed to ask, but didn't know when or how. Instead of focusing on the downfall of her friendship with Bethany, she focused on her new friendship with Tyler. He may not be her best friend yet, but he was a good substitute for now.

Chapter 10

"Hey!" A deep voice called from behind Amara. She stood in the bookstore's self-help section, browsing books on finding happiness, getting motivated, and embracing joy. Her lack of direction deepened with the realization that the life she loved was a mere memory.

Tyler walked toward her. His blue eyes lit up the room and his dimples made her smile.. His blond hair hid under the same black beanie he wore in the coffee shop, and tiny waves crested around the edges.

"Tyler." Her heart skipped and she clumsily placed the book back on the shelf. Amara automatically hugged him. It felt like an eternity since they paraded around the party store dressed up for Christmas.

"Are you hungry? I'd like to take you out for dinner tonight."

Amara blushed, wondering if this was a date. She hadn't been on a date in months, and the awkwardness of eating together sent butterflies flying inside her. "Like, an early dinner? It's only two," she said, glancing at her watch.

"Yeah, let's go out for dunch."

Amara giggled, briefly cupping the back of her neck with one hand.

She ran her fingers through her thick hair. "What's that?" She tilted her head to the side.

"Dunch. Lunch and Dinner. You have brunch, and you have dunch. Are you hungry for dunch?"

Amara laughed. She forgot how his goofiness erased all the prim and proper faces she wore. She continued to smile at him, taking in his long legs, smooth skin, and rosy lips.

They walked around the mall and eventually found an Italian restaurant to rest their feet and get comfortable.

"Can I get you a drink?" the waiter asked.

Amara shook her head. "Just a Shirley Temple, please."

"Make that two," Tyler said. Once the waiter left, he asked, "Why the Shirley Temple? I know you drink."

Amara blushed, remembering their first meeting when he had to drive her home. "Because I'm driving home. If I still lived in Providence and could get an Uber, I would have ordered a Manhattan."

"Ooh, sophisticated."

Amara's face went hot, and she wondered if sophisticated was a synonym for bitchy.

Amara sighed. She didn't want to ask about the wedding because her heart might burst, but she needed to know.

"Let's talk," Amara said, staring straight ahead.

"About…" Tyler smiled.

"The wedding. Tell me everything you know."

Tyler's body stiffened, and he pulled back in his seat. He looked around the room. Finally, he leaned in close to her as if telling her a secret. "I don't know much. I know the date, the location, and the date of the shower. That's it. Pinky promise." He held out his pinky with his other fingers curled into his palm.

Amara's lips rose and she embraced his finger in hers. "Pinky promise?"

"Yeah, I'm not involved. Someone tells me where to go, and I go, but I'm not doing anything with the planning. I told Ryan I was too busy. And the truth is, I don't care."

"So, tell me," Amara said, leaning her torso over the table to get closer to Tyler's face. "Where and when are all these things happening?". She needed to know, even though Bethany didn't appear to want Amara involved.

"The wedding is now in Jamaica on July twenty-fourth at the Wildtree Resort. The shower is at the Providence Harbor Inn on May first. The bachelorette party I haven't heard about, but the bachelor's party is on June thirtieth in Boston."

Amara bit her lip. She hated herself for not being there for her best friend. Her mind rapidly concocted a plan. "Can you find out about the bachelorette party? Date and location, if possible." *Maybe I can crash the bachelorette party and make amends.*

Tyler rubbed his chin and pulled his manicured eyebrows together. "How am I going to do that?"

"I don't know." Amara opened and closed her mouth and tapped her fingers on the tabletop. "Ryan's your brother. How hard is it to ask?"

"I'll try, but no promises." Tyler placed his elbow on the table and propped his head up with his fist. "Now that we aren't involved in the planning, I was hoping to learn more about you. Can we promise not to talk about the wedding anymore today?" His voice dropped to a whisper.

Amara wanted to stay grumpy. She was still reeling that Bethany and Ryan deleted her from their wedding, but Tyler was right. She didn't get to spend time with him often. It would be a shame if she remained hyper-focused on the wedding and didn't see what was in front of her.

"Promise," she replied.

After dunch, the sun was gone. The deep charcoal sky revealed puffy slate clouds that transformed into different shapes. The light from the moon disappeared, leaving the city's lights to brighten the roads. It wasn't even five, yet it felt like midnight.

Amara checked her phone and saw a text notification. "Tyler," Amara grabbed his hand to gain his attention and electricity traveled from her fingertips to her shoulder. She tried to drop his hand but his fingers tightened around hers. *C'mon, Amara. Be cool.* "Bethany texted me." She didn't add that it was in response to a text thread she started.

Tyler let go of her hand and leaned over her shoulder to see.

"It says 'I'm home from work tomorrow. Do you want to get together?'"

"Do you?" Tyler asked. He was so practical.

"Yeah. I mean, I'm pissed about what she did, but I would love to hear it from her. Plus, I owe her an apology for being rude. I think we have a lot to talk about."

"Then tell her yes. You're free, right?"

Amara nodded as she typed, her thumb flying across the screen.

After a series of dings and no attention paid to Tyler, Amara put her phone away, grinning like she just won Final Jeopardy.

"What's up?" Tyler pulled his hat tighter around his head.

"I'm going to sleep at Bethany's tonight, and we're going to spend the day together tomorrow."

With one text conversation, Amara's mind perked up. Her eyes sparkled, and she bounced in her seat.

Tyler fiddled with the buttons on his shirt and his lips tightened. He looked over Amara's shoulder and didn't respond. Amara felt tension build between them and frowned.

Tyler cleared his throat. "You know, I probably should get going anyway. There'll be traffic, and it's dark."

Amara nodded, recognizing the hurt across his face. She wanted to reach out and kiss him, to let him know that even though she prioritized Bethany over him, she really liked him. Instead, she hugged him. "Thanks for dunch. I want to do it again." She hoped that little carrot dangling in front of him was enough to keep him interested.

He gave her a loose hug and turned toward the parking garage.

Once out of sight, Amara walked to the beat of the background music playing in the mall, practically skipping. She zipped in and out of stores, buying pajamas and clothes for the next day. She swung by a department store on the way to Bethany's and grabbed toiletries and underwear. At least now she'd feel comfortable sitting in her old apartment with Bethany's new roommate.

Bethany's new roommate. Ryan. She stopped walking and flinched at the sudden car alarm in the distance. She placed her arms across her chest and hugged herself, rolling her shoulders up and down one at a time to relieve the tension in her neck. *Maybe this is a bad idea.* She crept toward her car, meticulous in her movements.

When she got to her old apartment, she froze behind her windshield. She wanted to get out of the car, but her legs stuck to the seat like bubblegum. She didn't want to appear eager, so she waited until she was comfortably late. *Please, please don't let this be a mistake.*

Amara knocked on the door. The door creaked open and Bethany stood on the other side. She looked the same. Her dark curly hair rested on her shoulders and she wore a flannel shirt Amara had given her the Christmas before.

"Hi." Bethany's tight smile pulled across her face and she held out her arms in greeting. "Come in."

Amara stepped into the hallway and dropped her belongings on the bench, which used to be filled with her shoes. "Hi." Amara stretched her arms out toward Bethany.

Bethany returned the hug with a gentle pat on Amara's left shoulder. They stood cheek to cheek. Amara pulled away and grabbed her belongings.

They walked to the living room and Amara observed the changes, purposefully trying not to make any snap judgments, even though it looked different. A leather couch replaced the comfy blue one Bethany's parents bought them when they first moved in. *Where did they get money for leather?* The photographs of Bethany and Amara were replaced by landscape photos and paintings. Amara wanted to ask where the photographs went, but thoughts of rejection paralyzed her.

Amara stretched out on the couch, pressing her back against the stiff pillows.

"Do you want a drink?" Bethany asked.

Amara nodded. "Water's fine. Thanks." She couldn't stop looking around, analyzing every nook and cranny.

Bethany emerged from the kitchen with two glasses of water and a side dish holding lemon slices. She placed them on the end table and sat on the edge of the couch cushion with her knees angled toward Amara. Amara scooted forward and placed her hands on her lap. She wanted to reach for the water but Bethany's posture brought her back to church when you moved your body according to tradition. Instead, Amara moved her shopping bags from the floor to the cushion next to her, like an old friend.

"So, how have you been?" Bethany asked. "It's been what...almost three months since we last hung out?"

Amara reminded herself that she needed to apologize and mend her relationship, not accuse Bethany of destroying her life. She took a deep breath. "Yeah, three months." The leather couch squeaked every time she fidgeted, which was often.

"What have you been up to?" Bethany picked lint off her skirt without breaking eye contact. The pleasantries killed Amara. *How long are we gonna play this game?*

"Let's see. I'm living with my parents back in my old bedroom. I sold my car. I wake at four-thirty every morning to open the bakery. I get home around four, in time to eat dinner and go to bed. It's great." Thick sarcasm dripped off Amara's words. *Basically, my life sucks. Thanks for being the one to start me down this path.*

Bethany's lips formed an 'o' and then transitioned into a tight grimace. They sat in silence for a moment. Bethany paused and leaned closer to Amara.

Amara took three gulps of water, feeling the icy liquid travel through her parched mouth. "How about you?" Amara tried to smile but it felt like a sneer.

Bethany's shoulders relaxed, and she took a sip of water. "Well, as you know, Ryan and I moved in together. He got a new job working for a real estate office on the shore. They promoted me to nurse supervisor. And we're planning the wedding."

Amara winced at the word wedding. She knew they had to go there, but she wasn't quite ready. She had to play her cards cool, holding them close so she couldn't get hurt. "How are the plans going? Did you order from the bakery? Do you have a date set?" *Too many questions. Now Bethany can skirt over the crucial details and focus on the stupid ones, like my dad's bakery.*

"Things are good. The venue's set. We're using your dad's shop for the shower."

Amara pretended like this was news to her. "The shower I was planning? I had it under control. Why are you using my dad's bakery, anyway?" Amara hoped Bethany wanted to crawl into the crack between the couch cushions and disappear.

"Yes, well, after our fight, I reached out to Mikayla and Ruby and they took over the plans. Sorry I didn't tell you." Bethany avoided eye contact. "And as for your dad's bakery, I thought it might be a good way to check in with you. Without making it too obvious." Bethany spun her engagement ring back and forth around her finger.

Me? You wanted to check in on me? I've been texting you for months and you never respond. I could have been dead on the side of the road and you never would have known. You're such a liar. Amara clenched her jaw and released the pressure. *One-two-three-four-five.* She inhaled and exhaled, feeling her body relax. "I was looking forward to planning it, you know. It was going to be beautiful. You would have loved it."

"Sorry, Amara. I thought it would be too much for one person. Tyler told us what you were planning, and Ryan and I decided to cancel before you lost your deposit." Bethany fiddled with the napkins, folding them into triangles, still not meeting Amara's gaze.

Is she looking for a thank you? And why didn't Tyler tell me? A sour taste filled Amara's mouth. "I'm really sorry for how I reacted in the bakery. I wasn't expecting you, and I was taken by surprise when you gave me back the check." Amara took a sip of lukewarm water to fill the void. "Am I invited to the wedding? Am I still your maid of honor? I would love it, Bethany. You're my best friend. Even if he isn't my favorite person, I should still be there." Amara hated herself for begging.

Bethany's mouth tightened, and her eyes welled with tears. Her chin quaked and her voice quivered. "I want you to be there. I want you to be in my wedding, I do. But I know how you feel about Ryan, and I know how you get when you drink. I can't have you making a scene on the happiest day of my life. I need you to be okay with him and my life choices. I love you, but Ryan has my heart."

Amara sighed inwardly. She felt like such an asshole. She should never have called Ryan a loser even though she still believed he was. Amara knew some things were better left unsaid but in that moment her mouth opened and the insults poured out like a waterfall. Now, they've had three months to stew on hurtful words, which embedded the shards of glass deeper. Maybe with time, they could learn to forgive each other.

"I miss you, Bethany. I miss our talks, our shenanigans, and our nights out. I'm sorry that I hurt you. I understand where you're coming from, and I hope you can trust me to be there. I won't disappoint you again."

"I miss you too, Amara. I wish things were different but my heart and my head are torn right now. You make me angry and frustrated sometimes, but you never disappoint me."

"I'm sorry." Amara leaned over and attempted a hug. Instead, the two women brushed cheeks. *Maybe seeing her is a good thing. Maybe this is what we need to move on.*

Once the hard conversation was over, Amara's body decreased in rigidity and tightness. Resentment and anger subsided after the girls let out their feelings, like laundry flapping in the breeze on a windy day. The apartment was different because Bethany moved on without her. It was now Bethany and Ryan's place.

Bethany hadn't agreed to let Amara back into the wedding party yet, tiptoeing around the topic every time Amara brought it up. When Amara sensed her indirect requests went too far, she pulled back, regaining her balance. It was a tightrope act to get Bethany to trust her again, but Amara had years of practice and observation.

"Where's Ryan?" Amara asked, now that it was nearing nine o'clock.

"I texted him and told him you were coming. We thought it would be better if he stayed with his parents tonight."

Amara bit her lip, unsure if she was glad or offended that Bethany didn't think they could be around each other. "Oh."

"It was easier. I knew we'd be up late, and he has work in the morning. I thought it would give us time to talk." Bethany's words ran together into one long sentence, and Amara knew she was being untruthful.

"Okay." Amara breathed a sigh and changed the subject. "What are you ordering from my parents?"

Bethany's eyes rounded like saucers. "We placed an order last week. I'm surprised your dad didn't tell you."

Yeah, me too. Amara weaved her fingers through her hair and pulled on the ends. Her heart decreased in size, knowing that everyone left her out of such an important decision. "Yeah, I've been busy," Amara lied.

"I'd like you to be at the shower." Bethany turned toward Amara. "If, of course, you want to be. It's already planned, so all you'd have to do is show up."

Everything felt weird to Amara. *First, I was planning it. Then, you canceled the reservation. Now, Mikayla and Ruby are planning it, yet you ask me to attend.* It felt like Bethany reopened the door to their friendship a crack, and Amara needed to squeeze back in silently.

"Sure." She wouldn't argue, although frustration revealed itself in her creased forehead and stiff posture.

"I'm so busy with wedding stuff right now. If I don't respond to your texts right away, it's nothing personal."

Amara squinted her eyes at Bethany, questioning the validity of Bethany's statement. "If I have questions about anything, can I ask Tyler? We were planning your shower originally."

"Sure, I don't see why not. I don't think he'll be much help, but he might hear something from the Rainey's."

Amara hated the backseat role Bethany gave her, but her stomach trembled at the thought of talking to Tyler again.

***

Amara had three missed calls from her parents the following morning. Amara had tossed her phone in her purse the night before, and the muffled ding hadn't woken her. The last call was hours ago.

She listened to each voicemail, all from her father. "Amaryllis, where are you? I went into your room to wake you, and you weren't there." *Oh no. I forgot to tell them I wasn't coming home.*

"Amaryllis, Henry's sick, and I need you at the bakery. Call me." His voice rose in volume and sped up. "Amara, when you get home, you must go straight to the bakery. I need your help." Amara imagined him slamming the red rotary phone sitting in their living room down.

Amara glanced at her watch. It was nine forty-five and the bakery opened almost three hours ago. Annoyance twisted on her face, her nose scrunching up and her eyes darting back and forth. She didn't want to call, but knew she needed to. Not only was it her job, but it was her parents, and she probably should have told them she wasn't coming home, even though she was a twenty-five-year-old woman.

She called the bakery.

"Hi, George."

"Amaryllis, where are you? We almost called the police to file a missing person's case!" Amara knew the bakery was empty; otherwise, he wouldn't raise his voice.

"I'm in Providence. With Bethany. I went to the mall yesterday and I bumped into her." *One little lie doesn't hurt.* "I stayed at her place. Sorry I didn't call."

He didn't respond for a moment. "I need you to come in to close the shop. Henry is out sick with the flu or something. We're behind for the shelter. I know it's your day off, but I need you to get here as soon as you can."

Amara's body froze. She worked twelve-hour days with no complaint. *Don't I deserve a day to myself?* "George, it's my day off."

"Amaryllis, this is a family business and you are family. I expect you to be here. We've been worried sick calling all morning. You owe us."

Ah, the no-phone-call card. "I'm an adult, Baba. I don't have to check in with you."

"My house, my rules. You want to do whatever you want? Get your own place. For now, I expect you to help."

Amara grasped the sides of her head to regain control. She didn't want to go but couldn't seem to stand up to him. "George." Her voice sounded stronger to her ears. "I don't know when I'll get there. It probably won't be until lunch but I will be there today."

"Fine. Noon and no later." He hung up the phone before she could argue.

She hated feeling responsible for the bakery. The shelter would survive without one day of bread. They probably had bags upon bags in the freezer they could defrost.

"Hey, Beth?" Amara called through the apartment. "I have to run. Apparently, there's a staffing emergency at the bakery."

Bethany stopped scrolling through the internet "Okay." She stood from the couch to say good-bye.

Amara touched her arm. "Hey. Do you still want me at the wedding? I'm only asking because I would need to find a dress."

An awkward silence settled on them and Amara dropped her arm. Bethany scratched her chin. "Can I get back to you?"

Amara flinched, shocked at her rudeness. "Sure." Even though they had a falling out, Amara thought they were on their way to repairing their friendship. *Wow. I see where I stand.*

"It's just that the wedding is so far away. There might be a limit at the resort for how many guests we have, and we've already sent out the invitations. We'll have to wait and see what the turnout is."

Sloppy seconds? I'm not sloppy seconds. Forget it. Not going.

Amara returned to her old bedroom and changed into her new clothes, ripping off the tags. *Maybe this was a mistake.* Their friendship remained fractured, despite Amara's attempts at wrapping it in gauze and securing it with band-aids.

She left the apartment, wishing she hadn't texted Bethany. She wondered if she would ever have her best friend back.

Chapter 11

Winter turned to spring. Daylight increased, the temperature warmed, and spots of green grass sporadically shot up from the brown, thawing ground. Amara and Bethany hadn't spoken beyond the obligatory "Happy Birthday" text for Amara's birthday five weeks ago.

Amara spent her birthday alone, which was something she would never have imagined herself doing, but somehow, she felt comfortable with it. She had sprawled across her bed before prime-time television was over, eating a bowl of cotton candy ice cream and a slice of red velvet cake Mama had baked that morning.

In Providence, she would've been out until two in the morning, dancing the night away at the clubs, kissing men, and getting woozy. She wondered if Bethany went out on her behalf. Probably not.

She and Tyler texted every few days, sending each other silly memes or photos. Without having any close friends in Connecticut, Amara found herself checking her phone every few minutes for a distraction. Tyler always made her smile.

Amara couldn't admit Bethany uninvited her to the wedding because it hurt too much and reignited feelings of inadequacy. She wanted to attend all the festivities leading up to the wedding, even though Bethany repeatedly stomped on her attempts to reconnect. No one had reached out to her about the bachelorette party, which shattered Amara. She wasn't part of the cool kids anymore and couldn't believe their inner circle from college hadn't attempted to connect or question why she wasn't involved.

Amara and Tyler video chatted a few times. Amara used the excuse that she needed to know the shower details, but secretly hoped the conversation would veer to other topics. Amara found herself confiding her inadequacies and fears to Tyler. Staying up with him until the middle of the night while her family slept created an intimacy that she didn't know she needed. Even though she couldn't get out of bed on time for work, she relished in the rebellious nature of her late-night phone calls. Tyler was the one positive thing going for her.

Amara had been living with her parents for almost five months, and with no fun or spontaneous experiences, her life flat-lined. She didn't know how much longer she could handle the isolation. She saved money every paycheck, hoping to get enough to find an apartment before looking for a real job. So far, she had close to five thousand dollars. It was enough for first, last, and security, but she knew it wasn't sustainable if she lived alone. She didn't want to stay in Connecticut, but was afraid to jump into full independence without a job waiting in the wings.

The shower was next weekend, and her father tasked her with driving the pastries and desserts to the event. Amara was thankful to have a purpose, knowing that walking in would be uncomfortable. Everyone probably knew the story of why she and Bethany weren't friends and why Amara was no longer involved with the wedding. Some of what they learned likely wasn't true, but they would have their opinions, anyway. At least if Amara carried the desserts, she could leave after she assessed the level of tension in the room.

Amara texted Tyler. **Next weekend, can we show up together? Please please pretty please?**

She included a heart-eyed emoji and praying hands.

Tyler quickly responded. **Sure. Do you want me to pick you up? I don't mind.**

Amara sat on that. Could she go without a getaway car? **What if it's terrible and I need to leave?** She bit her lip, waiting for a response. **Just say the word and I'll drive you home. Trust me, I'd love an excuse not to stay.**

He ended the text with an upside-down goofy face.

Her heart rate quickened at his reassurance. Amara laughed out loud and responded with a thumbs-up emoji.

***

Amara stood outside the bakery the following weekend, her long trench coat covering her black stockings and knee-length pencil skirt. She wore professional attire in case something went wrong and she needed to blend in with the staff. The starfish necklace sat above her bosom in the notch between her collar bones.

In both arms, she held three platters of kourabiedes and diples. The traditional wedding butter cookies pressed against the honey-flavored walnut pastry, and the presentation created a heart. Amara's arms felt like lead, ready to drop to the pavement and shatter into a million pieces. She wanted to check the time, but if she readjusted the weight of the pastries in her arms, they would slide and crash.

Henry and George worked inside, filling the display case and pouring coffee for the early morning rush. People sat at the tables facing the street, staring at Amara while she fumbled with the platters.

A few moments later, Henry pushed open the door. "Amara, do you want to come inside and wait?"

Amara shook her head, not wanting to make a scene or draw more attention to herself. It was a beautiful day, and she wore all black, like she was attending a funeral. Confusion swirled within her, and she wondered if her friendship was dying or already dead.

Amara still didn't know if Bethany wanted her at the wedding, and still, no one contacted her about the bachelorette party. Amara hoped it wasn't being planned by the bride.

"I'm good, Henry. He should be here any moment. It's a far drive from Boston, and he probably got lost." Amara's phone buzzed in her pocket. "Can you grab that?"

Henry reached in her jacket and pulled out her phone. "Want me to answer it?"

"Please." Amara tilted her head so Henry could place the phone against her ear. After a moment she raised her eyebrows at Henry and he placed the phone back in her pocket.

"That was George. Reminding me to take all the trays."

She readjusted her weight, momentarily releasing the pressure from her heels. Her feet were killing her.

A familiar car slowly rolled toward her. "He's here. Thanks for the help, Henry." Henry waved to the car and reentered the bakery.

Tyler pulled up against the sidewalk and opened the trunk. "Should these go here or behind the front seat?" He took the stack of desserts.

"They should fit on the floor under the seat just fine." Amara climbed into the passenger front seat, kicked off her shoes, and stretched her legs. "Thanks for the ride," she said over her shoulder.

"No problem. I didn't want to go alone either, so it worked out. We'll stick together."

"Did you know that I'm still not invited to the wedding?" Amara's voice raised in pitch at the end of her question, and the walnut sized ball of apprehension grew into a peach pit lodged in her throat. She dragged the starfish along the delicate chain.

"I hadn't heard," Tyler responded.

"She's using me for my food." Amara attempted to joke but it fell flat. "I'm trying to be patient because I said some hurtful things, but it's been over a month since we last spoke. Don't you think she would get over it by now?" It felt good to have someone to unload her feelings on.

"Don't be too upset. From what I heard, my parents are angry that the wedding is the same weekend as my grandmother's ninetieth birthday party. I think they planned the wedding first, and when my parents asked them to move it, they couldn't. When they asked for the birthday party to be moved, the nursing home told my parents that they couldn't approve another weekend. They're in a bind, but aren't talking about it because they don't want to put any more stress on Ryan and Bethany."

Amara scrunched up her nose. "Wow, that stinks," she said. "I hope it works out." She faced Tyler, admiring his straight nose and plump lips. "What are you going to do

"I think Ryan and Bethany are trying to change the officiating date from Saturday to Wednesday, so my parents and I can get to my grandmother's party for Friday. Ryan's going to miss it, but he's getting married. He has an excuse. They're having a hard time coordinating with everyone down there."

"Wow." It sounded like a mess. Amara wished they had used her as a sounding board, imagining Bethany panicked about the big day. "I hope it works out. Bethany deserves the best. So where is the wedding, and what are the dates again?"

"They want to move the date to July 21st. I'm flying down on the 19th and leaving the 22nd."

Amara thought about Jamaica, vacation, and weddings. *Maybe one day, I'll get married.*

"So, tell me something about you that I don't already know. We have some time." He threw her a lopsided grin while keeping his eyes on the road.

"You first," Amara said. She felt her blood swoosh through her veins like a waterslide, burning her limbs as it passed.

"Well, I wish you were coming to the wedding with me."

Suddenly Amara's chest closed in on itself. She wanted to go with him too, but knew if she showed up at the wedding, her friendship with Bethany would never repair itself. She fought the suffocation from the hot, stuffy car and kept her response light. "Me too."

Amara rolled down her window to clear out the dense air. She cleared her throat and changed the subject. "I grew up in a tiny town in Connecticut. My sister was born when I was thirteen years old. I left at seventeen for college and never came back. Until now."

"I already knew all of that. Tell me something else that makes you different from other girls."

I'm terrified that I will never find someone to love me. I'm afraid I'm not enough when I'm being me. If she said that, he'd be horrified at her honesty. Instead she stuck with something less personal.

"Well, I was best friends with Bethany, for forever, as you know. I didn't realize how alone I was until she kicked me out, and I literally had no one to call. If my parents were dead, I would have been so screwed. My parents were immigrants…I don't know if you knew that…and growing up, we were poor. Like food pantry poor. Things changed when Daphne, my sister, was born. My parents somehow got a loan from the bank and opened up the bakery. They put every single penny we had into that place. I remember night after night, seeing my parents exhausted, sitting at the table, my mother's head in her hands, defeated and stuck. They may have been living their dream, but it wasn't a good one."

Tyler looked at her and smiled.

"When I left for college, I knew that I never wanted to struggle like them. I learned that to survive, you had to act the part. If you look successful, people will treat you with respect. That became my focus."

Amara leaned back in her seat, unsure what he was thinking. Staring at his profile, she felt like a fraud. She wanted him to look at her and something.

Tyler reached across and touched Amara's hand. His warm smile melted her heart.

"Your turn," she said, her voice smiling at him.

"Let's see. I think I told you. My mom raised me when my parents split. When I was in high school, I made horrible choices…drugs, skipping school, sex. My mother freaked. She sent me to live with my dad, who wanted nothing to do with me. He had a new wife who came with a kid. I didn't know them, but was forced to live with them. Those years were rough. I was angry at my dad for leaving us, mad that he found a new family and never invited me in, and angry at my mom for giving up on me."

"Is that when you moved across the country?"

"Yeah. Looking back, it ended up being the best thing for me, though. My mother couldn't care for me the way my dad could. My mom was impulsive and unpredictable. Sometimes she would come home, and sometimes she wouldn't. Sometimes we'd have electricity, and sometimes we wouldn't. I didn't know how unsteady my life was until I moved in with my dad. At my dad's, we ate dinner together every night. They expected me to go to school every day. I had my own room, and they respected my privacy. It was a hard road to walk, but I eventually found my place."

"Did you and Ryan ever get along?" Amara asked.

"Nah." Tyler chuckled. "Ryan and I were never close. He was the golden child, and I was the black sheep. They constantly compared me to him. My dad didn't know who I was. It's better now, but I'm not really close to them, as you know. I prefer to stay away from the drama. I went to college, where I found myself and learned how to live according to my values. And now, here I am. With you. Going to a wedding shower for two people that probably don't even want us there." He threw a look at Amara. "No offense."

Amara laughed out loud. "You are so right! We're probably causing them so much stress right now."

"What about you? What are your parents like?"

Amara contemplated how to respond, scrunching her nose thinking. "I don't know if I would call them great parents, but my mom and dad are great people. They have hearts of gold and wouldn't hurt a fly. They're the type who would give the shirt off their back, even when that shirt was the only shirt they owned. You would love my mom. She cooks these meals that bring you straight back to Santorini, the island both her and my father's families are from. Her moussaka is to die for. It's a Greek eggplant lasagna with garlic and oregano and lamb. So good!" Amara licked her lips and her stomach growled.

Tyler grinned. "I've never tried it before but I've heard of it."

"If you ever come over, we'll have to have it." Amara's heart skipped a beat. *Oh no, did I just invite him over to meet Mama and Baba?* "Sorry," she stumbled, "I digress. My mom is kind and thoughtful and approachable and she's the one who has kept our family together."

"What about your dad?" Tyler asked.

"My dad thinks he's the one who keeps us together and my mom lets him believe it, but we all know the truth. My dad would do anything for his family, but he's so focused on providing that he misses out on our lives. He's tired and grumpy and most of the time I feel like an inconvenience to him. Or that my problems, no matter how small, are going to either cause an anger outburst or an hour-long lecture about how I should have done things differently. He's a good guy, but not a great father. I can never do right by him."

"I'm sorry," Tyler responded. "What about your sister?"

"She's thirteen years younger than me and I left when she was four, so there isn't much of a relationship there. Being home, it's improving though. She looks up to me and seeks out advice all the time. I feel like I'm finally getting to know her as a person."

"Well, they sound like a great family. Nothing more dysfunctional than anyone else's family. I'd like to meet them one day."

Amara smiled but didn't say anything. *Maybe one day.*

They transitioned to lighter topics and eventually pulled into the parking lot.

"Thanks for the ride, Tyler. I enjoyed it." Amara leaned forward, looked him in the eyes, and kissed his cheek. It was comforting to have someone to talk to who had no opinions about her situation.

He blushed and Amara's insides exploded. She scrambled out of the car to get the food.

They carried the platters of food into the hotel in silence. The lobby contained mid-century style furniture, all boxy and square. Amara had been there for a formal during college and knew exactly where to go. She smiled at the concierge and walked confidently down the hall, her heels clicking on the tile.

The door to the room was wide open, and Amara saw balloons in blue and pink dancing above the chairs surrounding the dance floor. A large sign hanging from the front of the room read "CONGRATULATIONS" and a cake sat in the corner with a bride and groom adorned on top. Amara found Ruby at the front of the room, directing guests to their tables. She pointed Amara and Tyler to the dessert table, where Amara arranged the pastries on an empty crystal platter next to the cake, keeping George's beautiful heart shape.

"Amara."

Amara's heart stopped as she recognized the voice. She turned and smiled widely.

"Bethany. Hi." The two women looked at each other, unsure whether a hug, a handshake, or a middle finger was most appropriate. They settled on an awkward half-hug, their shoulders banging together on one side.

"Let me take your coat," Bethany said, always the hostess.

Amara watched her walk away with her jacket. She felt naked without it and wrapped her arms around her torso.

"Hello, Amara," Ryan said, his voice high and soft.

"Hi, Ryan." She didn't make eye contact with him, and instead focused on the guests mingling throughout the room. "This place is beautiful." She didn't care, but needed to fill the silence with something.

Ryan mumbled agreement before distracting himself with another guest. His obligatory greeting with Amara had ended.

Amara found Tyler sitting at a table alone and joined him. He appeared to be eavesdropping on another conversation. *Are they talking about me? Who are those people? How do they know Bethany and Ryan? What if everyone knows?* Paranoia seemed to set in. "How long do we have to stay here?" she whispered, keeping her voice and eyes low.

He glanced at his watch. "I'd say ninety minutes, to be fair."

Amara nodded. She could survive ninety minutes.

The afternoon dragged on, and Amara helped herself to chardonnay. She needed something to ease the quiver in her stomach and goosebumps on her neck. Amara watched Bethany laugh with her friends and family, and isolation blanketed over her. Amara hadn't ever recalled being in this situation, where she so desperately wanted to be accepted. One glass turned to two, which turned to three.

Tyler looked at her empty wine glasses, which sat in a puddle of spilled wine on the white tablecloth. He placed a cloth napkin underneath, sopping up the excess. Amara saw pity in his eyes and she took one final swig to prove that she was in control.

Amara felt great. She chair-danced to the music, her hips popping, despite being cemented to the wooden chair. Her shoulders swayed ever so slightly. She felt the music take over her soul, and she stumbled to her feet.

"Tyler." Amara grabbed at his arm. "Do you wanna dance?"

Tyler's eyes popped and he lowered his voice. "Not now."

"Shouldn't you mingle with yer family?" She poked him in the arm with every word.

Tyler pulled his arm away, readjusting his chair. "I said hi. Do you want any food?"

"Nah, I'm good." She felt good. Her body warmed, making her feel wrapped in a blanket or in front of a fire. It started in her chest and traveled to her wobbly limbs. With a beaming smile and flushed face, she observed the blurred people across the room. The only thing clear was Tyler; everyone else faded into the background.

She glanced at her watch. "Has it been over ninety minutes?" she hissed and giggled. "Ninety was the magic number." Her flirty voice danced with temptation. Amara's hips swayed with the music and she raised her arms over her head.

Tyler's jaw clenched. "It's been about an hour, but I think you need to cool down a bit before we can leave. You've had a lot to drink in a short period."

Amara felt messy. Her askew limbs moved like a puppet. Her brain heard his words and saw his mouth move, but nothing worked together. "Thirty more minutes," she said, wagging her pointer finger at him like the tick-tock of a cuckoo clock.

Tyler shot her a glance. "I'm going to run to the bathroom." He slid a plate of crackers toward her. "Here. Have a snack." He leaned across the table and poured the pitcher of water into a clean crystal goblet. "And some water."

Amara watched his choppy and scattered steps walk away.

He disappeared into the hallway, and Amara felt naked again. She thought people were staring and giggling at her. Amara's body traveled from warm to hot, and annoyance crept into her mind. *Why am I bending over backward for Bethany? I did everything for her, and she didn't even care.* Anger shot through Amara's body like an arrow on fire. She stood abruptly, the room spinning. Amara felt the floor move beneath her feet and she grabbed the edge of the table to steady herself.

Her legs carried her to the dessert table where Bethany and Ryan stood, their heads close together, deep in conversation. It could have been a love chat. Or an argument. Amara couldn't tell.

"I'm gonna have one ah-these," she slurred. Bethany's eyes grew wide, like she knew what happened when she wasn't looking.

"Amara." Bethany clutched her upper arm and squeezed. Pain shot down to Amara's fingers.

"Ow." Amara frantically grabbed at the food tray.

"Amara." Bethany's low voice meant business. It transported Amara back to college when she threw up in the cab on the way home from a party.

Bethany glided Amara toward the exit. To a guest, they would appear to be engaged in conversation, but in reality, Amara was being dragged across the room.

Amara's head snapped backward like an owl searching for its prey. "No, my bag. I need muh bag." She had left her purse on the dessert table. She didn't need Bethany pushing her around. She needed to be in control. *My purse. My food. My life.*

Bethany ignored her request. Ryan appeared on the other side of Bethany and looped his arm through Amara's like they were skipping down the hall together. He didn't say a word, following Bethany's lead.

"No." Amara screamed. She dug her heels into the carpet and batted her arms, trying to free herself. Ryan let go, and Amara charged toward the dessert table, breaking free from Bethany's grasp. Her shiny black purse came in and out of focus.

She picked up speed, her feet moving without her consent, and her heel caught on a napkin, littered precariously on the ground. Her ankle gave way, and Amara flew headfirst into the table.

A hush fell over the crowd as everyone stared with a mix of shock and amusement.

Amara sat up, frosting in her hair, cake smeared across her arms, and her purse resting on her lap.

"Sorry. I needed my purse." She spat out the words like knives, stood up, and exited the room, pulling frosting from the tips of her hair.

Unmistakable hatred festered from Bethany as Amara walked by.

"Congratulations," Amara hissed. "Have a nice life."

As soon as she entered the empty hallway, tears burst out like a popped balloon. The magnitude of her actions crashed against her, knocking her into the wall.

She stumbled to Tyler's car and sat next to the wheelwell, hoping he'd find her soon. She didn't have her coat, but she didn't care. The warm breeze knocked the alcohol out of her, and Amara's abhorrence toward Bethany turned in on herself. She needed to go home and forget everything that had happened.

"Well, well, well," Tyler said, approaching the car. Amara couldn't see him through the waterfall of tears. She didn't know if he would scold her or comfort her. Amara's shoulders slumped forward, and she refused to look at him. Her make-up ran down her face, her black hair was speckled white, and her nylons had a hole the size of Montana. Her tear-stained cheeks comforted her shame. She was a horrible friend.

"I'm sorry." Amara wiped her tears. "I don't know what got into me."

Tyler crouched down next to her. "I do. It was an entire bottle of wine and no lunch. I know we don't know each other well, but I think you and Bethany have bigger issues than you not liking Ryan."

She heard him loud and clear, the buzz from the drinks disappearing like the destruction from a hurricane. Amara nodded, not knowing what the other issues were.

"Is everyone okay in there?" Not looking at him, she tilted her head toward the hotel.

"They'll be fine."

"Is she pissed at me?"

Tyler chuckled. "What do you think? You single-handedly destroyed her shower. Whatever benefit of the doubt she and Ryan gave you is probably gone."

One corner of her mouth raised in a sad smile. "I'm a horrible person," she groaned, banging her hands on the pavement and her head against the car. She wished the gravel would inflict permanent pain.

"It was quite funny, the chaos that followed. I grabbed your coat for you. I didn't even say goodbye. We can go."

Amara sobbed into her bent knees. She didn't care that she showed half the parking lot her black lace underwear.

"Do you want to go somewhere? To talk? Or do you want to go home?"

Amara huffed with anger. "I can't go home like this. My father would kill me."

"Let's go to my place. I'll drive you home tomorrow."

Amara looked at her watch. *How is it only one o'clock? How did I get wasted in a little over an hour?* "Thanks. Before we go, can I have a bottle of water?"

He ran back inside and emerged with an ice-cold bottle of water and a travel-sized packet of Tylenol. "Here, take this. It'll make you feel better."

In Amara's drunken haze, she fantasized that Tyler was taking her to his castle. In her vision, she sat on a throne, wearing a purple velvet cloak and a gem-encrusted crown, which sparkled against the rays of light. She imagined Tyler wielding a sword back and forth while fighting fire-breathing dragons to protect her. She sat in the car; her imagination playing out in her mind. Tyler had saved her.

When she opened her eyes, she was in Boston.

***

Amara's arm shook and she opened her eyes. She pushed herself up

164

against the soft couch and rose to a seated position. Tyler sat beside her holding her phone.

"Amara." His gentle voice lulled her back to reality. "Your phone. You have to call your dad. He's called three times now."

Amara reached over and listened to her voicemails. "What time is it?"

"Four-thirty."

"In the morning or at night?" Time was a concept that escaped her.

"At night. You've been sleeping since we got here."

Dizziness and head pounding wrapped its way around her like a tourniquet. Her joints ached and her mouth tasted like sandpaper. The earlier events crashed into her like a Mack truck speeding down the highway.

Her father's concerned voice rose in pitch at the end of each voicemail. She should have been home by now and forgot to call. *Again.* "Wish me luck."

The phone picked up on the first ring.

"Hi, Baba. I'm sorry I didn't call." She needed her voice to remain steady and closed her eyes to stop the room from spinning.

"Amaryllis, where are you? Is everything okay?"

Amara swallowed and traced her fingers along the curves of the couch. "Yes, yes. At the shower I bumped into a friend and decided to stay the night and catch up." She glanced at Tyler to see if he reacted to the word 'friend' but he remained indifferent.

"How was the shower?"

"Oh, the desserts were a hit. They couldn't stop talking about them."

Tyler stifled a laugh and Amara hit his leg to warn him to be quiet.

"Great! Did Bethany enjoy the heart I made?"

"Yes, Baba. She spoke highly of you." *But not me.*

"Wonderful! I will see you tomorrow then?" His voice carried appreciation. Amara cringed and pressed her head back against the

165

cushion.

"Yes, tomorrow. Bye, Baba." She hung up the phone before he could interject.

Amara placed her head in her hand. "Tyler, I'm a horrible person."

He rubbed her back. "No, you're not. You're trying to survive. Here, take this medicine. It'll help the headache."

Amara took the tablets and wished it would erase her past mistakes. *I can't believe I blew it. Again.*

Chapter 12

"Amaryllis," her father roared, while Amara sat on the couch with Daphne watching a movie. Amara jumped in surprise when he threw his phone and it crashed into her leg.

"What's wrong?" Amara grabbed at the phone, which had already darkened. She handed the phone back to him. "I can't see a thing."

Baba huffed as he jabbed his large fingers into the keypad. "Look," he said more gently as he handed Amara the phone.

It was a one-star review for the bakery. *Yikes.* Amara glanced at her father, uncertain if she should read it. Daphne pulled up close, trying to look over Amara's shoulder, her hot breath pushing against Amara's face. Amara readjusted and read the heading out loud.

"One Star. Never Again." Amara's stomach dropped, feeling somehow responsible based upon her father's reaction toward her. But she wasn't sure what she did. The past six months raced through her brain as customers' faces popped into her head. The shelter, Henry, Bethany. She hadn't started baking yet, so it couldn't be about the products. It had to be about customer service.

She continued reading out loud as if she were reading a telegram. Her family huddled around her, listening to every word. Anticipation and dismay rolled around their faces. Her father's expression held layers of disappointment and anger.

"I used the bakery for an important occasion in my life. The food itself was great, but the customer service was terrible. The person we dealt with was rude, inconsiderate to our special event, and made most guests feel uncomfortable. We've used the bakery in the past, but we will go somewhere else next time unless there is a change in staff. We work hard for our money and refuse to spend it on a business that treats us with disrespect. Never again. Using them for our wedding shower was the biggest regret of that day."

Amara's heart pounded against her chest. The person who wrote that was sneaky enough not to give specific information away, but Amara knew it was Bethany. Her jaw clenched and her armpits perspired. "Wow." Amara's voice withered into itself. She tried to swallow, but the rock lodged in her throat was too big.

"Explain. I know nothing of this." Baba's voice boomed against the small living room walls. Daphne pulled away from Amara and huddled into a ball on the corner of the couch, ricocheting her eyes between her sister and her father.

"I don't know, Baba." Amara tried to keep her voice steady, but her insecurities swirled around her words.

"Don't lie to me." He picked up the phone and threw it on the couch cushion, the blow absorbed by the fabric.

"Baba, I don't know. It must have been Bethany's shower." She didn't want to go into details. Her behavior embarrassed her and shame washed over her.

Her dad sighed deeply, sunk into the couch, and sighed again. "Tell me." Hurt and pain reflected in his eyes and shot out at her like arrows. "I need to know. This is my business."

Amara looked down at her fingers, not wanting to admit weaknesses or regrets in front of her little sister, but she didn't have a choice. "I brought the pastries, and I got drunk. I made a scene, and I fell on the cake, destroying it. She got mad. Obviously. And kicked me out. I haven't heard from her since. That's why I didn't come home that day."

"Amaryllis, this is my business." He spoke in Greek a mile a minute. Amara understood every word and Daphne looked on in horror. "You screw up like this, you tell me. My job is to fix all the screw-ups, but I look like a jerk when I don't know about them. That shower was a week ago. And now, because you didn't tell me, I have a scathing review online for everyone to see. Her father's gigantic legs paced the living room in five steps. He waved his phone in the air as if he were waving the white flag, in search of help. "Do you know how damaging this is to my reputation?" He sat on the chair and dropped his head into his hands. He pulled the ends of his short hair tight and his body slumped forward.

"I'm sorry. I didn't think it would affect you. It was between Bethany and me." Amara sputtered.

"No. You were representing us. You delivered food in my name. Even if you weren't in uniform, you were working." Her father stood up and stomped out of the room, slamming every door he passed.

"Amara," Daphne's eyes were wide. "I've never seen Baba this mad. I'm scared." The color drained from her face and her lips pressed down.

"It's okay. He'll be okay. I'll figure it out. Don't worry." Amara hugged her sister's shoulders. Amara didn't know how she would fix it, but she would. She had to.

Amara spent the night alone in her room. Although everyone was home, the house was silent. Each person was in a different corner, trying to survive the night. Amara couldn't believe Bethany screwed her like that. It was embarrassing, devastating, and low. *How can she destroy his life, like that? Sure, she leveled my life, but why drag my family into this? Especially when she knows this is my father's business?* She wanted to talk to Tyler, but needed to be alone with her thoughts.

Amara woke for work the following day, but the house remained dark. Usually, Baba ran around, making his lunch, grabbing coffee, and whistling in the kitchen. She contemplated knocking on their bedroom door, but decided against it. Amara continued her morning routine, despite the impending doom that grew with every minute.

The drive to work was quiet. She kept the radio off, lost in her thoughts. She wanted to talk to Henry about what happened, but she felt foolish for being so sloppy. Baba was right. This was no way to treat his business.

Amara unlocked the bakery door and found George elbow deep in dough. "George," she said. "You're here so early."

"I couldn't sleep," he grumbled.

Amara dropped her eyes and continued to the back, careful not to disturb him. He followed her and stood in the doorway. She felt his intense gaze remain on her and she changed her shoes. "Are you okay?" Fear flooded her.

George opened his mouth to speak and hesitated. He readjusted his hat and cleared his throat. With every delay, Amara's heart beat harder. *I don't think I want to know. Did I screw up again?* Amara searched her brain for other instances that may upset George, but she came up blank.

"Amaryllis, I hate to do this, but I have to. We no longer need your service." George's stiff words ricocheted around the room. Amara pictured him saying these exact words to other past employees.

Her arm extended halfway through her jacket sleeve and stopped. "What?"

"You're fired," he said bluntly. "You're not needed. You can go."

"But, Baba. That's not fair." She was talking to her father now. *I don't care if we are in the bakery or not.* Suddenly, she was six years old, and Baba had told her she couldn't have a lollipop before dinner. Her six-year-old self had stomped her feet and flopped on the floor, wailing at the world's injustice. Twenty-six-year-old Amara wanted to do the same, but she held her body upright and waited.

"Amaryllis, as an employee, you are no longer needed. You can collect your last paycheck next Friday." His voice was solid and even.

Amara picked up her bag and shoulder-checked him as she exited the shop. She drove home through blurry eyes, the lights from other cars casting diamonds in her vision.

Mama sat at the table, sipping tea. "Amara." She ran over and wiped Amara's cheeks. "What happened? Is everything okay?"

Amara shook her head. She couldn't speak, the emotion billowing up and overpowering her. She sobbed on the kitchen table while Mama moved around, pouring hot tea in a mug, and positioning it in front of her.

Amara looked into her mother's kind eyes. "Didn't Baba tell you?" she asked.

Mama shook her head. "About what?"

"Me." Amara wailed. "I'm a horrible daughter. I did something stupid at Bethany's shower, and Bethany wrote a one-star review because of me. Baba fired me from the bakery." Amara's utter shock turned to fury.

Her fingernails dug into her palms, creating crescent moons, as she fisted her hands under the table. The table rattled under the rhythm of her bouncing knees. Amara stood up from the table and paced past her mom. *What am I going to do?*

"No, he didn't tell me," her mother whispered. "I'm sure it will be fine." Amara saw concern flash behind Mama's eyes. She pinched her chin and offered comfort. "Here, have a cup of tea." She slid the sugar bowl to Amara. "You'll be okay."

Amara pulled her lips up but couldn't get further than a grimace. "No tea, Mama. I need to be alone." Amara stomped into her room and slammed the door.

When her father came home, he gave Amara the silent treatment. Amara felt like trash weighted down with seaweed sitting at the bottom of the ocean. She forgot how to respond to his passive-aggressive behavior, living away from home for years.

"Baba, would you like a drink?" Amara asked while setting the dinner table.

He didn't turn toward her or respond.

Amara got him a glass of water and placed it in front of his plate.

The family tip-toed around the subject of work, clearly seeing how angry he remained. Mama cooked tomato fritters, which was Baba's favorite meal, but he barely acknowledged it. Daphne shared funny school stories, and Amara and Mama forced laughter while Baba stayed stone-faced. Amara tried to be the perfect daughter, not causing any trouble. She cleared the table, did the dishes, and escaped to her room, locked away from the wrath of her dad.

The following day, she slept in late. There was no reason to wake up early. She drove Daphne to school and then returned home, determined to figure out her next move.

After a few days of silent treatment, Amara's parents came into her bland bedroom. Baba's demeanor softened, but his eyes remained hard as ice.

"Amaryllis," Mama started.

Amara turned to look at her.

Baba interrupted instantly. "We allowed you to move back on one condition. You help with the bakery and save money. It's been six months, and you're now unemployed. You should have enough money to move out. I want you out within the month."

Amara's mouth hung open, shocked at the business-like approach used to address family problems. "What?"

"George, don't you think that's a little harsh?" Mama asked. She placed her hand on his shoulder and his body stiffened. She pulled her hand away but remained close.

"No," he bellowed. "We've given her an opportunity to save enough money. We've given her the tools to be successful in her choices. She's already done enough to Loukoumades. It is time we see what she can do without us holding her hand." Baba looked directly at his wife. The lines across his forehead deepened like dried up river beds and the crow's feet around his eyes created a frowny face.

"George, she isn't ready." Mama's voice dropped to a hush but Amara heard her loud and clear.

Amara's throat thickened like molasses and it spread throughout her chest. Her shoulders slouched, as she tried to fade into the background. Amara looked down at her hands, shocked to hear that her mother found her incapable. They didn't believe she would make it. The realization stung her eyes and a hardness took over her body. "Fine."

"It's nothing personal. But you no longer have a job with us, so you need to go. You'll be fine," her father said.

Don't take it personal? Family is personal. Family should always accept and show compassion toward other family, no matter what. "Fine," Amara repeated, her voice rising in pitch.

"I think you'll find your way in the world," he said, and Amara laughed in anger.

"Come on, Baba! You don't mean that! You want me gone so you can focus on your business. That's all. You don't want me stirring up any more trouble for you."

"Amaryllis, this is my livelihood," he barked. "You're an adult. I'm not responsible for you anymore. I won't allow my livelihood to go down the toilet because you're too selfish to consider others. You are out by June thirtieth. End of story." He rose from the edge of her bed and stormed out of the room.

"Amara, I read the review. It was bad. We have a lot of damage control to do. Thankfully Henry has experience with dealing with the public, and he'll take on that responsibility. I'm sorry, but I have to support your father in this. I love you, but I think it's time for you to go and spread your wings."

Amara nodded, a stream of tears rolling down her cheek, and she walked to the door. She escorted her mom out of her room and closed the door before sliding down the wall. Her knees balled into her chest, and she sobbed. *I don't need them. I don't need anyone.*

The next few days were a blur. Amara didn't leave the house, get dressed, or shower. She couldn't eat, her stomach an electrical mess, and she refused to talk to her family. By the time Saturday rolled around, her matted hair and body odor almost comforted her.

Amara had received a few texts from Tyler asking her out to dinner, but she ignored them. She couldn't think, let alone have a conversation with him when her life was falling apart again. *I'm starting to recognize a pattern.*

"Ame?" Daphne's meek but uplifting voice called into her room. "Can I come in?" "Sure," Amara replied, her head buried into her pillow.

"I don't know what happened with Mama and Baba, but are you okay?" she eyed Amara's oily skin, greasy hair, and messy room.

"Mama and Baba kicked me out. I messed up, and they told me I have a month to find a new place to live." Anger tapped into Amara's words. She wanted to add that her parents were jerks for abandoning her, but she didn't want to bad mouth them in front of Daphne. Although it felt like they were leaving her, they weren't responsible for her.

"Oh. Where are you going to go?"

Amara shrugged, her face contorting like a broken mirror. "I don't know, but I'll figure it out." She didn't want to worry Daphne, plus there was nothing Daphne could do to help.

Daphne walked over and gave Amara a big hug, holding on tight. "Good luck," she said, and then she walked away.

Amara peeled herself out of her bed, the mattress dented by her figure, and stood in the bathroom examining her face. The puffy area around her eyes caused her eyeballs to disappear. Her cheeks were chapped from creating a crater in her pillow, and her dry lips begged for hydration. Amara climbed into the shower and cried, all her anger and frustration escaping her.

Hot water swirled around her, making it hard to breathe. Her skin prickled from the heat, and she forced herself to still, focusing on the pain with every intense, burning drop. Eventually, she stopped feeling, the tears stopped flowing, and she regained control. She turned off the water and wiped her face with a cool cloth.

She found clean clothes buried in the corner of her room and pulled them on. She texted Tyler. **Hi.**

Ding! **Hey! What's up?**

Nothing. Sorry I haven't been in touch. Can I come visit this weekend? Are you busy tonight?

Ding! **Come over tonight? That'd be awesome. I have no plans. Did you get my texts before?**

Amara called him to continue their conversation. "Hi," she said after he picked up.

"Hey," His smooth voice covered her body like melted chocolate.

"I'm sorry I haven't replied. It's been crazy here. There was a big issue with the bakery, but I don't want to talk about it. I'll tell you when I get there. I need some time to think." She spoke fast, eager to change the subject. "You sure tonight is good?"

"Of course. I can't wait to see you. I miss you."

Amara blushed, remembering the last time she saw Tyler. "Tyler, I'm really sorry. For the fiasco at the shower." Her recall was a hazy blur, but she knew she spent most of the weekend on his couch, nursing a hangover.

"It's okay." His enthusiasm took her by surprise and she found herself smiling.

"Are you always this optimistic?" Amara asked. "I ruined your weekend. You had to take care of me. I was a mess."

"Amara, you're a beautiful mess. I didn't mind. Scout's honor. It was nice having the apartment less quiet. Honestly, I missed you when you left." His voice quieted and Amara filled her lungs with a breath of relief.

"Thanks, Tyler."

For the first moment in a long time, she didn't feel like a tornado, mistakenly spiraling through people's lives, leaving havoc in her wake. "I'm gonna head out in a few, but I promise I'll fill you in later. See you in a few hours." Amara hung up the phone and held her hand against her chest, her heartbeat pulsing through her shirt.

Amara grabbed her backpack and filled it with clothes and toiletries. She called through the apartment to Daphne, "I'm going to a friend's house for the weekend," and left before Daphne could reply. Her beat-up Toyota carried her to Massachusetts. The speedometer maxed out at one-twenty and barely made it to sixty on the highway, but she still enjoyed the ride.

Amara had stopped caring about what everyone else wanted from her. She viewed this next move as another opportunity to find herself. Not her fake self to impress her boss, or her obedient self to please her parents, or her blunt self who risked her friendship for one truthful conversation. She needed to figure out a plan and be true to herself. She also needed to stop drinking.

She needed her clunker to escape Connecticut. She drove down the Mass Pike, staying in the right lane in case she couldn't keep up with the big guys. As she manually rolled down her window, her hair flew wild in the warm breeze.

Flying down the highway, she felt free, like maybe her life was just beginning.

Tyler lived outside of Boston, on the 128 loop. It was close enough to the city to feel the congestion, but far enough away to park your car on the street for free. Amara pulled onto his street, where the multi-family homes crunched together. She wedged her car between an SUV and a truck and manually checked the locks.

Amara felt lighter than she had all week. She bounced to Tyler's door, not realizing how badly she wanted to see him. She slung her backpack over her shoulder and pulled her hair into a ponytail before knocking.

The door swung open and he motioned for her to enter. "Come on in!"

The apartment looked the same as it had after the wedding shower, although the details were fuzzy that day. He pointed to the fridge. "Do you want a drink?"

"Water, please."

She made herself comfortable on his couch, settling into the worn cushion. She kicked off her shoes and pulled her legs up under her. "Thanks for having me up," she said. "I have to tell you what happened." Amara swallowed hard, mustering enough courage to tell him the whole truth.

Like a confessional, Amara spilled her story. She hid nothing because Tyler deserved her honesty. He watched her humiliate herself in front of his family, and he still took her home to take care of her. She hadn't understood how the repercussions of her actions could impact the bakery, but it did. "Now I'm jobless and homeless again," she summarized.

Tyler sat quietly, his gentle eyes encouraging her to continue. When Amara told Tyler her parents had kicked her out, she cried. Hot tears rolled down her smooth complexion and he wiped them away with his thumb and forefinger.

"What do I do?" Her voice cracked as she struggled to hide her emotion.

He kissed her under both eyes, and her heart fluttered, contradicting the shame monster growing inside her. "I don't know, but I'll help you figure it out. How long are you here for?"

Amara laughed. *Forever?* "Is it okay if I go home on Sunday?"

"Of course," Tyler said. "I have no plans."

They spent the afternoon cozy on the couch, watching movies. Tyler appeared involved with the film while Amara reengaged with her thoughts, circling between embarrassment, shame, and anger. He reached over and grabbed her hand, intertwining his fingers with hers. Under the closeness of their skin, sparks ignited.

Amara shifted her weight and leaned into him, her head resting on his firm bicep. He raised his arm and pulled her closer to him. She leaned into his chest and smelled his cologne. Her body tingled with sparks. She tried to focus on the movie, but his lips touched hers, and they ended up in his bedroom.

Even though her mind was a jumbled mess, something clicked inside her. Amaryllis, the girl who went after the world, was back in charge. She took in every movement of Tyler's body and absorbed it into her own. They moved as one, and Amara's stress evaporated with each kiss, completely freeing her. Amara relished every feeling, knowing it could go away in an instant.

***

That night, Amara and Tyler ate pizza in his living room and brainstormed ideas to solve her problems.

"Let's see. How much money do you have saved?" he asked, pulling out a notepad and paper. "If you don't mind telling me, of course."

"I have a little less than ten thousand in the bank."

"Okay." Tyler tapped his pencil against his lip. "It's so hard to know what comes first. Should you look for a job and then an apartment? Or look for an apartment and then a job?"

Amara shrugged. "Ideally, I'd like to get settled in an apartment, and then work. But if I do that, I'm putting my finances at risk. And I can't get evicted my first month."

"Where do you want to live?" Tyler asked.

Amara loved Providence, but she knew she couldn't afford solo living there. She also didn't want to find a random roommate who could make her life hell. "I love Providence, but I'm willing to give it up for something cheaper." Six months ago, she never would have uttered those words. Amara laughed at the irony of her situation. She was in the same place as she was six months ago.

Tyler pulled up a map of New England on his computer, and they zoomed into different towns around Providence that could be affordable.

"Woodstock, was that too small for you?" Tyler asked.

"Yes, I need a grocery store in my town."

"Okay, job. What's your degree again? Would you want to go back to a bank?"

"Finance. And I don't know. I would until I got myself settled and established." She didn't love the bank, but she knew what she was doing. Or she thought she did. "Do you think they would hire me knowing I got fired?"

Tyler raised his shoulders. "Worth a shot. If you applied in Massachusetts instead of Rhode Island, they might never know."

"So, do you think I should apply for a job first?" Amara asked.

"Yes. Job first. If you need to stay here until you get an apartment, you can."

Amara stared at him, noticing the outline of his nose, the intensity of his eyes, and the firmness of his jaw. "No, no, I can't do that."

"You can if you need to. I like you, and it wouldn't be perfect, but we could make it work for a short time."

Amara looked away because the passion behind his eyes made her dizzy. *Would you really let me stay here?* The commitment attached to that action scared her. *What if I screw it up?*

Amara ignored his comment and opened her phone. "Okay, it looks like I'm searching for a job now. Can you help me with my resume?"

Tyler grabbed a pen and paper. "Where do you want to start? The cover letter? I'm all yours this weekend."

Amara heard the flirtation behind his words and her head snapped away from her phone. He looked at her and smiled with his eyes. She touched his hand and said, "Thank you."

Amara's mushy brain struggled to keep everything straight, but Tyler helped create an impeccable resume with no mention of getting fired or anyone who could spill the beans.

Amara and Tyler searched for jobs outside of Providence, in surrounding Rhode Island towns, and over the border in Massachusetts. She sent off her resume to four banks and applied for various positions. At this point, she didn't care what she was doing as long as she got a paycheck.

They browsed apartment listings within the general area, too. Amara found that a studio apartment at least ten miles outside of the city was enough of a price drop to afford comfortably, pending a job.

They worked tirelessly that weekend, taking the occasional breaks to make love, eat food, and watch movies. By the time Sunday rolled around, she felt human again. Having Tyler next to her made her feel capable.

"How are you so good at this?" Amara asked over breakfast.

"Good at what?" Tyler hadn't showered yet, and his long blond bangs hung over one eye. His t-shirt hung loosely over his gym shorts, and Amara smelled a hint of musk on his skin.

"This mess." She waved her hands up and down at herself.

"You're easy," he said, smiling. "No, really, I learned a lot from my mom. After my parents split, she was out of control. Someone had to make sure we survived. I learned how to cook dinner, how to manage her money so the bills were paid, and how to solve her life problems. I've been practicing since I was a little kid."

Amara smiled up at him and kissed him on the lips. "Thank you for not thinking I'm a total loser. I got kicked out, fired, and have no friends. My life right now sucks, but I'm so happy to be here with you." She kissed him again, deeply, and her toes tingled.

"You're not a loser. You're kind and capable. You're beautiful. If all those things hadn't happened, you wouldn't be here." Tyler ran his fingers up and down her arm and she shivered. "Think about that. All that bad stuff led to a great weekend." Amara nodded, feeling a little lighter.

She didn't want to go home to her parent's house but knew she had nowhere else to go. Random moments from her past traveled through her mind like a merry-go-round. As each memory came into focus, another one took its place. Vision of her first meal with Bethany in their apartment, parasailing during spring break, pledging the sorority, eating pasta sides for weeks because that's all they could afford, shopping for formals, partying on the weekends, the first night she met Ryan, losing her job, seeing Bethany at the bakery, and falling into the cake faded into black.

"Tyler," Amara started, her voice full of concern. "Since you're so good at problem-solving, what would you do about Bethany? Do you think I'll ever be friends with her again? She was my only friend. Really. I hate the idea of losing her over a stupid guy." She threw a glance at him. "No offense."

Tyler shrugged. "None taken!"

"Do I ignore her? Do I approach her about the review? What do I do?"

Tyler looked distracted by his thoughts. "I don't know. I think you should lie low and let her cool off. If you want, I can fish around for information and let you know what I find out."

Amara nodded, biting her lip until she tasted blood. "Please."

"If this were a movie, you'd show up at the wedding. You'd apologize, she'd apologize, and life would go back to normal."

Amara chuckled. *Were you reading my mind? That was my plan with the bachelorette party, but that plans flew out the window with the cake debacle.* "Yeah, not gonna happen."

"Mona is the gossip queen. I'm sure she's heard something from Ryan by now. I'll find out." Tyler kissed her on the lips.

"The thing is, I never liked Ryan, and I never thought he was good enough for her. When he came into the picture, I slowly lost my best friend. Either she was working or with him, and she made excuses when I questioned her about it. But I've learned that it's none of my business. It's her life. All I can do is live mine and be there for her when she needs me…if she decides she ever needs me again."

Tyler nodded. "Definitely don't do anything. Don't contact her or ask about the wedding. Let me do some sleuthing."

"Thanks, Ty. Do you mind if I call you that?"

"Only my mother calls me that, but for you, I'll make an exception." He kissed her gently on the top of the head and pulled her against him.

"My parents call me Amaryllis. It's my real name. I hated it when I was a kid. My classmates would call me Armadillo or Amadeus. I was always so embarrassed by my Greek culture and my parent's lack of English. When I was twelve, I changed my name to Amara." She laughed. "Not legally, but on all my papers and everything. I had just started Middle School, so no one knew me as Amaryllis. It stuck. I hated that name, but if you want to call me that, you can."

Tyler kissed her again. "Because I'm special?"

"Yes, you are special. You're the most special person I know." She kissed him again. Her life was in shambles, but she never felt so alive.
***

Amara spent the next week in Woodstock, humming aloud, swaying her hips, and researching her next steps. Her parents looked at her funny, like they wanted to ask where she was over the weekend, but it wasn't their business. Amara kept her secret and continued to focus on finding an apartment and a job.

She felt happy for the first time in almost a year. The last time she felt this excited about life was when she received her acceptance letter to college. She was finally getting out of Woodstock for good.

The day she received her acceptance letter, she was babysitting Daphne while her parents closed up the bakery for the day. Amara had only applied to a handful of colleges because the fees were too expensive to apply to every school she visited. She resented her parents for not having enough money for her to pursue every college she dreamed about. She struggled to narrow down her top five choices, so her parents did what they thought was best. They allowed Amara to apply to two schools she wanted and her parents selected the rest.

During her senior year of high school, a large, white, glowing envelope waited for her, with her name in cursive on the address label. Amara ripped it open, her heart pounding in her ears. "Daphne!" Amara felt desperate to share her excitement with someone, even if it was a five-year-old girl who couldn't understand the magnitude of the moment.

Papers spilled onto the floor, and Amara scrambled to pick them up before Daphne could interfere. She flipped through, searching for the cover letter addressed to her. Amara squealed, clapping her hands, and Daphne did the same. Amara scooped up her little sister and swung her around the room. "I'm in. I'm in."

Daphne clapped her hands, loving the vestibular high Amara had provided. "More, Ame," she exclaimed. Instead, Amara turned on the radio and blasted pop music. The two girls danced without a care in the world.

On that day, Amara had felt free to pursue the life she wanted. What she had thought she wanted was admiration for being admitted to college, and to become someone her parents could be proud of.

Today, she found herself at the same crossroads, but with a chance to walk another path. She was finally free to choose the life she wanted, and today, she wanted to build a life completely on her own, unafraid of other people's judgements and opinions.

Today, she chose to live a life she could be proud of, but to do that she had to be real. Her authenticity needed to start with herself.

Chapter 13

Tyler kept Amara motivated, sending her daily texts, checking in, and showing that he cared. He sent her random job or apartment classifieds, some of which she applied for and some she tossed.

By the time Friday rolled around, she had applied for fifteen jobs in various towns north of Providence. She wanted to be closer to Tyler, so she focused on locations between Providence and Boston. Tyler advised her to apply at small hometown banks, since they probably wouldn't check her work history.

By the following Monday, she had four interviews lined up. Two weeks ago, she had felt like her life was over, and she didn't deserve anything positive in her life. Now, there was a world of possibility right in front of her. She saw the harsh world from a different light, which was much more rewarding.

Amara texted Tyler. **EEK! I have four interviews this week! All on Wednesday!**

He quickly responded. **I knew you could do it! Good luck! Want to come over next weekend so we can celebrate?**

Amara blushed, sensing his touch from the last time she saw him.

She responded with a big red heart.

When interview day came, Amara desperately wanted to go shopping, but she refrained from spending money she didn't have. Instead, she tore open her closet and pulled out her most competent outfit. She wanted to send the right impression. Not too fancy or uppity, and not too casual. She tried to be professional but approachable. She settled on black linen pants, black heels, and a white button-down shirt. Staring in the mirror, she braided her hair in one thick braid down the middle of her back. She put on mascara and Chapstick, refusing to overdo it.

She climbed into her beat-up car and chugged to Plainville, a small town about twenty-five minutes north of Providence. The independent bank blended into a cute downtown strip. Amara noticed the old homes, the free parking, and the people shopping amongst the stores. The quaint town reminded her of Woodstock, and she shuddered, questioning whether this was a good idea.

Amara entered the bank and introduced herself to the receptionist. She sat in the oversized, cozy leather chair in the lobby, waiting to hear her name.

"Amaryllis?" a petite woman called from the door behind Amara. Amara stood wearing a grin plastered across her face. She made eye contact, stuck out her hand in greeting, and followed the woman.

"My name is Martha. Nice to meet you."

Her gentle voice and encouraging eyes put Amara at ease. "Nice to meet you too. The bank is lovely," she complimented with a smile.

The job itself was for a head teller, which was a supervisory role. They traveled through the bank to a small conference room with a square table.

"So, tell me," Martha said. "Why would you be a good fit here?"

"Well." Amara paused to clarify her thoughts. If she had been asked this question six months ago, the self-compliments would have rolled off her tongue like melted butter. Life had knocked her off her pedestal and she struggled to pull herself up from the dirt and grime. "I'm a hard worker. Organization is my strength, especially when it comes to time and responsibilities. Not only can I manage my day but I can delegate appropriately, which makes me extremely efficient. Also, I love numbers so much, I got a degree in finance." Amara flashed Martha a smile but Martha did not smile in return. Amara's confidence wavered and she swallowed loudly.

"Why are you applying here for this position?"

Amara looked at her, visions of responses flashing through her mind. Tania's scowling face documenting every weakness, Gail encouraging Amara to apply and then firing her on the spot, and Mallory teaching her a job she already knew. Years of experience and those three moments jumped out at her.

Martha looked up from her laptop and Amara smiled again.

"I lived in Providence for years, working for a bank. I worked my way up the ranks and I loved it. But my parents own a Greek bakery in Connecticut and they needed my help, so I decided to move closer to them to help when possible. Now that they don't need the help, I have relocated and would like to return to the banking industry." Amara prayed that Martha was satisfied.

Martha seemed to believe her story, nodding in sympathy when Amara explained how they baked every night for the homeless shelter and needed someone to transport the goods. Amara painted herself as the hero, saving her family's business from bankruptcy.

Amara felt terrible lying, but couldn't risk not getting this job. After fifteen minutes of what felt more like a conversation than an interview, Martha stood and shook Amara's hand one more time.

"Amaryllis, thank you for coming in. You should hear from us within the week."

"Thank you, I look forward to hearing from you." Amara smiled and swallowed her confidence. She walked out of the bank and struggled with keeping her excitement to herself. When she got into her beat-up car, she cranked the radio with dance music, and drove to her next interview.

Amara felt worthy again, even though she had created a fictional persona. Regardless of her termination, she was an outstanding employee, and any of these banks should be happy to have her. Amara drove around the little New England town to kill time and explore her potential new residence.

Her life shifted drastically within the past year. She recognized her progress with self-acceptance, but knew she had a long way to go. Things that used to make her happy no longer seemed important. It was what it was. She had screwed up more times than she could count on both hands, but at least she was trying to fix it.

***

"The rent is seven hundred a month," the old man said, peering at Amara over his glasses.

Amara looked around the large single room, imagining a bed, sofa, and small table. *Would there be room for it all?* She wouldn't know until she moved in.

"Sam, what about heat and hot water?" asked Tyler.

Amara smiled at Tyler, thankful he was with her. It could cost her a fortune if she agreed to the wrong apartment.

"Yep, yep. Both included. Snow removal and parking included, too. Washer and dryer free in the basement."

Tyler nodded. Amara noted the cobwebs in the corner, the overall darkness, the four small windows on two walls, and the antique fixtures in the bathroom.

"Can we let you know later today?" Tyler asked.

"Sure, but I want someone moving in within the next ten days, and I have two more appointments tomorrow. Let me know as soon as you can, Amaryllis."

The three adults squeezed out of the tiny apartment, walking single file down the old hallway. The house was probably over a century old, and the musty smell couldn't hide the history. Amara held her breath until they were outside.

"I don't know," she said to Tyler as they sped away. "It's a place to live, but I don't know if I can make it my own."

"It's month to month, right? It can always be a right-now apartment until something better comes along."

Amara bit her lip. "It's tiny."

"It's just you. Do you need a lot of space?"

"Well, I have a lot of stuff," Amara countered.

"That's what storage is for."

Amara folded her arms and stared at Tyler, considering his suggestion. They had looked at half a dozen studio and one-bedroom apartments. Nothing was up to her standards, but with her budget being so small, her standards needed to disappear. She knew that, but struggled to make it a reality.

"What's up with your name?" Tyler asked. "I saw Amaryllis on your resume, and then this guy called you that, too. Is that what you're putting down on your applications?"

"Yeah, because it's my name. It's like I'm starting over, and a new name is a perfect chance to recreate myself. Plus, I thought if I put down Amaryllis instead of Amara for the job positions, they would be less likely to track my history."

Tyler chuckled. "Okay, Amaryllis." He had only used her real name a few times before, and the extra syllable stuck to his tongue.

Amara laughed. "It's not Am-aryllis. It's Ah-maryllis. Like Amara, but longer."

"Ah-maryllis-Ah-maryllis," Tyler sang.

They drove up to his apartment to discuss and consider her choices.

"Congrats on getting the job! When do you start?"

"Thanks. In two Mondays."

"Was that the bank in Plainville?"

"Yeah, I guess Martha liked what she heard."

"When do you have to be out of your parents?"

Amara picked at her fingers. "In two Mondays."

"And when do you want to be moved into an apartment?"

"Honestly," she spoke rapidly, "by next Monday. I need time to get settled."

Tyler pulled out a piece of paper and made a chart. **Job,-check**, he wrote, along with the date of her first day in big numbers.

Next to **Job**, he wrote **Apartment** and listed four places they saw. Amara considered her commute to work, commute to Tyler, and price. No apartment was perfect, and they each had a huge negative. They were either too pricey, too small and dingy, or too far from work.

"That one." She impulsively pointed at the third item on the list. **Old Victorian.** Besides it, Tyler had written: **third floor, washer/dryer in basement, heat and hot water included, large driveway, large yard, walking distance to the park, walking distance into town/work, extra-large studio/attic-$1400.**

"You sure? That one was one of the most expensive. And can you handle walking up two flights every time you want to come or go? Think of groceries, furniture, work stuff," he listed.

"Yes. It was clean, it had a lot of windows, and was private. It felt like a home, and the landlord was nice. What was his name again? Monty?"

Tyler had gone with her for every appointment. "Yeah, Monty. I think his wife's name was Deborah. They live in the house, too. Are you sure you want to deal with that?"

Amara waved her hands. "Yes. If you asked me five years ago, I would have said hell no, but I'm different now. I've done a lot of growing up. I'm not planning on sleeping all day and partying all night or having tons of people over. You're my only friend right now. I feel better having them there, in case something happens or if something breaks."

"I think he had a lot of rules, too," Tyler said. "No painting, for one." Amara waved him off. "It's fine. I don't care. I can afford it, it was cute, and it didn't feel like a dungeon. I liked the neighborhood and I could walk to the downtown shops. It might make me get outside more and exercise. It'll be fine."

Tyler scanned the choices of the other apartments. For needing something so soon, it was slim pickings. "How did you hear about this place again?" he asked.

"When I accepted the position at the bank, I told Cassie, my new manager, that I couldn't start right away because I needed to find housing. She told me her uncle had an extra apartment available. I want to take it," she persuaded. "It came recommended. Plus, I think I'm a good tenant, and maybe being on his good side will help me move ahead with work."

Tyler grinned. "Okay, it looks like we have a winner." He circled **Old Victorian** and checked off **Apartment**.

Amara giggled and threw her arms around his neck. "Thank you for all your help! I couldn't have done it without you." She kissed him deeply and pulled away. "Should we call Monty?"

***

Amara's mind moved like lightning. Every time she sat down to do something, another thought burst through, distracting her and causing her brain to splinter. She needed to get ready for her first day of work, and wanted to look organized and confident.

When she called Monty and Deborah, she convinced them to let her move in earlier for a prorated rate. She used Cassie's name as leverage, and Monty said she could move in as soon as she signed the lease.

Amara barely read it and scribbled on the dotted line. It was official. **It's official!** She sat in her car and texted Tyler. He responded with a sunglasses smiley face. To celebrate, Amara drove to the nearest shopping plaza and made her first purchase: a welcome mat for the front door. It had three sets of flip flops and said, 'WELCOME' along the top and 'Catch you on the Flip Side' along the bottom. It was goofy but perfect for her first place.

She drove home to Woodstock to gather her things. When she moved back in with her parents, she had one suitcase and one box of belongings. Six months later, her room overflowed with random knick-knacks, new clothes, and furniture. Amara decided that if it didn't fit in her car, she wasn't taking it. She didn't want to ask her father for any help, and she didn't want him to see her struggle with furniture she couldn't carry.

When Amara pulled up, the Corolla sat in the driveway and the porch door was wide open. Amara checked her watch. It was nine-thirty in the morning on a Thursday. *Why is Mama home?* Amara's heart rate quickened in anticipation of a scene. She prayed her father was at the bakery.

Her mom sat in the kitchen, stacks of paper surrounding her on the table.

"Mama," Amara said. "What are you doing here?" Amara's smile faded as her mother looked up with tear-stained cheeks and puffy eyes. "What's wrong?"

"Your father's selling the bakery." Her voice quivered and she blew her nose.

"What?" Amara dropped her purse on the floor and rushed to her mother. "Why? Over one stupid review?"

"No, the review was the final straw. We have been floundering for a few years, barely making ends meet. We're old, Amaryllis. He wants to retire, and he's tired of working seventy hours a week."

"You're not that old," Amara exclaimed.

"We already spoke with Henry. He'll purchase the bakery. We'll still be involved, but the day-to-day operations won't be our responsibility. It will ease a lot of stress, and we will be home more for Daphne."

Amara's mouth fell open, and she blinked a few times, trying to make sense of her mother's words. "But you love the bakery. The bakery is who you are, and it's how the community knows you!"

Mama winced, and her chin trembled. "It will still be who we are and what the community sees, but we won't be the owners."

Responsibility for her parents' decision sat on Amara's shoulders. She may not have caused their entire problem, but she was a factor that solidified the final decision. "Oh, Mama."

Amara sat, unable to move. Anger billowed up inside her like a hurricane. *Damn it, Bethany!*

Amara grabbed her purse and keys. "I'll be back in a few hours." She knew what she needed to do.

***

Bang!-Bang!-Bang! Amara slammed her fist into the door with authority. "Bethany, I know you're in there. I need to talk to you." Amara's voice had an edge that surprised her. She didn't know if Bethany was home because her schedule was so inconsistent, but Amara needed to try.

The door opened a hair, and a single eye stare out at her. She saw the freckles glide across his nose and the spiky brown hair stick through the crack. "Ryan, open up," Amara said sternly.

The door opened. "Hello, Amara," he said sarcastically. "Come in."

Amara pushed the door open, sending Ryan slightly back on his heels, and she barreled past him into the kitchen. "Bethany," she yelled.

"She'll be right out. What brings you here?" Ryan's eyes hardened and his lips curled into a sneer.

"Shouldn't you be working?" Amara snapped.

"I am. I'm working from home today, if it's any of your business." He didn't elaborate, and Amara didn't care. She sat at the table and faced the door, waiting for Bethany to emerge.

Bethany strolled in, looking ten years older. She also wore a hardened gaze and kept her posture upright. Her arms crossed against her chest. "Amara. Funny finding you here. What do you want?"

"I need to know. Why did you write that review about my parents? I get why you're angry, but why drag my parents into it? It's their livelihood, Bethany." Amara stood up from the chair, tripping toward the door. She found herself directly in front of Bethany's face.

"I don't know what you're talking about," Bethany spat. "Get out of my face." She stormed past Amara and stood next to Ryan.

"The review online. It completely killed them!"

Bethany rolled her eyes. "Ryan, do you know what she's talking about?"

Ryan half-shrugged. He protectively wrapped his arms around Bethany. "I may have heard about a review that went out after our shower, but I don't know who wrote it."

Amara stared into his calculating eyes. "He's lying." Amara spun to face him. She pointed her index finger and poked him in the shoulder. "He did it! Bethany, my parents might lose the bakery because of that stupid review. One critical review in a small town can suffocate a business."

Ryan's lips curled in the corners. "Maybe, Amara, you shouldn't drink while on the job."

Amara saw a flash of red and there was no turning back. She hated him more than she had ever hated anyone. "Bethany, you're too good for him. Take the blinders off, Bethany. He doesn't deserve you. If he treats strangers like this, how will he treat you?" Amara tore through them and slammed the front door behind her. She couldn't see through the hot tears that drained down her face.

Amara sat in her car for what felt like hours. She couldn't leave. Her cloudy head and tornado of emotions spiraled out of control. She needed a solution before she saw her parents again.

Amara considered calling Tyler, but she couldn't. Ryan and Tyler were technically family, and Amara didn't want to run her mouth and risk losing her boyfriend. *Is he my boyfriend?* She didn't know. Behind the closed windows, the blistering sun beat down on her face and the heat enveloped her. She couldn't breathe but felt comforted by the smothering air filling her lungs.

I need to talk to Bethany without Ryan around. There has to be a way to fix this.

From the corner of Amara's eye, Bethany left the apartment, quickly racing down the sidewalk. It almost looked like she was in a panic, her little legs hurrying, while her upper body remained stiff. Amara pulled sunglasses over her eyes and waited for Bethany's car to pass. Amara pulled out behind her, keeping her distance. Her heart rate slowed when she realized Bethany wouldn't recognize the beat-up red coupe Amara now drove.

She followed Bethany to the grocery store and watched her climb out of the car and enter the store. Amara pulled into a spot directly next to Bethany's car and waited.

Thirty minutes later, Bethany emerged with a cart full of bags. Amara had calmed her mind and composed herself from her earlier outburst. She climbed out of her car. "Bethany, we need to talk."

"I can't. I have to get this food home and in the freezer. I have ice cream."

"Fine. Go home. Put the food away and then meet me at the bookstore. We can sit and talk in the café."

"I can't." Bethany's voice cracked and lowered to a whisper. "I can't."

"Bethany, you owe me a conversation. Tell Ryan you forgot something, or you have to run to the bank. Tell him anything, but meet me at the bookstore. All I need is ten minutes."

Bethany looked conflicted. Her eyes darted to the bags of food in the backseat and then to Amara's car. "What happened to your car?"

"You know, just downsizing. My best friend kicked me out, and I was broke and homeless. The BMW didn't quite fit my image anymore."

Bethany's face dropped and tears filled behind her eyes.

"I'm joking." Amara's voice softened. "Please, come meet me. We need to talk."

Bethany nodded and threw her arms around Amara. "Okay. Give me a half-hour. I'll text you if I can't make it."

Amara nodded and watched Bethany fly out of the parking lot.

At the bookstore, Amara waited by the stack of self-help books. She browsed the bookshelf while monitoring the door. She checked her watch repeatedly, but time seemed to stand still.

The bell rang above the door, and Amara glanced up. Bethany entered, her feet moving a mile a minute. Amara stepped in front of the registers and waved with a half-hearted smile. They made their way over to the café.

"Can I get you a coffee?" Amara asked.

Bethany nodded. "Thanks."

They settled into two plaid armchairs and placed their handbags on the end table in between them.

"I'm sorry," Amara said. "For interfering with your life. But as your best friend, I need to look out for you, like I did with Ronnie Mac that first year of college. You would do the same for me. I'm sorry if I came off as bitchy."

Bethany took a sip of coffee and swallowed. "I've really missed you," she said. "It's been weird without you."

"I'm sorry for the shower. I drank too much that day, and I made a scene. That wasn't fair to you."

Bethany nodded. "I'm sorry for ignoring your texts. That was kind of bitchy too."

Amara shrugged. "I don't know what it is about Ryan, but I don't believe he's right for you." Amara carefully used "I" instead of "you" statements in case Bethany felt attacked. "I believe you deserve someone who will take care of you. I'd hate to see you get hurt. I tried to tell you, but when you kicked me out and ignored me it practically killed me."

"I'm sorry," Bethany whispered. "I didn't know what to do. Ryan told me to let you go. I didn't want to lose him."

Amara gazed into Bethany's eyes, refusing to look away. "Can I ask you an honest question?"

Bethany nodded.

"What do you see in him?"

Bethany giggled and shifted in her seat.

"No, seriously. What makes him so special? Because I've tried, and I can't find any endearing qualities." Amara stopped herself, careful not to overstep with criticism.

Bethany gazed past Amara's right shoulder. "When I first met him, he was funny. He was goofy and charming. I liked the fact that he was young but old-fashioned, like 'open the car door' type of old-fashioned. He seemed innocent, less jaded about life. I liked the idea that I could shape him into the man I needed him to be."

Amara couldn't stop herself. "Oh yeah? And how did that work out for you?" Her words were harsh but her tone was comforting.

Bethany's eyes cowered. "Not great. Everything changed after he moved in. He's controlling, checks my phone all the time, and I have to check in with him anytime I leave the house. If someone calls or texts and he doesn't like it, he deletes the messages. He doesn't like me leaving the house without him. Like right now, I told him I forgot the eggs, and all he wants for dinner is meatloaf. I have to get back before he wonders where I am." Bethany checked her watch and quietly cried big, round tears.

"Bethany, look at your life. This is not what you wanted. You wanted to find someone who would treat you with respect. This isn't respect. If you marry him, your life is over as you know it. It's going to get worse."

Bethany continued to sob, wiping tears away with the back of her hand. "I'm so sorry about that review. I didn't know, and I would never have dragged your parents' name through the mud. I love your parents."

Amara nodded. She believed her. Bethany's phone buzzed, and she jumped in her seat like a rocket launching into space. "I have to go get those eggs. I'll try to contact you in the next few days when Ryan is working."

Bethany grabbed her bag and reached over to give Amara a weak hug, their arms barely acknowledging each other. Bethany dropped away from Amara and glided out the door.

Not only had Amara lost her best friend, but her best friend lost herself, and there was nothing Amara could do.

***

"What can I do?" Amara asked Tyler as they carried boxes in and out of the U-Haul.

"About what?" he asked.

Amara rolled her eyes at Tyler for not keeping up with all the drama in her life. "About my parents. About Bethany. I need that handy chart you made me, laying out all my options."

They continued to work, emptying the truck, dragging boxes up the two flights of stairs, and dropping them in the area that might end up being the bedroom. They both gasped from exertion. Amara wiped her wet hair from her eyes and pulled her damp t-shirt away from her abdomen, welcoming the flow of air under her shirt.

"I need to help them both, but I don't know how," Amara said.

Tyler chugged a bottle of water.

"My dad's a man of few words, and all he said was that it was time to move on. He told me Henry was the perfect person to take over the business."

"Maybe he is."

Amara sat on the cool floor. "No, he doesn't know how to run a Greek bakery." Amara bit her lip and readjusted her ponytail. "And, Bethany can't marry Ryan. She just can't. He's the worst person for her."

Tyler nodded. "It sounds like you can't do anything about either situation, and neither situation concerns you."

Amara stopped mid-step and kicked her hip out, adjusting the box on one side. "But they're both making huge mistakes. I have to do something."

Tyler threw his arms up in the air and rested the box on the counter. "You just got a new apartment and a new job. You should probably focus on you. Let's get you settled and secure in this new life of yours before you go solving everyone else's problems."

Amara felt hurt by his nonchalance. She put the box on the floor. "Tyler, I've been worrying about myself and only myself for my entire life. It's time I help others when they need it."

"But they didn't ask for your help, did they?"

She shook her head, her body too tired to argue her point. She entered the small apartment and dropped another box near the door.

"So, you should sit back and mind your own business. That's how you got into this mess at the shower. You stuck your nose into their marriage, and it backfired."

Amara pulled back and tightened her arms across her chest. Her eyes dropped to her toes as the unsettled air between them lingered like unexpected snow squalls at dusk. "Have you talked to Ryan?" she asked.

"No, because he and I don't talk, remember? I talked to my dad, and the wedding is still happening. Everyone has their flights, and the resort is full. You need to let her make her own choices. If you don't, she's going to push you out even more."

"Ha." Amara scoffed. "Or Ryan will, the little weasel."

Tyler nodded. "Or Ryan will."

"I don't know how you can be related to him," Amara said, accusing him of not sticking with her.

"I'm not related to him at all. That's why we have no relationship. I choose not to know him because I don't like him. I'm only in the wedding as a formality."

Finally, he agrees Ryan's a jerk. "Did you know he tracks her every move? He screens her calls and deletes her messages?" She faced him and saw uncertainty in his eyes.

"No, who said that?"

Amara looked up at the ceiling. "Bethany told me. I convinced her to sneak away and meet me at the bookstore. She had less than ten minutes because Ryan was keeping time. All those times I texted her I thought she was ignoring me. She hadn't even seen them." Amara shook her head. "He's bad for her, but I think she feels trapped and pressured to get married because it's only a few weeks away."

Amara knew she could be overbearing with her opinions. She didn't want to push Tyler away either, so she quieted the voice in her head and started opening boxes. "Thanks for your help," she said, changing the subject.

She noticed Tyler's body loosen. He took off his shirt, and his muscular abdomen glistened under a layer of sweat. They both lay on the chilled wooden floor, staring up at the ceiling.

Amara yanked her tank top to her bra line, the coolness from the floor zapping her skin. They remained as two statues frozen to the floor, with boxes full of surprises surrounding them. She grabbed his hand and interlaced their fingers. Maybe Tyler was right. Even though everyone else's lives were falling apart, her life deserved to finally fall together.

Chapter 14

The following week was a blur. Amara woke up and thought of herself as Amaryllis, a successful businesswoman who had her life together. She put on her signature attire of black and white and walked into the bank in her two-inch heeled black leather boots. *I am accomplished. I am successful. I am respected.* She held her head high and her shoulders back.

The first few days of work consisted of watching training videos, shadowing, and meeting with management. Amara's confidence rose with each transition because she already knew how to do this. If nothing else, she was moving up in the world, bolstering her resume for the next best thing, if the next best thing ever knocked on her door.

Amara came home from work to her cozy apartment. She flung the curtains open and collapsed on the loveseat next to her bed. She loved her new apartment because it was hers. She hadn't ever lived alone, and it was a welcome change. Amara finally felt like a grown-up.

See, Tyler is right. Maybe it's none of my business what happens to them. Amara tried to embrace that thought, but images of their lives teetering toward collapse pressed close against her heart.

Amara still didn't understand why her parents wanted to sell. *Sure, that review may have hurt business slightly, but it wasn't enough to kill their finances.* It made little sense.

Amara thought about her parents and how selfless they were. She remembered feeling shocked when she learned they gave free food every night to the shelter. They weren't bringing the leftovers; they were actively baking full platters and bringing them to those in need. That act, day after day, must have eaten into their profits.

Amara grabbed her laptop and searched for whatever information she could find. *How do homeless shelters work? How do they get funded? How much does the state reimburse?*

Then she searched for everything related to running a bakery. *How much does it cost to make those desserts? How much does overhead cost?* She knew she could have asked her parents, but they were too proud to share any details with her, and Amara was too insecure about showing interest.

Things clicked together as the puzzle pieces transitioned into place. *This is why they ran out of money.*

Amara pulled open her email and blind-carbon copied multiple email addresses into the recipient line. She didn't know who to contact, so she emailed them all. Amara needed people to know how much her parents did for the community. She knew she was overstepping boundaries, but she was their daughter and a previous employee. Her parents were giving up on their dream, and Amara couldn't watch it happen.

Then she texted Henry and asked if they could meet up for lunch on Saturday. She needed to sit down with him and get as much information as possible about her parents' business. Amara's heart jumped like a gymnast.

She needed to apologize to her parents for constantly disappointing them, and also thank them for all they sacrificed.

***

"Tell me, Amaryllis, how long has the bakery been donating food to the shelter?" Marcy Matthews asked, holding her microphone towards Amara. Amara, Henry, and Marcy stood outside the shelter in the nearly empty parking lot. Amara glanced at Henry, encouraging him to answer for her. *I'm so glad Henry is on board. If this slips between my fingers or ends poorly, it's not all my fault.*

Henry reached over and stood beside Amara. "We've been donating every day for almost two years, and no matter the weather, we always delivered. We're like the post office." He smiled at the camera. The curtains on the first floor of the building waved as people stuck their heads in between the panels. A news van stood behind Amara and the production crew milled around her.

"Thank you, Henry," Marcy said, her large straight teeth taking up most of her mouth. "Whose idea was it to deliver?"

Henry continued. "Actually, it was George and Katerina's idea. Loukoumades Bakery was doing well, and they wanted to give thanks to the programs that kept them afloat when they needed support. They never used a shelter, but often used a food bank. Since the food bank only took nonperishables, they donated to the shelter."

Amara flinched, hearing the history spoken out loud for millions of people to hear. *My parents are going to kill me.* She hoped the recap of their financial needs didn't anger them when they say the newscast.

"Will your family do this forever? It's very generous of them, but I can understand the expense of feeding an extra group of people for free." Marcy held out her microphone to Amara and then transitioned to Henry.

Henry started to answer, but Amara jumped in front of him. "Uh, actually, they won't be. Anymore. They're selling the bakery." She refused to acknowledge that the bakery was going to Henry.

"Are there other Greek bakeries in the area?" Marcy asked.

Amara shook her head. "No, the next closest bakeries are in

Worcester, outside of Hartford, and Providence. We've been the only one in this area for the last eleven years."

"Well," Marcy said, looking directly into the camera. "Without the bakery, what will the community do? And not just the customers, but all the people who benefited from their generosity?"

"That's a good question," Amara agreed.

Henry stepped in front of Amara. "The person who takes over the bakery will continue their charitable work." Amara noticed that Henry did not admit he was buying the bakery. *Is it not a done deal?* Henry continued to look in the camera. "Their good deeds will not be forgotten." *Great, now it sounds like Mama and Baba died. I really hope this works.*

Marcy wrapped up the story with a quick summary for those who tuned in late. "Loukoumades Bakery has been providing support to a local homeless shelter for two years. They are a secret benefactor, so to speak. This is another story of finding goodness in the world, and giving back to the community."

Marcy smiled until production yelled, "Cut!"

Amara and Henry shook hands and thanked the news crew for taking the time to meet and showcase the bakery's story.

"Henry, I have to go. The story's going to air at six tonight, right?"

"Yes, six and eleven. You did lovely."

Amara hugged him. "Thank you for being here."

Her hands trembled as she drove home. *I hope I didn't screw up again. Now, we wait.*

***

Amara clicked off the television set in her parents living room and looked from Baba to Mama. She tried to contain her pride but it stretched across her lips, her smile practically touching her ears. "Well?" She raised her eyebrows and rounded her eyes. "What do you think?" She tapped her toe against the coffee table and bit her cuticles.

Baba looked at her. "Amaryllis, you exploited us."

Amara pulled her head back, hurt by his interpretation of kindness. "No, I helped you."

"Helped how? By drawing attention to the shelter? We didn't do it for praise. We did it because it was the right thing to do."

"Baba, you didn't deserve that one-star review. People need to know how amazing you and Mama are. You deserve a ten-star review. You've sacrificed yourself and secretly helped our community for years. You deserve that recognition."

"It is no one's business what we do with our talents, time, or money," he replied.

Amara ran to her mom and held her hands. "Mama, what do you think?"

She nodded, staring at her lap. Her gaze met Amara's, and she sighed before speaking. "I think whoever buys the bakery will make a difference in the world in their own way."

Amara retreated to her chair and sat with her head slumped down. "I wanted to help." Her barely audible voice quivered.

She basically dragged Henry to the interview, afraid to do it alone. With Henry there, she thought her parents would be more accepting of the interview and the attention, but she thought wrong.

"Amaryllis, I wish you hadn't." Baba walked out of the room.

"Mama." She turned her attention to her mother. "What will you do once you sell?"

She shrugged. "We haven't figured out a plan yet. We weren't there for you the way we should have been, and now you're an adult. When Daphne needs us, we want to be there for her. We don't want to make that mistake twice."

Amara swallowed back a sob.

"We have enough money in savings to enjoy life for a little while. Your father will still work for Henry and consult."

"But Mama, a British man running a Greek bakery? That's a contradiction! What will he bring to the business?"

Mama placed her hands in her lap. "He will be the brains of the business, and your father will be the baker. Running a bakery is too much work for us. We want to be a part of it, but we need to step back. It isn't healthy for us or our family."

Amara nodded. "Do you think Baba is upset with me?"

Mama shook her head. "No, not at all. He's just surprised."

They sat there in silence for a few minutes. Amara left, feeling like everything she did was self-destructing in her hands. She wondered what was going to crumble next.

She had driven to her parents' house, knowing when the newscast would air. She wanted to applaud her parents and showcase how much they meant to her. She wanted the world to know how much they did for the community. Instead, she somehow betrayed their confidence. Either sharing their history of needing help or breaking the confidentiality of helping the shelter had rubbed Baba wrong.

***

Back at her apartment, Tyler waited for her in the driveway. The mid-summer sunset revealed a haze of watermelon, violet, and indigo. She gave Tyler a big hug. "I'm so happy you're here."

He kissed her forehead and handed her a small bouquet of wildflowers.

"These are beautiful." She brought them close to her nose and inhaled.

They walked up the two flights of stairs, Amara slightly panting by the end, and placed the flowers in a vase. "Are you getting excited about the wedding?" she asked.

"The wedding? Nah. The vacation? Yes. I only wish you were coming with me."

"So, what happened with the reception? Were people able to change their plans?" She hadn't spoken to Bethany since the bookstore two weeks ago, but it felt like a million years ago.

"I heard that my immediate family and Bethany's family would be there, plus a few friends that got off work. My parents and I are leaving the day after the wedding to go to my grandma's party. Are you still coming to that with me?"

Amara nodded and smiled. "Of course. Can we hide from your parents? I feel like they hate me because of the shower fiasco."

Tyler chuckled. "I'll keep you safe. We can make an appearance and then leave." He wrapped her in a hug.

"Does it have to be ninety minutes?" She chuckled.

"We'll just play it by ear. Tell me you want to go to Disney World, and we'll go."

Amara looked into his eyes. "Disney World, huh? I'd like to go there one day."

Tyler rubbed her shoulders. "That'll be our code word. If things get weird, we'll go. I promise," he said into her hair. "Don't worry. Once they get to know you, they'll fall in love with you."

Amara breathed in his familiar sandalwood cologne. "Thank you," she whispered.

"So, what happened with your parents today?"

Amara pulled away from him. "Ugh, my dad looked so disappointed in me. I don't know what happened. He said it was no one's business what he did with his talents, time, or money. I did it because he needed positive press after the one-star review, and they deserve the recognition. They've sacrificed so much! But he left the room, never returned, and didn't even say goodbye to me."

Tyler hugged her tighter. He rubbed her hair and caressed her head, kissing her forehead. "It'll be okay."

They spent the next two days together, wrapped in each other's arms and legs, cuddling under the blankets. Monday morning rolled around, and Amara kissed Tyler one last time before his trip to Jamaica. "Have a great time. Call me when you get home."

She watched him drive away, the sun rising over the horizon, grateful that at least one thing in her life was good.

On Wednesday, her mom called in a panic. "Amaryllis, we need you."

Amara left work early, telling Cassie there was a family emergency. She hopped in her car and drove back to Connecticut, her mind racing. Mama didn't share why, but Amara could hear the chaos in her voice. She sounded breathy and high-pitched, unable to communicate what was wrong.

The drive from Plainville was about five minutes longer than her previous apartment, so she pushed down on the gas pedal, watching the speedometer rise. She drove to the bakery, unable to find parking. Cars lined both sides of the street, and the occasional news van hid amongst the alleys. Amara drove around the block, finally settling on the drugstore parking lot. She raced down the sidewalk, a line of people waiting inside and snaking around the block.

Amara entered through the back. "Mama? Baba? Henry?" Nothing appeared unusual except for the overflowing sink full of dirty pans, the spilled syrup on the floor, and opened containers of pistachios and walnuts. She pushed the swinging doors open and found the store jammed with people. George was filling the empty display case with melomakarona and baklava. Her mother stood at the register pushing numbers and pulling receipts, and Henry organized the crowd. In the corner, a cameraman stood with Marcy Matthews. Amara waved and smiled, unsure if she should help her parents or thank Marcy for visiting.

"Amaryllis," George growled. "Help your mother take orders. This is all we have left for the day." He turned and exited the room.

It was difficult to hear with all the conversations happening at once. Henry walked around with sample-sized kataifi and loukoumades to prevent the waiting guests from complaining. The line stretched past four stores down the sidewalk. Then, Henry carried a large, empty jar labeled "Donations" and weaved through the crowd.

"Help support the shelters in Connecticut. Help support the food banks. Your donation will go to the statewide programs that help people down on their luck. It sets them up with a life coach, job interviews, and housing. It gives them access to the food bank, daycare, and translation services. Your donations will help those in need." His voice rose over the crowd as he walked through the line. His bucket slowly filled with dollar bills. Amara never realized Henry was such a showman.

Marcy's cameraman videoed Henry as he worked through the crowd. Amara knew that the bakery's future was now in Henry's hands and his persuasion to show the public how necessary Loukoumades Bakery was to the community.

Amara worked for hours alongside her parents and Henry, until the entire shop emptied. Crumbs filled the corners of the trays. Muddy footprints dotted the tile floor, and the trash cans overflowed with napkins and bakery bags. The place was a mess, but at least they could sit and catch their breath for a moment.

When three o'clock hit, Henry locked the door, and they all sighed an overwhelming breath of relief.

"What was that?" Amara exclaimed. "What just happened? That was insane!"

George sighed. "It's been brewing since Saturday. Sunday, we sold out by eleven. Monday, we sold out by one, and yesterday and today, the news people were here. I have never been that busy. Ever. I am exhausted."

"Since Saturday, Baba? Why didn't you call me? I could have helped."

"We had it under control until yesterday, and then when things got crazy again this morning, we needed you. Thank you for coming,

Amaryllis."

The four of them sat there, their bodies broken. Blisters on Amara's feet blew up under her dress boots. She flexed her calves and her sore muscles screamed out in pain. The bakery's future still hung precariously by a thread, but the constant media could only help.

Amara smiled, not understanding how things flipped so fast. "Is tomorrow going to be like this, too?"

Mama chuckled. "Funny that you ask. Tomorrow we're closed because we have an interview on the Connecticut Morning Show to talk about the bakery and how we've helped our community. It's unreal. We've made more money over the past four days than we had made in the past month. I don't think it's sustainable."

Henry nodded, smoothing his polo shirt. "I don't know, Katerina. It's just the three of us."

Amara looked at him, taking in his salt-and-pepper hair, round glasses, and stocky build. There was no way they could manage this volume. "Henry, you killed it out there. I didn't know you were such a salesman."

Henry adjusted his glasses and brushed back his hair. "Well, it's easy when you're passionate about something."

Amara jumped up from her seat, hugging both parents in a bear hug. "Congratulations. We did it. You got the recognition you deserve."

George cleared his throat. "I must admit, I'm pleased that the shelter is getting what they need, and I think education and advocacy are important for the state programs to survive. Sorry, Amaryllis, if I reacted poorly the other night."

Amara widened her eyes and touched his hand. "We all have our days, George. Whatever you need, I'm here to help." For the first time in a long time, she meant it.

***

By the time Friday rolled around, Amara's parents were on every news channel in Connecticut promoting their story, business, and generosity. The shelter director gave a testimony about how the bakery lightened the lives of so many. They wanted to blend into the background, but they were local celebrities.

"Amaryllis," Mama said into the phone. "We need you. Can you help us this weekend?"

"Mama, I can't. I have a birthday party to go to tomorrow, but I can come down early Sunday morning."

"Thank you, that will help. We have all this publicity and no employees to keep up with the demand." Her voice dropped, and guilt draped over Amara throughout the drawn-out silence.

"I promise I'll be there early Sunday, Mama."

She hung up the phone and picked out her outfit for her date with Tyler. Amara's heart quickened, and her hands shook while thinking about seeing his family again. Fear that Ryan's mother would make a scene clouded Amara's thoughts. Amara imagined Mrs. Rainey pointing at Amara and announcing her as 'the girl who ruined the shower.' Mrs. Rainey would demand she leave while throwing food at her as she exited the room.

Amara picked out a black sundress with black leather sandals. She grabbed a black headband and clutch and piled them on the chair between her bed and the couch. She waited for Tyler to call, but time stood still.

Her phone rang at nine-thirty. "Hey!" she sang, recognizing the number on display.

"Hi. I missed you," Tyler purred. Amara's breathing quickened as she pictured his tanned body.

"How was it? How was the wedding?" Amara hoped Bethany had a beautiful day, but also secretly hoped it was a disaster.

"You won't believe this." He sounded happy, but the words he chose made Amara feel like something terrible had happened.

"Um, party's canceled?" she asked, hoping to spend time alone with him after not seeing him for a week.

"Nah, still on. But they canceled the wedding!"

Amara choked on her iced tea. She coughed, trying to catch her breath.

Tyler chuckled.

"What?" She leaned forward, desperate to learn more.

"We got there, and all was well. There was no rehearsal dinner because everyone flew in at different times, so we didn't see them until the wedding day. The morning of the wedding, Ryan sent a mass text, and it said, 'I regret to inform you the wedding has been canceled. Enjoy your stay anyway.'"

Amara furrowed her brow. "What twenty-two-year-old says, 'I regret to inform you?' Who does that?"

"Ryan does. Of course, we were all confused. We were dressed and on the way to the ceremony. We bumped into Bethany's parents in the courtyard. They told us Bethany decided she didn't want to get married unless she was one hundred percent sure, and right now, she wasn't."

"No way."

"Yes! My parents were livid. Ryan stayed with them instead of in Bethany's room, and we all flew out this morning. The whole thing was a disaster. I'm glad they didn't get married, especially after everything you told me." She wished Tyler was there in person. She wanted to high-five him and clink beers in celebration.

"Yes." Amara cried. "I tried telling her from the beginning he was bad news. The last time I saw her she cried and confessed how controlling he was. I haven't heard from her since. I hope she's okay."

"I think she's still in Jamaica with her family. Ryan was supposed to come home next week after their honeymoon, but he came home with us. Maybe she'll go alone or bring her sister or something."

"I hope so. She deserves some fun," Amara said. "What are we doing tomorrow?"

"I'm picking you up in twenty-four hours. The party starts at eleven, and hopefully, we'll be home by four at the latest. I'm going to make you a fancy dinner with salad and bread and wine, and we're going to watch movies, tell stories, and laugh all night long. Amongst other things."

Amara giggled. "That sounds perfect, but what about your parents and Ryan?" Amara's confidence wavered at the thought of seeing them.

"Don't worry about it. The last thing Mona wants is to talk about the wedding, so I'm sure she won't even say hi to us."

"Okay." *I hope so.* "The entire day sounds perfect."

Amara said good night and lay in her bed, wondering if she should call Bethany. She decided to wait a week and call once Bethany returned from her trip.

That would give her a week to focus on saving her parent's bakery.

***

"I'm so nervous," Amara said, sliding her sweaty palms over her black sundress. She forgot to wear a slip under her skirt, and the static clung to her pantyhose. "Ugh, I hate this dress." She yanked at the sides.

"You look great," Tyler said, turning off the car and kissing her.

"No, I can't wear this. It's driving me crazy." Amara kicked off her shoes, reached up under her skirt, and pulled her hose off. "So much better!" She balled the hose in her palm and tossed it at her feet.

They pulled into the nursing home parking lot and Amara recognized Ryan's car. She followed Tyler into the party room, greeting staff and residents outside.

The large room contained two dozen people, all wearing their Sunday best. Amara recognized Tyler's dad and Mona and Ryan. She ducked behind Tyler's broad shoulders, hoping they didn't see her. She avoided eye contact with peering eyes as much as possible. *What if everyone recognizes me as the drunk girl who ruined the cake?* "Please protect me," she whispered to Tyler and he squeezed her hand.

Tyler's grandmother sat on the couch and a variety of family members surrounded her. Mr. and Mrs. Rainey stood in the corner, and Ryan fluttered around the room with an air of arrogance in his interactions with others. He held his chin high and hands loosely clasped behind his back. His booming laugh and voice traveled throughout the room.

Tyler leaned down and kissed his grandmother on the cheek. "Grammy, this is Amaryllis," he said.

Grammy's face lit up. She wore bright pink lips and rosy cheeks from too much blush, but her eyes were full of warmth and compassion. Amara smiled and shook her hand.

Tyler and Amara passed Tyler's father and step-mother. Amara said hello and smiled brightly, before excusing herself to use the bathroom. She splashed water on her face and counted to one hundred. When she emerged from the restroom, she needed Tyler to be near people that knew nothing about her.

She found him chatting with Ryan, and her heart sank. She didn't want to have awkward conversations or pretend everything was great. Instead of saying hello, she stood near enough to hear their conversation but not close enough to be invited in. She kept herself busy, looking at the photographs and paintings on the wall.

Ryan explained to a group of people around their age that Bethany wasn't ready to settle down and get married. He sounded glum but agreed that maybe they rushed things. They hadn't even known each other a year when they got engaged, moved in together, and almost married. "It was like my life was in super-speed mode, and somehow I missed all the signs that we wouldn't make it." Amara almost felt sorry for him, but then she remembered how he sabotaged her parents. *Karma.*

Embedded in the group, Tyler patted Ryan on the shoulder and reassured him it would get better.

Ryan said he was moving back home to his parent's basement while Bethany was away.

Amara frowned, feeling bad for Bethany's situation. *What's she going to do now?*

Tyler looked over and caught Amara glancing at them. "Hi." He pulled her over and wrapped his arm around her shoulder, hugging her tight.

"Hi, Amara," Ryan said, confusion clouding his face. "Wait, are you two together?"

Tyler nodded, beaming. "We are. We met at the engagement-birthday party and reconnected when I helped her plan the shower that never happened. We've been inseparable since."

Amara blushed. She wasn't sure if it was because of embarrassment or flattery, but she leaned into him and squeezed his waist.

Tyler kissed her and asked, "Do you want a drink?"

Feeling overwhelmed by his public display of affection, she nodded and followed him to the refreshments table.

Amara chuckled and playfully slapped him on the chest. "Were you trying to make him jealous?"

"You know it. He may have lost a great girl, but he helped me find my perfect partner."

Amara continued to giggle, taking a sip of soda. "You are one of a kind, Ty."

"You're perfect for me, Amaryllis."

***

Driving back to her apartment, Amara felt relaxed and content. "Thanks for bringing me," she said. "Your family's nice. I thought they hated me."

"They did," Tyler said, "but once they saw how happy you made me feel, they realized it was none of their business what was going on with you and Bethany."

"Thank you for everything. For standing up for me, not backing down, and pushing me out of my comfort zone." She meant every word.

"You are one of the kindest people I know. I know you would do it for me, so I would do it for you."

Amara thought about his statement and whether she would reciprocate or run away if the roles were reversed. Even though Ryan and Bethany's relationship was not her business, she stood up for her friend. She stood up for her parents, proving that they deserved respect and support from the community. She hadn't yet needed to stand up for Tyler, but she knew she would fight for him if an ex-girlfriend arrived on the scene.

Amara felt like a renewed and rejuvenated version of herself. She couldn't believe how she had destroyed her life six months ago yet somehow figured out how to put the pieces together in a better way.

***

Amara drove back to the bakery the following day and fought the masses of people who came for their Greek pastries. People traveled from all over New England and New York to try the delicious goods and be a part of history, stuffing the donation jar with money. Over the past week, her parents donated over three thousand dollars to Connecticut's food banks and shelters.

Henry hustled the crowd, Mama and Amara worked the counter, and George baked like a machine. Daphne emptied the trash cans, cleaned tables, and swept the floor. Loukoumades Bakery was a family affair. It was the exact repeat of the week before, and Amara didn't know how they could survive their sudden popularity.

That night, all five of them sat down to discuss the shop's future. Amara hadn't had time to think about her parent's situation, and she didn't even know what they wanted or if it was a problem Amara could fix.

"What do we do?" her father asked no one in particular. "I'm tired, and I need a break, but there is no break."

"Baba, do you still want to sell?"

He sighed and hesitated. "Yes, I think so. But it has to go to Henry, and I still have to be involved."

"No offense to Henry," Amara said, glancing at his pasty white face and freckles before turning to back to her dad, "but do you think he would be an appropriate face for the business?"

Henry pulled away from the table, his brows creased and eyes blinking. "Amaryllis, what do you mean?"

"It's a Greek business, and you aren't Greek. What do you know about the traditions and culture, and what makes our food so special?"

"I've worked here for years and am considered part of your family." He readjusted the round frames on his eyes and rubbed his jaw.

"Yes, we know that. But the public doesn't. If it becomes public knowledge, which it will with all this media, people will question our credibility. You can't have that. That's like business suicide."

"Amaryllis, if we sell, which we want to, it will have to go to Henry. He agreed to keep the atmosphere and menu the same There is no one else. It is the only way for us to stay involved."

"Mama, what do you think?"

"I agree with your father," she said. "Your sister has suffered. We barely know her, and she's raising herself. She needs her parents. She's going to high school, and we only have four years left. She's still learning right from wrong and how to stand up to peer pressure. We're currently married to the shop. If selling allows us more time with Daphne and you, we need to sell."

Daphne swallowed, rubbed her temples, and moved away from the table. No one acknowledged her movement because they were too concerned with the bakery's future.

"But Baba, what if you and Henry became partners instead? Wouldn't that make more sense? Then nothing changes, but you can cut back your hours, and Henry could make most of the decisions with your guidance."

Her father looked around the shop, eyeing all the memorabilia hanging on the walls. He glanced toward the phone, which hung next to the corkboard holding their first dollar made. He scanned the empty display case and the family photo hanging behind the register. His family, Henry included, stared back at him, waiting for an answer.

"Amaryllis, I'm tired. I need a change."

"Baba, do not give up on your dream. This is your dream right here, and it's exploding! Because of you and Mama and your kindness, people are out here supporting you and your generosity. Don't give up on it."

"Amaryllis, I promise you, the business will thrive," Henry defended. "I have an entire background in the food industry, and I've been working in bakeries for decades."

Amara tapped her long fingers on the table. "Fine. This started as a family thing, and it will stay in the family. Henry, you'll be in charge of the shop. George, you'll bake, and I'll sort the books. My degree is in finance, and I've worked in banking since college. I know a thing or two about money and business."

Confidence grew like a weed within Amara, and suddenly she didn't know who was speaking. "Baba, you can't sell. You can make Henry a partner if you must, but it can't be split down the middle. It has to be a two-third one-third split. Sorry, Henry." She threw a glance at Henry. "We'll split the business three ways, but Baba, I don't want it. You can keep my third. So that would be a third to Henry and two-thirds to you. We'll be a team. Does that sound good?"

Henry's face scrunched up, processing the math or the change in plans; Amara wasn't sure. "How is that even fair?" he asked. "I've given this place the last two years of my life. Amaryllis, while you've been gallivanting in Providence, living your best life. Why should you get the same as I?"

"Because, Henry, it's my family, and I won't let them give their livelihood away to anyone. You are a wonderful partner, but you aren't Greek, and you don't know the traditions, the history, or the love behind what my parents have built here."

"That is ridiculous," he exclaimed.

"You'll be in charge of the shop. I'll be in charge of the finances. Baba, it will list us both on all accounts. Nothing will change, except that you and Mama will have more free time."

"But Amara, you have a job," Mama interjected. "How are you going to do that? You live an hour away."

Amara sighed. Her current situation wasn't ideal. She wished she had thought of this scenario before she accepted the job at the bank. "You're right, but my rent is month to month. I don't want to move home, but I could move north, maybe outside of Worcester." She thought about Tyler, considering the distance to Boston. *It will be fine.* "I'll drive down three to four days a week to balance the books, make purchase orders, and manage advertising and publicity. It'll be perfect."

Henry sighed, his face getting red and his body straight.

"We need to think about it," Baba said. "But it's something to consider."

Mama kissed Baba on the cheek. "I knew you didn't want to sell," she said. "You were doing it out of necessity, but maybe there really is another solution." She took his hand and squeezed.

Amara, Daphne, Baba, and Mama drove back to the house, and Amara treated her family to homemade souvlaki. Daphne sat at the table, asking about the shop.

"I'm so tired," Mama said.

"Same." Baba kicked off his shoes and plopped into the armchair. Daphne and Amara cleared the table while their parents rested in the other room. "Daphne, what do you think? Should Mama and Baba sell the shop to Henry? Or should they make him a partner?"

Daphne shrugged, her gaze on her hands in her lap and her shoulders tense. It was clear she felt uncomfortable in these adult discussions. "I don't know."

Amara sat down in front of her. "Do you feel like Mama and Baba are never home or here for you?"

Daphne glanced backward out the kitchen door. She dropped her voice. "I've been on my own since the fifth grade. Mama calls at seven every morning to remind me to get up for school. I have breakfast, get ready, and catch the bus. Thankfully someone is here when I get home, but they're so tired I try to stay out of their hair or cause trouble. I play sports after school, shower, eat dinner, and then hole up in my room to do homework. Weekends are better, but I still wake up alone and manage my time until dinner. It's not like I need to know them. They're parents. But they don't know me either."

Amara pulled away, surprised by Daphne's honesty. It was almost like she had never voiced her feelings before, and her thoughts and emotions poured out like a broken hose.

"Okay, so is it right to assume you'd like them home more?"

Daphne nodded.

"Then it's settled," she said.

Amara marched into the living room and made an announcement. "Baba? Mama? Daphne and I just spoke, and she agrees that working fewer hours would be beneficial. Consider your health, your happiness, and your relationship with your family. Also consider your dream. You're too young to retire."

"Amara we've gone over this. I'm ready."

"Baba, you say you are, but you're not. You're frustrated with me. I revealed your secret to the world and ruined your reputation. Don't confuse your disappointment in me with your disappointment in the business." Amara's eyes filled with tears. "I don't care about the percentage, but please don't sell or make it a fifty-fifty split. You've worked too hard to give half your livelihood away. I'll be there to help no matter what. We can do a trial run. I can start at Loukoumades in September. Baba, this is the right thing to do. I promise I won't let you down again."

He smiled up at her. "You never have."

Amara took a step backward, her head jerked back, and her forehead creased. "Really? I feel like I'm always letting you down."

Her dad leaned forward in his chair and pursed his lips. "Never. I'm sorry if I made you feel that way. It's not easy being a father, Amara. I mean, it's hard for both parents, but men hold the responsibility of providing for the family. All I ever wanted to do was provide and be a good example for you."

"Do you remember when I tried to make you baklava for your birthday? There was syrup everywhere, and the baklava was so soggy and over-sweetened, we couldn't eat it. Instead of saying thank you, you threw it in the trash and wouldn't let me leave the kitchen until I cleaned every last mixing bowl and pan. I remember crying over the sink while I scrubbed the dishes. Mama was with Daphne at the park, I think. I was a little older than Daphne is now, Baba, and you killed my curiosity to have any interest in our culture."

He put his glasses on and leaned forward. "I'm sorry."

Amara waved him off and continued. "Then you started the bakery, and I was afraid to step into the kitchen when you were around. I was always in the way or messing things up. I honestly felt like the way to make you happy was to keep my distance because if I weren't near you, I couldn't upset you."

Baba wiped his eyes. "I remember that day, Amara. I've made many mistakes throughout the years. Did you know that Papou's dad died when he was twelve, and he had to be the man of the house because he was the oldest?"

Amara shook her head, unfamiliar with the story.

"His mother couldn't take care of all the kids or pay the bills, so his father had to get a job when he was just a child. He ended up quitting school. That family needed to survive with a roof over their head and food on the table, and nothing else mattered. My papou passed down that work ethic and focus to your papou, who eventually passed it down to me. We worked to get ahead in this country to provide a good life for you and your sister. That day with the baklava, I was more concerned with the number of ingredients and money thrown in the trash. I didn't consider your feelings. What you did was thoughtful, but all I saw was our bank balance. During a time in our life when we relied on assistance from others to survive, I felt like a failure. But I never considered you a failure. I'm sorry I crushed your spirits."

"It's okay, Baba. It's in the past. Maybe you can teach me how to make baklava now that we're partners. If, of course, you want to be partners with me."

He breathed in and held his breath before releasing the air. "Sure."

"Mama?"

Her mom nodded. "Why not."

Amara kissed them on the forehead. "I'm looking forward to working beside you!" She spat in her palm and held it out for a shake. Her father laughed, spit in his hand, and shook hers vigorously.

***

A few days later, Amara called Bethany. Amara debated for hours whether texting would be more appropriate for the first contact since their meeting in the bookstore. She opted for the phone. Amara imagined Bethany holding her phone, wondering if she should answer. It rang five times before Amara heard Bethany's voice.

"Hello?" Bethany asked, obviously knowing it was Amara on the other end.

"Hi Beth, it's Amara. Can you talk?" She had prepared herself for rejection and held her breath, waiting for the call to disconnect.

"Sure, I have a few minutes. What's up?"

Amara tried to talk, but her parched throat stopped the words. She coughed into her elbow and sipped water. "I wanted to apologize for the last time I saw you when I called Ryan a piece of shit. That was uncalled for, and I was completely out of line."

"It's fine," Bethany responded. "I was pissed, but you gave me a lot to consider. I don't know if you heard, but I didn't marry Ryan."

Amara pretended she didn't know, and she didn't want to distract Bethany with news about Tyler. "What? What happened?" Her voice rose and fell in all the right places.

"You were right. We'd barely been together, and he was so needy and insecure that he tried to control me. You probably helped me more than you know, so thank you."

"When did you call off the wedding?"

"I called it off the night before. It was a small group, and word traveled fast. My mom, sister, and I stayed for the honeymoon, and I think everyone else left."

"Oh, my." Amara's hand flew to her face for effect, even though Bethany couldn't see. "What did he say?"

"First, he tried to convince me I had cold feet. Then he got angry and blamed me for ruining his vacation. It was all wrong. I wish I had listened to you from the beginning."

"I can't even believe it! Did you get back today?" Amara didn't know the answer.

"Yesterday. I was afraid to come home because I didn't know if he would be here, but all his stuff was gone. Poof! It's like he completely disappeared from my life."

"Oh, Bethany, I'm so sorry." Amara was sorry that her friend experienced heartache.

"Do you want to come over? I have a charming oversized studio in a beautiful Victorian home about twenty minutes north of Providence. I'd love to have you if you don't want to sleep at your place tonight." Amara wanted to be there for her friend.

"You know, that'd be great."

An hour later, Bethany knocked on Amara's door.

***

"Ty, baby, can you help me with this box?" Amara called through the apartment.

She was starting over again, this time near Worcester. She was a half-hour from her parents and the shop, forty minutes from Bethany, and forty-five minutes from Tyler. Her new location forced her to stand on her two feet, but allowed her to lean on her friends and family when she needed extra support.

Tyler opened the boxes on the floor and started pulling out kitchen gadgets. "Where do these go?"

Amara shrugged. "Wherever. Thanks."

"When does Bethany officially take over your lease?" he asked.

Amara turned and hugged him, wrapping her arms around his thick torso. "I think she has to be out of her place by the end of the month. Monty was upset when I told him I was moving out because I had only been there a month. When I told him Bethany wanted to move in, he reluctantly agreed. After he checked her references, credit, and work history, I think he was fine with it. Thankfully, I hadn't fully unpacked all the boxes."

Amara's new apartment was twice as large, with an updated kitchen and a washer and dryer in the unit. It was a step up from the third-floor Victorian.

"Are you excited to be starting over again?" Tyler asked.

Amara nodded. "Yeah, it's a fresh start. I'm happy I was able to give Bethany a place to stay when she needed it most. I consider it my olive branch."

"How is everything with Bethany?"

Amara shrugged. "As back to normal as it can be. I feel like a different person. I call it 'pre-Tyler' and 'post-Tyler.' When I met you, I was in a horrible place, and somehow you stuck by me while I figured out my life." Amara kissed him deeply. "I like who I am now. Way more than who I was. I wasn't a good friend to Bethany. We developed this unhealthy codependency, and I probably should have moved out years ago. She and I had blended into one, and when Ryan came into the picture, it threw me. My other half was gone, and I was alone. I was jealous and also hated him. I deserved everything that happened."

"So, are things still weird?" Tyler asked. "I assume you told her about us?"

Amara nodded. "Yeah, I did. She seemed happy but surprised. Things are uncomfortable since we spent most of the year not talking. It'll take some time to grow back together."

Tyler nodded. "It will. So, when's your last day at work?"

Amara sat on the couch and kicked her feet on the ottoman. "Friday. I heard they're giving a donation to the shelter since they heard the story about the bakery. It was all over the news, even here." She laughed. "I might send them a thank you platter with all my dad's desserts."

Tyler scooted next to her. She loved having him close. A knock on the door pulled Amara to her feet. "Pizza."

She opened her wallet and pulled out some cash for the delivery man. A folded rectangular paper slipped out with the bills and fluttered to the floor. Amara took the pizza, placed it on the counter, and picked up the paper. She unfolded and read the fortune from the weekend of Bethany's party. "Hey, Tyler?"

"Pizza. I'm starving." He rubbed his hands together.

"Check it out." She waved the paper at him. "The weekend after Bethany and Ryan's engagement I got Chinese food. This was my fortune. 'Some dream of fortunes, other dream of cookies.' Seems a bit psychic, doesn't it?"

She secured the fortune to her refrigerator.

"Seems to me like your fortune came true." Tyler kissed her on the forehead. "Let's eat. I'm starving!"

They spent the rest of the day hanging out in her empty apartment eating pizza and setting up the wi-fi to watch movies.

In her room, Amara and Tyler sat on the mattress pressed against one corner of the room. A trash bag full of clothes sat in another corner, and stacked boxes climbed the walls. "I can't believe this is my fourth address in one year."

Tyler nodded. "You were on a journey. Do you think this is it?" he asked.

Amara grabbed his arm, placed it around her neck and snuggled into him. "This is it. I feel happy right now, and there is no other place—well, besides your place—that I would rather be."

He held her against the uncomfortable, lumpy mattress, kissing her lips until they fell asleep.

***

"Hi, this is Amaryllis Leventis. I'm calling from Loukoumades Bakery. We would like to set up a schedule to deliver food to your soup kitchen," she said into the landline attached to the shop. George prepared more galaktoboureko, and Henry helped customers behind the counter.

Amara took a bite of the syrupy custard pastry. "George, this tastes amazing. You must teach us the recipe."

George winked. "I guess it's time."

Henry had accepted the lawyer's offer of a forty-sixty split, with Henry owning almost half. Amara didn't think it was an intelligent move but knew it wasn't her choice. She would be there to help her parents as best she could.

"George, what time is Daphne's game?" Amara called into the back room.

"Four o'clock today," he hollered back.

"Perfect. I'll be there."

"Ride with your mother. You know she doesn't enjoy driving at night."

Amara tried to see Daphne two or three afternoons a week, and so far, that little effort was enough to tighten their bond. Their family felt like a family, and they were together for the good times, the bad times, and the boring times.

Amara picked up her phone and read a text from Tyler. **What are you doing this weekend?**

"Hey, Baba," Amara called. "Are you doing anything on Saturday?"

"Nothing."

Amara thumbed a message to Tyler. **Do you want to come to Connecticut for dinner on Saturday? I think it's time you meet my family.**

Ding! **Moussaka?**

I'll ask!

"Baba, I'll cook you, Mama, and Daphne dinner. I'm bringing a special guest."

Her father stuck his head out of the doorway and winked, smiling brightly. Amara smiled back and giggled. Loukoumades Bakery had delivered each of them good luck, prosperity, and happiness.

It was time they celebrated their past, present, and future together.

The End.

***

If you fell in love with Amara and Bethany, check out the short story The Girls' Trip.

A spring break trip to Daytona Beach sends Bethany White and her five sorority sisters on an adventure they'll never forget. From lost luggage to facing fears, meeting men, and a bathing suit malfunction, the six girls are on a wild ride. Join Bethany and Amara that will forever solidify their friendship...or will it?

https://www.linktr.ee/edhackett

About the Author

E.D Hackett is a Speech-language pathologist by day and a writer by night. Writing has always been a passion to her and she recently decided to jump into writing head first. She has one self-published novel that investigates the layers of self-expectations, family expectations, following your dreams, disappointing others, and finding true love and true happiness. She hopes that her novels create a safe and cozy environment for her readers to fall into and explore.

Her husband and kids are her strength. Her husband has always encouraged her to follow her dreams, no matter what her dreams are.

She lives in New England but in her heart, she feels that she belongs in Ireland. She loves to read, write, knit, and cook.

Please stay in touch through her newsletter, social media, or email at e.d_hackettwrites@yahoo.com or email.edy@edhackettwrites.com.

You can connect with me on:

🌐 http://edhackettwrites.com

📘 https://www.facebook.com/edhackettwrites

🔗 https://www.instagram.com/e.d_hackettwrites

🔗 https://linktr.ee/Edhackett

🔗 https://www.goodreads.com/author/show/20864221.E_D_ Hackett

Subscribe to my newsletter:

✉ http://www.edhackettwrites.com/contact

Also by E.D. Hackett

The Havoc in My Head

She had all she expected to achieve. But a surprise hidden in her head was about to change everything…

Ashley Martin has it all. With a high-paying job, a devoted husband, and impeccable children, the ambitious woman is living the dream life she envisioned for herself. So determined to maintain her perfect existence, she hides her odd vision problems, headaches, and confusion… until one morning she wakes up blind.

Diagnosed with a brain tumor, the terrified professional faces two difficult surgeries and a year-long recovery. And as she struggles to cope with her sudden reversal of fortune, Ashley begins to see truths she never had before.

Can this tenacious woman reclaim her health and redirect her happiness?

The Havoc in My Head is a powerful and moving women's fiction novel. If you like deeply personal journeys, overcoming impossible hurdles, and inspirational turnarounds, then you'll love E.D. Hackett's tale of extreme courage.

An Unfinished Story

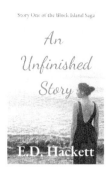

Complete strangers. A bustling B&B. Can two women help each other find their dreams?

Boston. Joanie Wilson has played it safe her whole life. But her fifteen years of loyalty to the newspaper seem like they count for nothing when her boss announces the business's impending sale. And though she doesn't really enjoy her job, the frightened reporter fights to save it by accepting a remote assignment to write articles on local flavor.

Block Island, RI. Carly Davis longs to live on her own terms. But with her father deceased and her mother's dementia dominating her world, the gregarious young woman feels trapped into running the family's bed-and-breakfast. So when a desperate journalist arrives and swaps her rent for assistance with the property, Carly seizes the chance to finally take a deep breath.

As Joanie becomes immersed in the relaxed atmosphere and meets a handsome police officer, she wonders if her need for safety is costing her happiness. And as Carly grows close to her big-city tenant, she sees a new future opening before her.

Will this accidental friendship trigger the changes both women crave?

An Unfinished Story is the charming first book in The Block Island Saga women's fiction series. If you like relatable characters, sweet romances, and beautiful settings, then you'll love E.D. Hackett's escape to paradise.

Story Two of the Block Island Saga

Hope Hanna Murphy

E.D. Hackett

Hope Hanna Murphy

She sacrificed too much for them. When her real ancestry shatters her world, will she ever reclaim happiness?

Carly Davis was sure getting away from the island would help. Elated after finally freeing herself from running her late family's inn, her fresh start in Maine fizzles in the aftermath of a failed relationship. And her luck sours further still when an innocent DNA test reveals at least one of her parents had been deceiving her for decades.

Furious she gave up the best years of her life to support people she wasn't even related to, the distraught woman returns home to seek answers about her actual origins. But with her dear friend's sister marrying a guy who is suddenly Carly's cousin, the angry adoptee fears the truth could leave her more alone than ever...

Will she find the joy she so desperately craves, or will her true heritage only bring new sorrow?

Hope Hanna Murphy is the enchanting second book in The Block Island Saga women's fiction series. If you like optimistic stories, conflicted characters, and the strength of community, then you'll love E.D. Hackett's tale of courage.